To the memory
of the Prince Regent,
who changed the face of Brighton
for ever.

## Acknowledgements

As well as my typist Elisabeth Francis, and my ever-supportive partner, Faith O'Reilly, I would like to thank Jonathan MacFarlane for useful advice about Real Estate agencies.

# Chapter 1

'Hi Dany!
What a surprise! I thought you'd left the country.'

She had managed to push herself to the bar of the pub in Balham where I was working. She was looking good.

'A pint of lager.'

If she hadn't changed it would be the first of many. She was a head shorter than me, all bone and muscle. I remembered she was very fit, worked out regularly, played in her university women's rugby team and could drink most men under the table. When she was off duty, of course. When we worked in pubs together neither of us had touched a drop.

'I'd like to talk to you. Meet me tomorrow morning for coffee at the big bookshop in the high street? You know the one. Eleven o'clock.' She was just in time to take possession of a corner table before three amazonic types joined her.

She was back and forth to replenish glasses during the evening, served this time by one of my fellow barpersons. Her name was Michaela, Mickey to most people. We had always had a great time together, she and I. Attraction of opposites maybe. I guess she had Nordic blood somewhere along the line because she was as fair as I was dark, with almost white straight hair, which she occasionally allowed to grow longer than a couple of inches before having it all chopped off again, and light blue eyes. I never knew what she was studying, she never talked about it and I probably wouldn't have understood anyway. She used to say to me "You're bright, you know, Dany. All those languages you speak. Haven't you ever thought of going to college?" No I hadn't. I was bored by school, so college would be a really painful experience. Sure, I spoke many languages fluently, picked up here and there, but that had been easy, probably since my parents and grandparents had spoken French, English and Italian to me from the moment I was born. My current girlfriend Ellie had suggested gently when we first met that perhaps qualifications of some kind might give me more opportunities. "Opportunities for what?" I asked. The only opportunities I needed were to travel and have good sex from time to time. I'd always been able to work my passage and pulling when I wanted had never been a problem.

Michaela left soon after eleven, bright as a button with her bleary-eyed friends trailing behind her. 'See you tomorrow Dany,' she called. 'Don't forget, I have an interesting proposition for you.'

As a matter of fact, I could do with a change. Since I'd come back from France the previous summer, I'd felt very low. I'd loved deeply, and lost, irrevocably, and I would rather have done without that pain. The scars hadn't healed in spite of Ellie's tender loving care. I hadn't told her the truth, she thought I had simply got mixed up with a bad crowd when I left her for a while to go on one of my periodic European walk-abouts. Fortunately she'd had other interests at the time – sacred dancing in Scotland. She'd been so excited by that she didn't press me for more details of the circumstances which led me to a kind of breakdown. Which is just as well, since I didn't understand what it was all about myself. I was still fragile, it was almost as if I'd had a major operation to remove my most vital organs. I was empty. I returned to the pub in Balham where I was known as efficient and popular, because I couldn't face any major challenges. Ellie and I weren't lovers any more – we ought to have separated but I didn't have the heart to move and she was too kind to throw me out, although she could have done better than saddle herself with this morose flatmate who could offer her nothing.

That night in bed in her elegant flat in Clapham, I told her about Michaela.

'It could be a good thing' she said. 'You need to break loose from me, Dany.'

'And you, Ellie?'

'I could do with a complete change. Of job, of city, of mind. I've been wondering about Edinburgh. I'm tired of the Central Office of Information. I could sell this place for an awful lot of money. Sleep well.'

She kissed me goodnight and turned over.

\*\*\*\*

The bookshop wasn't a place I would choose to have coffee. The drinks were expensive and served in cups which were far too big. I had dressed with care to cheer myself up and to honour what seemed like the first day of Spring. My best jeans, a pale green shirt and a brand new denim jacket I had been saving for the good weather. It was gratifying that more than one woman gave me an appreciative look as I took my seat beside Michaela, who was already half way through a huge mug of hot chocolate.

'Wow!' she exclaimed. 'You look absolutely great.'

She was stunning. A designer outfit down to the shoes and handbag. An impeccable cut and subtle, muted colours. Expensive good taste written all over it.

'Have you inherited a fortune?' I asked.

'Not a fortune, but a considerable amount.'

She filled me in on her recent history. After finishing her degree, with a result no better than to be expected, considering how little time she had spent on her studies, she went to stay with her great aunt in Brighton and Hove. Well, Hove actually. Great Aunt Miranda had been married to a millionaire, a marriage of convenience between very good friends with their own life styles. Her husband died of Aids before the development of modern drugs. Miranda continued to have affairs, as she had always, without any real commitment, in continual mourning for the only person she had truly loved. Then her favourite great niece, Michaela moved in whilst deciding what she wanted out of life. In fact, what she wanted at that moment was to do nothing except drag her feet with a part-time job in a café, which left her a lot of time to play with Miranda. Until Miranda had a stroke. She recovered fairly well from general paralysis but needed the constant care of a live-in companion. She gave Michaela a generous allowance before she had a second stroke.

'It was just a year ago,' said Mickey. 'She left me everything. It's been awful sorting through the papers. I found lots of love letters. I suppose I shouldn't have read them but I couldn't resist. She broke quite a few hearts. I'm not surprised. I have a photo of her taken with my Uncle Samuel just before his illness. Aren't they just beautiful?'

She fished an envelope out of her Gucci bag.

'I carry this around all the time. They were a fantastic couple. They were both always so good to me. I do miss her so much.' There was a catch in her voice.

Miranda and Samuel were smiling at each other rather than looking straight at the camera. Handsome profiles. There was a tenderness, a complicity between them that almost took your breath away.

'They look very…..' I searched for the right word. 'Very wise.' I wasn't sure what I meant by that. Wisdom wasn't something I had often encountered.

'Oh, they were.'

She took the photo back, put it away carefully, then stared into the dregs of her chocolate. Since she didn't seem inclined to speak I was the one who broke the silence.

'I'm sorry.' Perhaps it was a stupid thing to say to a woman who had just inherited a fortune but she was so forlorn that clearly the money wasn't that important, I thought. Not quite true, I discovered.

'Anyway, there we are. I'm the proud owner of a beautiful big house as well as innumerable investments and savings.'

I was beginning to wonder where I fitted into all this.

'So you'll be off on a world cruise, or buy your own yacht or something. No need to ever work again.'

'Not at all. I can't fritter the money away. It wouldn't be fair to Samuel and Miranda.'

'I don't know much about stocks and shares. Don't they just keep on making money anyway?'

This wasn't the conversation I'd imagined having.

'It's not like that. Anyway I want to set up a business. In Brighton. I shall stay in the house.'

Where was this leading, I wondered. Was she going to open a guest house or something? Hardly her style, and certainly not mine. I waited.

'I'm going into real estate.'

My mouth dropped open.

'I've rented a shop to set up as an estate agent. Selling and renting. Property management.'

It was time for me to leave, if she'd bought a pub I would have perhaps been interested.

'Would you like to come and work for me? Don't say no immediately. I can tell by the expression on your face you're going to refuse. Sleep on it. Meet me tomorrow at the same time. Promise?'

'Just tell me one thing. Do you know what you're doing?'

'Oh yes. I studied law after all. Property law was my specialisation, and I've followed a course for setting up a small business.'

'O.K., tell me a second thing then, why employ me, of all people?'

'Because I like you. Last night I remembered the good times we'd had. I trust you. You're a straight on person, Dany. You can speak lots of languages, which could be helpful.'

'You're assuming I'm a free agent.'

'You always were, aren't you still?'

'I'll let you know tomorrow,' was my only response.

'Wonderful!' She leaned over the table to give me a great hug almost knocking over her mug. 'You'll move in with me. There's a separate apartment, so we won't be in each other's way if we don't want to be. I've taken over Miranda's old room. We open shop in a couple of weeks. I've put out plenty of advertisements, asking for properties.'

'I didn't tell you the most important fact. We're going to concentrate on finding homes for women. We won't exclude men, that would be silly. Homes for women will be our speciality. It's like women taxi-drivers, there's a definite niche. That's where you will be helpful. I won't make you sit inside all the time. We can take it in turns to go and look and take clients round. It will be such fun. Shall we discuss your salary?'

I shrugged.

'Name a figure. You'll have rent-free accommodation, of course.'

I hadn't a clue. I tried out what seemed an outrageous sum, just for fun.

'Oh, I don't think that's enough.'

She doubled it and promised commission on top.

'I'm going back home tomorrow. Can you come?'

'I have to give notice at the pub. It's a relatively informal arrangement, a week will do.'

'Splendid. Then we can have a week to organise ourselves. And,' she added with a broad grin, 'to buy you some new clothes.'

## Chapter 2

My apartment in Mickey's house was the most beautiful place I'd ever lived in. Big windows giving on to a fantastic garden. I'd mainly lived in cities with very little in the way of outside space – Ellie's place had overlooked Clapham Common, a very public park. This was private peace, trees, shrubs, a vast lawn and flowerbeds overflowing with spring flowers. There was a small terrace, all my own, with a little table and chairs where I could look towards the sea. As soon as I settled in Mickey asked me how much I would sell the house for and how much for the apartment alone.

'You said you weren't going to sell!' I protested.

'I'm not. This is practice for you. How much?'

I made an attempt at both figures. She fell about laughing.

'Oh Dany, where have you been this last year?'

'In limbo.'

'You must have been. I wouldn't take offers lower than......' She named sums which made my jaw drop.

'You're not serious?'

'Oh yes I am. I think you'd better leave the valuation to me until you get real.

'Look Mickey, you can see I'm hopeless. I told you I'd be no good.'

'You will, I promise.'

'I realise that you could rent my apartment for three or four times whatever I could afford to pay, so why don't you do it and employ a couple of pretty eighteen year olds in the office whilst I find a little studio somewhere.'

She was aghast.

'No, no. I don't want somebody else living here, some stranger who wouldn't understand about Samuel and Miranda and me. I don't want to work with anyone I don't feel completely at ease with. Its' very, very important to me. Don't let me down. You can't imagine how excited I was to come across you again. I'd been vaguely hoping I might, but I was just over the moon when it happened.'

She was wringing her hands and gazing at me imploringly, making me feel even more uncomfortable. I mean, we had been good friends, not exactly soul mates. I had forgotten all about her – out of sight out of mind. Probably mainly because my mind had been, still was, full of images of someone else. I had to make it clear what she wanted from me besides my professional assistance.

'Mickey, were you in love with me?'

'Good heavens no.'

The emphatic way she said this was not flattering. However, it was reassuring.

'I've usually fallen in love with most unsuitable types. It's just a physical/chemical thing, isn't it? Doesn't last. Exciting, of course. You weren't in love with me either.' This was a statement of fact, needing no answer.

At least that was out of the way, even if I was still unsure of my role in her life. We were sitting in her kitchen, the doors open onto a large patch of herbs. She obviously used these in cooking as there were bunches of them hanging from the ceiling, and jars, lots of jars of crushed leaves, all carefully labelled, lining shelves, stored away in a glass-fronted dresser. There were roots too, and dried flower heads. It was like being in an old farmhouse, especially as the furniture was worn, even slightly worm-eaten. Quite different from my smart, modern kitchen upstairs. In fact downstairs and upstairs seemed worlds apart.

'Miranda enjoyed cooking?' I asked.

'Cooking?' She was puzzled. 'Not particularly, why?'

'The herbs.'

'Oh, they are medicinal. She could cure anything. Well, most things. I was learning. If you have a headache, don't take a pill, just ask me. Not everything you see here grows in the garden. You have to go out and look in the hedge-rows and fields. Would you like a herbal infusion before we go out shopping? I have plants to calm you down, others to make your heart beat faster. What do you fancy?'

'Nothing right now. Thank you. Perhaps we might have a coffee later?'

'As you like.' She was disappointed.

Shopping was for me. I allowed myself to be treated as a sort of gigolo. After all, Ellie was much better off than I was, so I had been used to living partly at her expense. I had usually bought my own clothes, though. This time we trawled through the most expensive boutiques until we were both satisfied. Mickey had a great colour sense, advising me what looked best against my olive skin, (the best way I can describe the result of my very diluted African blood.) Neither of us worried about the bills, which must have been considerable.

14

We took a taxi to the new office. It was not far away, very central in one of the streets leading away from the Royal Pavilion, that camp oriental palace, converted from a simple house by a decadent prince for his beloved mistress. This area was gay Brighton.

Mickey's agency was painted in the palest lavender, mauve in some lights, white in others. The chairs were upholstered in white leather, the desks glass and steel. Even the filing cabinets were elegant pieces of furniture. Already the windows were full of advertisements, one window for lettings, the other for sales. The response to the shop had been most satisfactory.

'Welcome to *"Her Place"*. Do you like it? I hope so, it's a very interesting neighbourhood.'

I was glad of my new clothes. My normal old denims wouldn't have fitted in. Did I like it? No, but perhaps I'd get used to it.

'Very smart,' was my only comment.

She explained the contents of the drawers, went through the files on the computer. To try to cheer me up during the winter, Ellie had given me my very own laptop. I was hardly computer literate, had steadfastly turned my back on modern technology, but to please Mickey I played around looking up useless information on the web. There was a person I desperately wanted to get in touch with, so I tried every avenue I could think of to trace her. It wasn't any use since I had little to go on except that her name was Anita and she came from Louisiana. Although I didn't find her, I learnt a lot about the Mississippi delta. I was dreaming about Anita (which I still did as often as most men are supposed to think about sex, which is every few minutes), listening with half an ear to Mickey describing Home Information Packs, when the 'phone rang. We both looked at it. I wasn't going to move. After six rings Mickey picked it up.

*"Her Place"*. Michaela speaking.'

She listened.

'We aren't actually opening until Monday. I will come and look at your property if you like, though, so that we can have the details ready. When would suit you?'

She kept listening. I played with one of her beautifully sharpened pencils. People don't often use pencils these days, I thought.

'Tonight is rather difficult. Are you sure you can't manage tomorrow morning?'

A very brief pause.

'Alright. 6.30. What is the exact address?'

A very long pause whilst she seized my pencil and scribbled frantically on a piece of her headed notepaper.

'You'll be waiting at the gate? See you later then.' She put the receiver down, frowning. 'Of course there's no problem about going this evening. I didn't want to be pressured, that's all. I didn't like the sound of her. She was very anxious. Nervous. She frowned again. 'Almost frightened.' She shrugged. 'Still, we'd better have a look,'

We took my new clothes home. Mickey said she needed to meditate before we went out again. Meditation can mean many different things. She didn't explain. I explored the garden with all its secret corners. There was a lily pond on the east side, a rose garden on the west, the south was the cottage garden with the herbs, and to the north, the side I could see from the smaller window in my bedroom, there was the lawn and shrubbery with large trees beyond. Although the lawn was immaculate, the bushes were quite untended growing into each other to form an almost impenetrable hedge. There was a gap in the corner marking the entrance to a pathway which went round a big circle through the trees, or so I thought, until I realised it was a spiral ending back amongst the shrubs in a space which was perfectly round and white, in the centre of which stood a small white building. Marble, they must be marble, I thought. Even in the darkness of the surrounding bushes they glowed. Treading very carefully, I tiptoed across the circle to open the door. It wouldn't budge.

Locked, I supposed, though there was no sign of a keyhole. There was perfect silence. Not a leaf stirred. I tried the door again, pushing harder, even knocking on the smooth surface, even though I would have died of fright if anyone had answered. There was a slight rustling in the leaves behind me, that was all.

As I wound my way round the little path, clouds passed over the sun, big black clouds, out of a blue sky giving the wood a sinister appearance. My heart was beating fast. I went up to my room and lay on the bed to calm down. I must have drifted into that half-awake half-asleep state when reality begins to slip. Images of the shrubbery, and the copse beyond became mixed up with memories of the chestnut woods in France, the bright white house faded into a mellow stone cottage. When I knocked at the door this time it was opened by Anita.

I sat up. One of my reasons for coming here, was to get over last year, so I was disturbed that the vision I'd just had of Anita's face was the clearest for months. Perhaps that was a final appearance before she went away. I prayed it would be the case.

I looked through my wardrobe. Mickey had been wildly generous in buying me several sets of everything – trousers, jackets, shirts, even shoes and socks. I chose sandy coloured linen with a pale green and brown striped shirt, suitably spring like for an April evening. I felt better looking at my reflection in the wall-length mirror. Smart she'd wanted, and smart she got. Would that woman inspire you with confidence, I asked myself. The answer was most definitely yes. I would prove to be a good side-kick after all, if I kept my mouth shut and didn't display my ignorance.

Sitting side by side in Mickey's BMW we were a handsome pair. We were complementary – she pale and fair in a skirt and jacket so dark green that it looked almost black, me even more dark and southern in my faded chic. We were heading out of the city on the A23. We hadn't spoken much after her meditation. I hadn't wanted to bring up the subject of the white circle and she appeared to prefer not to enter into meaningless conversations after her communion with herself or the universe. I ventured a question.

'Are we going far?'

'It's a cottage towards the village of Steyning' she replied, swinging suddenly off the main road to London. 'The directions were a bit complicated.' She took an almost immediate left turn. 'I hope this is the right way.' She pulled into the entrance to a field where I was entranced to see a flock of sheep with tiny lambs wagging their tails and leaping straight into the air, all four feet leaving the ground at once. I had never seen such a thing before, being a city girl.

'Look at these directions.' She passed me a piece of paper. Her writing was small and neat, not like mine. I realised I'd have to learn to write more legibly for this job. 'We've come this far, I think. She pointed to the appropriate line. 'Do you agree?'

'Seems fine' I reassured her.

'You direct me from now on.' She looked at her watch. 'We have fifteen minutes. I like to be dead on time.'

Dead on time is what we most certainly will be, I thought, or dead anyway, if she continues to drive at such speed on these narrow winding roads. It was a miracle that we met nothing coming in the opposite direction, not even a tractor. The directions were precise down to almost every tree, which I would have found confusing on my own since I couldn't tell one tree from another. "A small clump of elms" was no different from "a group of sycamores". When I said as much to Mickey her rather tart reply was that she'd better not send me into the country on my own. She took a sharp bend, almost running into a tall woman standing in the lane. Her sudden halt jerked me painfully against the seat belt. It was 6.30 precisely.

'Lady Loxley? So pleased to meet you.' She extended her hand which the other ignored.

'You nearly didn't, I was lucky not to be squashed flat. Do you always drive like that?'

'I don't like to be late. I've passed my advanced driving test so I'm always safe.'

I could hardly agree with this last statement, advanced driving test or not.

The woman grunted 'Come in. I don't have much time as I explained to you. I have to catch the train to London then the plane to Rome. Half an hour will have to do.'

Her voice was unpleasant, guttural, staccato, I understood why Mickey had taken against her. She was stiff, expensively dressed in a classic timeless way. Well combed, well manicured, a good deal older than either of us, going into a gaunt rather than comfortable middle age. Desiccated was the word that came to mind. And tense. Mind you, hardly surprising since she'd almost come to a very nasty end outside her own gate.

The house was ancient. A place with continuous history. Not all good, it couldn't have been, there had been nasty goings-on since the twelfth century when she claimed the foundation stones were laid for the original priory.

'It's gone a bit to rack and ruing since my mother died. I've been too busy to take charge, I can't afford to spend much time in England and my brother won't have anything to do with it. My mother disinherited him you see. I'll give him something from the sale, though he doesn't deserve it. It's the only inheritance he'll get. He certainly needs the money. Just feel free to wander. You know more about these things than I do I suppose' she added doubtfully staring at our youthful figures.

We didn't exactly wander, she was too agitated for us to do that. We made notes about the old fireplaces, the oak kitchen dressers, the low beams (worm eaten, an added bonus for some), the flagged floors, the surprising en-suite bathrooms to the five vast bedrooms, the enormous refectory turned into a living room big enough to give concerts in, and the locked door, the original smoke darkened door, leading, we were told, into the old lady's study.

'It's crammed with all kinds of things I haven't had the chance to sort out. When you have an interested customer then I will come with a friend to sift through. Perhaps you would arrange for the rest of the house to be cleared and the furniture sold? Some of it is worth a bit. There are plenty of antique dealers in Brighton aren't there?'

We had a trot around the grounds. They had by no means gone to "rack and ruin". They were on the contrary very well maintained. If Mickey's garden was big, then this was enormous. A lake, water lilies, statues.

'There's two acres of woodland and some paddocks. I'm afraid I really do have to go now. Here's my card with my phone and e-mail. I hope to hear from you very soon. It's worth a lot isn't it?'

'It certainly is. For that reason it may take a while to find a buyer. But we will, we certainly will. It wasn't your family home by the way?'

'Oh dear no. My mother bought it twenty years ago when my father died. From some friends. We hardly ever came here, my brother and I.'

'The gardener, whoever he is, will keep on working here? It will make a great deal of difference when clients visit.'

'Oh yes. I'm sure. That's not my responsibility. The gardens were used for gatherings. I expect that will continue. I'll give you the keys when we lock up, there's only one set. There are other gates through the wall which surrounds the land except the paddocks. People come and go,' she said vaguely.

'You realise that if "people come and go", we can't take responsibility for the property.' Mickey looked her straight in the eye.

'Of course. I'm not asking you to take responsibility, just to sell it,' she snapped.

'I'll need you to sign a declaration to that effect. As well as a contract with us. You should do it before handing over the keys.'

'I've told you, I haven't time for such things. Do you want to take this on or not?'

'Have you put it with other agents?'

'Of course not. I've told you. One set of keys.' She had closed the front door and we were walking towards the gate. 'My taxi is due. I'd be grateful if you would wait until he's left before you drive away.' She was pushing us into the road as we heard the engine of an approaching car.

'Why choose "*Her Place*" instead of a bigger agency with wider contacts?'

An old fashioned black cab stopped, reversed into the driveway before she finally slammed the gate shut, locked it and dangled the keys in front of Mickey's nose.

'I have reason to believe that your Aunt was an old friend of my mother. Are you going to take these or not?'

Mickey took them. Lady Loxley got in beside the driver and the black cab drove away. Instead of following him, Mickey followed the lane in the other direction, dawdling now, enjoying the landscape, until we came to an inviting pub where we had shepherd's pie washed down by a pint of beer. Mickey was thoughtful.

'I like that woman even less after meeting her. I'll get a whacking great commission on the sale though. I won't even bother to ask you what it's worth, you'll have no idea. How are you liking the job?'

'So far so good.' I finished my pint and bought us another.

# Chapter 3

Ellie came to stay with me for the weekend. It suited Mickey very well as she was busy and, in any case, would be spending Saturday night in Hastings at some kind of conference. She was surprisingly particular about guests in the house, asking for a character reference. She invited Ellie for a cup of tea as soon as she arrived, so she could conduct a sort of interview, which made me most uncomfortable. If she trusted me, surely she didn't think I would open her home to all and sundry during her absence. I was embarrassed for the sophisticated, cultured woman I still loved. Whatever test had been set, she obviously passed it with flying colours, since Mickey hugged her with great warmth, pronouncing that she could come and stay whenever she wanted. I didn't like this condescending, lady of the house attitude at all. Ellie was her normal calm self, more amused than angry. I was very glad to see her, I needed her advice. I said as much to her as we sat on the beach eating fish and chips.

'What do you think?' There was a soft breeze, the sea was flat calm, the palest, almost translucent blue.

'What do you think?' I repeated. Is it going to work for me?'

'My dear. I can't answer that.'

'Do you like her? Do you like Mickey?'

'Yes. Do you?'

'I don't know. I thought I did. She seems to have turned into a Miss Know-all and bossy with it.'

'Well, she does know her job, I hope, and you don't, so you have to listen and take orders.'

Ellie had a career, Ellie had bosses who had bosses, was a boss who gave orders herself. More than once she'd come home from the office furious with the way she had been treated. She had to put up with it to "get on". I didn't. There were lots of things I could do without having to learn much, jobs I could leave if I couldn't stand my employer's attitude.

'Let's put our feet in the water. It's too cold to swim, but I'm not coming down to the coast for the weekend without paddling on the sea'

Hand in hand we made our way across the pebbles, took our shoes off, joined hands again and wet our toes. It was low tide so there was even a strip of sand. The cold, clear waves lapped gently round our ankles. Behind us men with buckets and spades were digging for lugworms. Ellie's hand was warm, her fingers curved round mine with the gentlest of pressure. I had a moment of panic.

'Ellie, I want to come home with you. I don't want you to leave me. It's so good us being here together.'

She smiled. 'You poor baby! Of course you can come if you want to.'

Poor baby! Those words were enough to bring me to my senses. I let go of her hand and splashed back to find my shoes.

'O.K. I'll give it a try. See how it goes.' I was 29 years old for goodness sake.

We walked along the front as far as the Marina. It was getting dark as we returned towards the pier. Windows were alight in "luxury" apartments, chandeliers glinting in some. "For Sale" signs had sprouted from all the façades, many with "sold" splashed across, half of the rest proclaimed "under offer". So many different agents' names. I guessed Mickey had her boards prepared too, although I hadn't seen them.

'Hm! You're already taking a professional interest!'

I knew she was teasing. Maybe I was getting into the habit though. I switched my gaze to the left.

'Oh Ellie, just look at that moon.'

Full and clear it made a pathway of light across the black sea.

We leaned on the railings, transfixed. We could almost see the craters.

'You know we danced in the moonlight in Scotland.' She had a far-away look. 'Circle dances all night long.'

I didn't like the sound of it. I could still be jealous. This might be our last weekend together for some time. Not for ever, I wouldn't believe for ever.

'I have a better suggestion for tonight. An empty house, a balmy night. What are we hanging around for?'

\*\*\*\*

We were sitting on my little terrace sipping cold white wine, soft music playing, nothing that needed our attention. I was stroking the back of Ellie's neck, when a voice called up from below

'Hello! Are you all upstairs?'

I leaned over the balustrade, much put out. A young man looked up at me, more a boy really. I found the switch which operated the outside light. Suddenly illuminated he screwed up his eyes and covered them with his hands.

'I say don't do that! Mickey, I'm sorry I'm late. I thought you were going to be in the garden so I came in the back way and got a bit lost. Please turn the light off, Mickey.'

I obliged.

'Thanks. Shall I come up or are you coming down?'

'Neither.' I leaned out further. 'Mickey isn't here. I'm her tenant.'

There was a moment's silence.

'She's not here! But it's the full moon!' He didn't believe me.

'No she's not here. Please go away, whoever you are. She's in Hastings' I added to emphasise my point.

'In Hastings! Oh no! Of course, now I remember – can you switch the light on again so I can see my watch?'

'It's half past eleven' I informed him.

'Oh no! I'll never get to Hastings in time. Oh no!'

'I don't know what your problem is, nor am I interested. Will you please leave. You have interrupted a very important, private moment. And if you say "Oh no!" once more I'll drop a bottle on your head.'

'Why don't you ask him up for a drink' whispered Ellie. 'He seems very distressed.'

'No way!' I addressed the visitor once more. 'Haven't you gone yet?'

'I'm going, I'm going.' He reflected for a minute. 'Will you tell Mickey Ray was here and to let him know definitely about May 1st? E-mail me. I'll be in touch anyway, but if you tell her you actually saw me, that I was actually here, it will be better than me just saying I turned up, she might think I was pretending. Will you promise to tell her?'

Was he afraid of her? I began to feel sorry for him. Perhaps Ellie was right, I should ask him up for a drink, now I was quite sure he was harmless.

'I promise. Do you want to have a drink with us?'

'Oh no! I mean, no thank you' he corrected himself hastily in case I fulfilled my threat to drop a bottle on his head if he said "oh no" once more. 'No, no. I couldn't do that. Thank you. That's very kind. Thank you. Well, goodnight. I'm sorry to have bothered you.'

'I'll turn the light on for you,'

'Oh no! Thank you. The moonlight will do fine.'

It was true. There was no need for artificial light. He disappeared, presumably the way he had come, through the garden on the North side.

Needless to say, the romantic mood was broken, but not completely destroyed. The air was still mild and fragrant, the distant sea still glittered. The music was still playing, and Ellie still looked lovely. To cap it all, in the shrubbery a bird began to sing.

'A nightingale!' I said. Unfortunately, that brought back bittersweet memories.

'A blackbird' corrected Ellie. 'They sometimes sing at night too.'

A blackbird. A good old English blackbird, not a Mediterranean nightingale. So that was all right. I put my arm round Ellie's waist and led her to the bedroom.

We got up late the next day and took a bus along the coast. It was still brilliantly sunny, though slightly cooler with a fresh breeze from the English Channel, so we stopped off at the highest point of the line of chalk cliffs at the edge of the South Downs and walked, an activity I wasn't used to, up and down ridges pitted with rabbit holes. By the time we took the bus home my feet were sore, my calves aching, so I was somewhat irritable, whereas Ellie was exhilarated, her eyes shining.

'Thank you for a wonderful weekend' she said when I left her at the station. 'I hope this works out for you, my darling.

I'm going to be very busy for a while, I'm going away for the next few weekends, then I have a month's holiday in the Shetland Isles. I want you to keep my key, so if you feel like coming home, please do, even if I'm not there.'

It was sweet of her to pretend that I had a home in Clapham.

'I'd better be quick or I'll miss the train. I have a lot of paperwork to prepare for a presentation tomorrow. Love you, Dany.' She gave me a quick hug, then was off through the barrier on to the platform.

'Love you too!' I called after her.

I walked towards the promenade, against the streams of day-trippers with their red faces exposed too rashly to the sun and salt air, confident that the cool wind would stop them being burnt. Fractious children trailed their feet, hating the prospect of next day's school. The traffic was crawling, almost at a standstill. If hundreds of families had flocked here on the trains, hundreds more had brought their cars. As far as the eye could see a line of metal roofs stretched out towards a distant metropolis. All of it depressed me, the irrevocable parting, the frantic people, the noisy cars. My feet hurt more than ever. I looked for the nearest taxi rank.

\*\*\*\*

Mickey's BMW was in the drive, the kitchen light was on, so I decided to announce my presence, although I really wanted to go to bed to catch up on the sleep I'd lost the previous night. I guessed that Ellie might be nodding off over her papers. Would she be dreaming of my hands on her body, my lips on her breasts, our coming together as we used to before? Before Anita.

'Hey Dany! What have you been up to? Come and have a herb tea. I've just made an infusion. Smell!'

She held a steaming bowl under my nose. It was like wet hay.

'No thanks. Coffee?'

'Decaf?'

'If you don't have anything else. Before you say anything, I do know that caffeine is supposed to keep you awake, but I like the hit.'

She pursed her lips as she pulled out an espresso machine.

'It's your choice.'

It certainly was. She wasn't going to dictate what I drank, nor when I drank it. To be extra provocative, I asked 'Do you have any whisky? That's a very good nightcap, especially when combined with strong coffee.'

'No. I don't. I do have this, though'

She produced a bottle of virulent green liquid.

'It's distilled wild grasses with added plants. I can't tell you what, it's a secret. I'll have a glass too. I'm glad you mentioned it.'

I hadn't of course. Before I could refuse she'd poured two small measures and pushed one towards me.

'Sip it slowly, it's quite strong. I believe it's well matured. Miranda made it.'

Strong wasn't the word. It was like rocket juice.

'Are you sure this won't corrode our insides?' I could hardly speak. Maybe it had already done irreparable harm to my vocal chords.

'Perhaps we should add water,' she conceded. She brought two larger glasses, poured the firewater into them, topped them up with mineral water. The mixture immediately turned cloudy.

'Is this stuff absinthe?' The tipple that was the ruin of many a nineteenth century Frenchman. 'If so, I believe you have to burn a sugar lump over it or something.'

'I don't know. Miranda's still is through in the utility room. I haven't used it yet.'

An interesting woman, Miranda. Distilling illegal alcohol, maybe in the herb garden she also grew illegal substances.

'I'd like to see this still.'

'The utility room is too untidy at the moment. I have to sort things out in there. Later, maybe.'

I wondered what else might be stored in there. Everything one might need in a kitchen was here around us. A washing machine, dishwasher, enormous American-style fridge freezer, large eye-level oven.

Mickey pushed her glass away. 'Perhaps we'd better not drink this. It may not be what I think it is. The label is a bit illegible.' She frowned. 'I'll put it away until I've looked it up in the book.'

'The book?'

'Her book of recipes.'

She changed the subject.

'You didn't tell me how you've spent the last couple of days.'

Mind your own business, I thought. But then she was only being friendly, wasn't she?

'Ellie and I went out to the country. Yesterday we stayed around town, came back here, sat on my terrace. By the way, a young man was looking for you. About half-past eleven. I told him you were in Hastings.'

She stared.

'What did he want?'

'I don't know.' From the expression on her face I guessed he might have come for some of Miranda's illegal substances. Perhaps part of the fortune was from drug-dealing.

'He said his name was Ray. He'll e-mail you. He insisted I tell you I'd seen him. He was mixed up about something. Burbled on about the full moon. Said you must let him know about the first of May in case he makes another mistake.'

'He's a complete idiot.' She was very annoyed. 'I was wrong about him. I sometimes am. Miranda never was. I'd better tell him to drop it until he's older.'

'His response to that will probably be "Oh no!"'

I expected her to say more, she didn't. Instead she yawned.

'I'll be off to bed now. I was awake all last night. We leave here at 8 in the morning. I'll take the mini, it's easier

28

to park. And I've had "*Her Place*" painted on its side. I might have to drive customers around. Goodnight.'

# Chapter 4

The phone rang almost immediately we stepped through the door.

'I'll answer this then you can do the next.' She picked up the receiver. '*Her Place*, Michaela speaking how can I help you?'

An appointment was made for later in the day.

We were each working through the website, making separate decisions so that we could compare notes afterwards, when our first live buyer arrived. A man. A middle-aged man in an expensive suit. There was something about him immediately off-putting.

'Good-morning. How can we help you?'

He leered at her.

'I don't think you would appreciate the answer I would like to give to that question.'

She stiffened, so did I.

Seeing his bad beginning, he continued hastily. 'I'm sorry. I wasn't prepared to find such charming young ladies. I'm looking for a cosy apartment, even a small house in a discreet area. Very discreet.' He winked at me.

Who, or what does he think we are, I wondered. A provider of love-nests for the mistresses of wealthy businessmen?

It would seem that's exactly what he did think.

'"*Her Place*" must be the right agency for my needs. Something exclusive, luxurious. Money is no object.'

I hope she's worth it, I thought. But then, he had the kind of face that would need money to back it up if he wanted to catch a woman of style.

'We have two or three places on our books which may suit.' Mickey was cool, professional. I couldn't tell whether she wished him out of the door or considered him a good customer.

'If you'd like to come through to the back room, I'll show you the descriptions and we can discuss the matter.'

At the mention of a back room his eyes gleamed.

'Danielle, would you listen to all the messages and answer the ones which seem the most important?'

'Danielle, Michaela, pretty names.' He rolled them around his tongue appreciatively.

'What's your name, is that pretty too?' It just slipped out, I couldn't help it.

He hesitated. 'Jiminy Cricket. Mr. Cricket.'

He must be lying. What a ridiculous pseudonym. I couldn't meet Mickey's eye.

'Please come through, Mr. Cricket, and I'll show you what I have. No double entendre intended.'

She ushered him into the second office and shut the door. She'd thought of everything. Most offices had several assistants talking at once with little or no privacy. I couldn't even see them through the heavily frosted glass, let alone hear them. Obediently I turned on the answer phone. There were so many messages the tape was full. Most left a number to ring back, nothing more. There were four extensive ones, all selling. Women's voices. I rang back. The only person at home lived just round the corner, on the front. I told her one of us would come round at two o'clock that afternoon. Mickey might trust me to do that on my own. She had already spent nearly half an hour with Jiminy Cricket. Was that gong to be the norm or was it because he was our first customer? Heaven forbid that the back room might serve other purposes. There was an awful lot I didn't know about Mickey.

I was saved from further speculation by the appearance of a pale, thin, shabby looking girl.

'Hello, I'm Danielle. How can I help you?'

'I'm looking for a room.'

'To rent or buy?'

'To rent, to rent.' She seemed completely shocked by the word "buy". She was twisting her hands anxiously. 'Immediately if possible.'

'We don't have much to rent at the moment, I'm afraid.' I guessed she couldn't afford much.

'Just a room, anywhere.'

'A room would be difficult. A studio?'

'Isn't that a room?'

'Well, yes. With a kitchen, usually a shower room attached.' A bed-sit we used to call it. An L-shaped room where the occupant spent many lonely hours cut off from her neighbours.

'The cheapest you have.'

Of course, I wouldn't have imagined anything else.

Mickey emerged at last with a somewhat chastened-looking Jiminy.

'Danielle, I'm taking Mr. Cricket to look at some properties. I'll be back soon. She gave the newcomer a brilliant smile. 'Hello. I'm Michaela. Danielle will look after you.'

Danielle is already looking after her, I thought with some annoyance.

'Perhaps we could go in your car, Mr. Cricket, since you've managed to park it right outside. If you left it any longer you would certainly get a fine.' She breezed out.

Mr. Cricket's expensively tailored suit was not lost on the girl. 'You probably don't have anything in my price range.'

'Let's see. Make yourself comfortable.' I clicked on to studios. 'Do you have a job?' Most of these newly furbished little gems would have required a good salary every month.

'I've just left one. I'm looking for another. Is it any of your business?'

'I'm afraid it is.' I sympathised with her defensiveness. In fact, I sympathised with her altogether. It could easily have been me the other side of the desk. 'You'll need to pay a month's rent in advance plus a returnable sum in case of damage.' She must be familiar with this procedure. 'You'll need references.'

'I'll get them.'

'You'll need them before you move in. The owners must have guarantees.'

'I'll bring them this afternoon.'

'And the money?'

'I'll find it.'

'For this afternoon? Don't forget we have to clear a cheque.'

'Tomorrow. What is there in your list?'

Nothing, I thought grimly. I thought I had exhausted the possibilities when I came to a bottom line which read *"Details of room to let in large house for right person in left hand bottom drawer of desk"*.

'Just a moment.' I opened the appropriate drawer. It contained a large envelope, which I removed. Inside was a coloured picture of a beautiful room, with an accompanying typewritten sheet. 'Excuse me while I read this through.' I would have passed her the photo immediately, if I hadn't been afraid of raising false hopes. The writing was as follows: *"Room vacant in shared house. Women only. MUST be right person. Rent negotiable. No deposit necessary. Non-smoker, vegetarian, tolerant sociable young woman needed to share in renovating garden and home and subsequently maintaining them. Any religion, any race provided that she will accept all other beliefs. Ability to cook an advantage, clean driving licence desirable. Essential to love animals and children."* It sounded more like a job advert. I passed it over.

'Does this sound like you?'

She shrugged. 'It could. Yeah, a lot of it. I'm willing to give up meat, I couldn't care less what other people get up to. Animals and children I can take or leave. I like cooking, I can't drive.'

I leaned back. 'How old are you?'

'Eighteen.'

'What's happened to you? Why are you so desperate?'

'It doesn't say on this paper that you have to interview me.' Her tone was hostile.

'No. Shall I ring to make you an appointment?'

She nodded.

What's your name by the way?'

'Tracey.'

The call was answered by Giulietta. Her English was not good. I tried Italian. We got on much better. Yes, it would be O.K. for Tracey to go round straight away. They were eight women, five children, three dogs and two cats. Not everyone was at home, but it didn't matter.

'It's out at Preston Park.' I wrote down the address. 'It will take you about half an hour to walk from here. A little more. I'll keep the details in case you don't like it or they don't like you.

'I'll like it. I'll make sure they like me.'

'You know how to find your way?'

'No problem.'

'Can I have a contact address for you?'

'You've got it right there.' She indicated the sheet in my hand.

'That's not.....' She had left before I could finish. She almost collided with Mickey in the doorway.

'Jiminy's made an offer. I'm about to ring the vendor.'

'What a slimeball!'

'He's all right really. Heart of gold underneath it all.'

'Are we going to get a lot of men like him, who want to set up their bit of fluff in a cute pad?'

'She's his mistress not "his bit of fluff".' He's head over heels besotted with her. She's a young Albanian. Quite a history, brought to England under false pretences, forced into prostitution, escaped, employed as a sort of au pair by friends of his. He's going to give her an allowance and send her to a language school.'

'In return for what?'

'What do you expect? Love, devotion and exciting sex'.

'He's married of course.'

'Twenty-five years. Four children. Loves his wife, couldn't leave her.'

'You certainly learnt a lot.'

'He talks non-stop. Can't wait to get her down here.'

'And then make more and more "business trips" to this city of sin.'

'You sound very disapproving. We have to be completely objective, you know.'

'Sell anything to anybody for the right price?'

'What do you think business is about? Anyhow, I told you, he has a heart of gold.'

And a bank balance to match, I thought.

'What's his real name?'

'Whose?'

'Jiminy Cricket.'

'That's the name we'll be using.' Her tone was final. For the rest of the morning I answered the phone whilst Mickey checked e-mails, and updated the website. At one o'clock she sent me round to the local deli for sandwiches, declaring that we should both be around at lunchtime when working women might be likely to pop in. It felt like a moment's liberation, so I took as long as I could to get there. It was obviously a popular place – the queue stretched almost into the street. Mickey had been precise with her order, an avocado and salad ciabatta, which I subsequently learned was what she had every day. Me, I liked a change. I studied the menu board as I neared the counter.

'What would you like today?'

The voice sounded vaguely familiar. The young man in the white overall waiting for my request was surely the same who had stood beneath my terrace. Although I hadn't seen details of his face, the shape, the demeanour was the same. I asked cautiously 'Do you have Roquefort and watercress on rye bread?'

'Oh no!' was the immediate spontaneous answer.

'Ray?'

He was puzzled. 'Do I know you?'

'Not really. We've sort of met.' The queue was building up again, so I told him what I really wanted, no more games.

'I gave Michaela your message,' I assured him as I took my packages.

'Ah! Yes!' He looked over his shoulder furtively. 'Thanks.'

'You know that boy who came looking for you works in the deli?' We were sipping the coffee she had made in my absence.

'Yes.'

'Why don't you just talk to each other instead of bothering with e-mails and stuff?'

'There are things you just don't talk about in public.'

'Like what?'

She didn't answer. I assumed it was because her mouth was full of ciabatta, so when she had finished chewing I asked again, 'What don't you talk about in public?'

'One day I'll tell you, not yet.'

My suspicions about drug dealing returned. This Albanian of Jiminy Cricket's must have been forced into dependency on heroin, could it be that Mickey had agreed to supply her? There was no point in asking, she would be bound to lie. I had to admit that Mickey herself didn't look like an addict. She was positively blooming with health. Ray too had a kind of dewy freshness.

'It's quarter to two. You should make a move if you're doing the visit you talked about.'

Surprise, surprise, she had agreed to send me round to the woman on the sea front.

'Take measurements of the rooms. Make a note of fixtures and fittings. Find out if she has a share of the free-hold. Is there access to any private garden at the back? How much does she pay for maintenance per year? Actually I have typed a list to remind you.'

'I don't need that!' I was offended.

'Take it anyway. You never know. Here's your notebook. How good are you at taking photos?'

She dangled a camera in front of me.

'I'd have to have a lesson with that, I haven't worked with one quite like it.'

I wasn't going to admit I'd never had a camera, never been interested in photography.

'O.K. maybe another appointment. If she's keen to sell we want to get the publicity ready.'

# Chapter 5

The apartment I was to see was the ground floor of an immense house. I rang one of eight doorbells. There being only four floors and the separate basement, I guessed there were two apartments on each floor, which turned out to be true, one at the back, one at the front. My lady lived at the back. She had large windows from her sitting room opening onto an enclosed communal garden. She was old, very old, I thought. Very wrinkled skin, a neck like a tortoise, hardly any solid flesh anywhere, all folds and pouches hanging from a frail skeleton. Her voice hadn't prepared me for that. Didn't very old people have this wavering voice, their diction impaired by a lack of teeth? When this lady spoke it was energetically and she had plenty of teeth, real or false. She had taken precautions when she let me in; as well as cross-examining me through the interphone system, she peered at me through the spy hole in her front door as I waited in the hallway. She seemed to have an intricate system of locks and bolts.

'You look honest, she declared. 'Show me your credentials.'

I wasn't certain what my credentials were, but a flash of the notebook with "*Her Place*" on the cover and at the top of my paper, satisfied her.

'We have burglars in here regularly. All kind of dubious callers. You could get murdered for a few pounds. It's mainly drugs they need it for, you know. Would you like a glass of sherry? What's your name did you say? Daniella?'

'Danielle. No thank you. Have you ever been robbed, Lady Bestwood?' When she gave me her name that morning, I had wondered whether we were going to have rather a high percentage of titled clients.

'No. I take care. I could protect myself, anyway, with this.' She delved behind a sofa to bring out a sword.

'It was my husband's dress sword. He was in the military. I could do some damage with it.'

She pointed it at my heart.

'Indeed. Should we perhaps talk about the sale?'

'If you like.' She put the sword down. 'I've lived here for years. It's very pleasant. We have parties in the garden all summer. The first is on Mayday. We have a Maypole and dance. Jim and Ernest who live over there opposite me' she gestured across the neat lawn, 'work in the theatre. Ernest designs and Jim makes props, so they organise it.' We've got a good crew, get on well together. Isabelle two doors down from me used to be a cook, prepared meals for the crowned heads of Europe, she likes to keep her hand in and gives us a slap-up feast. It's a bit simpler these days because she is eighty-five after all. We all contribute money, except me. I'm always guest of honour. I'm very old, you see.'

I did.

'They pulled out all the stops for my hundredth.' She sighed nostalgically. 'I'll be sad to leave them. I think I have to be looked after now, though. I can't do the things I used to. I have a girl come in to clean, Social Services keep an eye on me, but I have decided the moment has come to go and live with my daughter in Spain. I'm not keen on her present husband, he's her fourth, you know, but he may not last long.'

'He's ill?' I asked sympathetically.

'Good gracious, no. None of them has lasted long. She gets rid of them pretty quickly.'

The finality of her tone suggested poison rather than divorce.

'I'll miss my great grandson. He's a poppet. Sees me right. Comes in every day after work. Brings me little titbits. He lives upstairs. I don't want to rely on him, he's too young. Just twenty. He has his own life to lead. To tell you the truth,' she dropped her voice as if someone might be listening 'he's the one who's dependent on me. His parents are no good, his mother, my granddaughter had him when she was 40, he was a surprise, a terrible shock. His father disappeared, and my daughter, who was going through a particularly nasty divorce, wanted nothing to do with it. Poor Raymond! No wonder he's still wet behind the ears!'

All this sounded uncannily familiar.

'Where does Raymond work?'

'The little delicatessen. It's very convenient but I don't know how long he'll stick it. He's always being kicked out of jobs, doing something wrong. Sir Henry and I sent him to a good school, well, not one of the best you know, we couldn't afford that, but an adequate boarding school. Several actually, he kept being expelled. Not his fault. Easily led by others, bright enough to stay out of trouble. In the end he managed to scrape a few qualifications together, not enough to be any use. I worry what will happen when I'm gone, can't be long now, so that's why I want to wean him off. I have to say, my husband couldn't stand him. Couldn't stand the girls either if it came to that, neither my daughter nor my granddaughter. He had hopes for Raymond as the first boy in the family but they were soon dashed. Said he could see he was going to be a cissy even when he was a few months old.'

A cissy? I was intrigued. What did that mean? Was his grandfather convinced he was going to be gay from that early age?

'A crybaby. No spunk. Frightened of shadows. I kept saying he was sensitive. What good would that do him, my husband said. Dear old Henry, didn't have a sensitive bone in his body.'

I was suddenly aware how much time I'd spent with this fascinating woman.

'Excuse me, I'll just take the measurements of your rooms. My colleague will be back to take photos.'

'I'll look forward to that. Is she as handsome as you?' Her eyes twinkled. I had the impression that in spite of her age, she saw everything.

'She's a very attractive woman,' was my response to this unexpected compliment. I busied myself over room sizes and original fixtures and fittings, then ran through Mickey's list of questions, including the last which was her price.

'Oh, I've no idea. That's up to you. I don't really care. I don't need much money. I have enough already to keep me to the end of my days, even if I pay my daughter a handsome rent for looking after me. I don't want to leave her anything, she's had enough from us already, one way or another. She got plenty from all those husbands. She'd only spend it on booze and cigarettes. Smokes like a chimney. Probably she'll die before I do, she's eighty this year. I'll be the one looking after her not her after me. She has servants, though, cooks and cleaners and all that. I didn't want to leave money to my granddaughter either. She's made her bed she can lie on it. She made several beds. It'll go to Raymond. I'll put it in trust. He's not responsible enough to handle it yet. I already bought him that little studio upstairs. Very cheap. Worth a lot now, I suppose.'

I closed my notebook.

'Thank you very much, Lady Bestwood. Michaela will give you a call.'

'My name is Davina. I sincerely hope it won't be the last time I see you young lady.' She took my hand. 'You remind me of someone I was very close to years ago. One of Sir Henry's subordinates. We were very intimate for a couple of years. I was a good looker when I was young and she was a Greek god.' There were tears in her eyes. 'And I mean god not goddess.' She blinked rapidly. 'She was killed in the war.'

'I'm sorry. I must go.' I withdrew my hand gently.

Mickey was fuming. Her afternoon had been dreadful. She'd been plagued by time-wasters. Three of the people with whom I had left messages had rung back requesting visits as soon as possible. I ought to have been there, a maximum of half an hour was enough for what I had to do. Half an hour away, it was most unprofessional to spend so much time over a simple job. I listened to the tirade in silence, then said quietly

'I'm sorry Mickey, I told you I'd be no good at this. I'm more interested in people than money. I'm giving you my notice. I'll pay you back the advance salary as soon as I can and I'll look for somewhere to rent. I don't think you have anything cheap enough for me on your list.'

She looked at me open-mouthed, then burst into tears.

'Oh Dany, I'm so sorry. That was awful. I can be a terrible bitch. I'm a bit overwrought at the moment, it's not your fault. Too much stress. Don't leave. It's only the first day. Give me a chance.'

You didn't give me much chance, I thought. You didn't make allowances for my inexperience. Stress or no stress, I will not be treated in that way.

I said 'It's not going to work between us.'

'Yes, it will, I promise. I'm working at controlling my temper. I won't shout at you any more.'

In spite of my deep misgivings, her distress was getting through to me. 'Please Dany, I need you. I don't know what I'll do if you quit.'

Now I'm a pushover for women who need me. It's a serious flaw in my character, but that's the way it is. Usually it's been lovers who have ensnared me in that way. I couldn't make out what Mickey's particular need was. It wasn't physical, it wasn't emotional and it most certainly wasn't financial, so what was it?

I'll make us a cup of tea and you can tell me about your afternoon.'

She hoped her appealing smile was irresistible.

Whilst we were drinking our tea, I described Lady

Bestwood's apartment emphasising its grand proportions, the fact that it was at the back of the house, therefore quiet, and that it opened on to communal gardens where a friendly group of residents got together to have fun. I kept the account of her family to myself, including Ray.

'Sounds pretty good. What price did she say she wanted?'

'She didn't.'

'She'll probably be pleased at what I tell her.'

I don't think she'll care a damn I thought.

****

When we'd closed up shop we visited two of three women with whom Mickey had made appointments.

'I don't want to make a habit of evening calls.' We were in the mini speeding towards a council estate on the eastern edge of the city. 'It's only because I couldn't leave the office earlier.' There was still the faintest hint of reproach. We drove down from the racecourse with its panoramic view of the coast and entered a complicated system of small roads. Some of the houses were very pretty, others were partly obscured by the rubbish piled in the front garden – broken-down furniture, rusty car parts and such like. We drew up at a sort of urban cottage, a porch, roses in bud round the door, a bed of bright tulips, in stark contrast with the neighbours on either side, whose grasses were growing luxuriously round old toys and rusty, discarded kitchen apparatus.

Mickey had brought her camera. She skilfully positioned it to avoid anything except the romantic façade, golden in the evening sun.

'So far so good for the front.' She announced. 'Who knows what we'll find at the back?' We scrunched up a little path of pebbles, separated from the flower bed by rows of neat wooden pegs. There was no bell, only a brass knocker in the shape of a horseshoe. Mickey rapped firmly.

The woman was probably in her late forties. She and I instantly recognised each other as two of a kind, even in my business outfit. She was wearing faded jeans and an equally faded denim shirt. She was tall, thin with short curly hair ever so slightly greying, at the temples. Perhaps she would become a friend.

'Hello Miss Browning. I'm Michaela and this is Danielle.'

'Roz. I told you my name was Roz Browning. Hello, Michaela, hello Danielle.'

'Dany. Hello Roz.' Her handshake was firm, her smile warm. The inside of this bijou residence didn't match Roz. There was a lot of pink, a collection of porcelain dogs, antique furniture and few books.

'You have a pretty house, why do you want to sell?' Important to ascertain the drawbacks before we went any further. I guessed the fly in the ointment might be the neighbours.

'It's not my house. It's nobody's house at the moment. It was Patrick's. I'm acting as his executor. I was his solicitor. He wants the money to go to cancer research.'

I'm so sorry' Mickey murmured. 'Was he in a hospice?' I don't know why she asked that, something to say, I suppose, to get over a difficult moment.

'He didn't die of cancer. He was beaten up when he was walking home from a club. Whoever it was did it, and they haven't yet found out, though they think it was probably a gang from London looking for trouble, left him lying in the bushes. He died on the way to hospital the next day. He was a good man, a very dear friend.'

'And a brilliant gardener.' I wanted to give this dismal conversation a positive turn.

'Yes he was. He was also very popular with the folks round here, would you believe. He was cheerful, helpful, so nobody cared a damn that he was gay. Denis next door has been weeding and trimming since Patrick died some weeks ago, Denis who won't lift a finger to care for his own land. He told me it was out of respect for Patrick.'

There was a long silence before Mickey suggested I take some measurements whilst she took photos.

'I have the details, everything you will need, including the furniture which is also for sale. Shall we look round?'

The whole house was as pristine as the living room. Someone, possibly Roz, had been dusting and polishing recently. The cream painted kitchen with blue and white tiles opened on to a back garden as charming as the front. There was a minute patio with just room for a table and chair. It wouldn't be difficult for Mickey to make it all look most desirable. However.....

'That's right, I'm aware of the problem.' Roz was slightly amused. I've worked in this city for many years. Yes, only a few properties are privately owned. Patrick lived here with his parents who took the opportunity to buy when it was offered. He stayed on when they died. Parts of the estate are pretty rough. It's getting better. A good invest-ment, I would say, Michaela. You wait, in a couple of years, you'll be able to describe it as a garden suburb, with prices to match. There'll be creeping gentrification everywhere. Here's my card.'

She gave it to me, ignoring Mickey's outstretched hand. To her she gave a large envelope.

'The particulars. All you could wish for and more. A suggested price. An executor's sale, always a bargain for the buyer, isn't it? Don't hesitate to contact me if you have any questions.'

Mickey preceded me to the car. I lingered deliberately.

'Good to meet you.'

'Good to meet you too, Dany. You have my card. Give me a call. Maybe we could have a drink sometime.'

Oh yes, maybe we could.

'She was a bit smooth, I thought.' Mickey had been fidg-eting during Roz's last speech.

'She was simply doing her job. Please slow down, Mickey.'

'We're going to be late if I do.'

On the contrary, she went faster. There was a flash.

'Oh damn, damn, damn. I'd forgotten the speed cameras along this road.'

We were heading towards another estate to the North of the city this time, even bigger and more confusing than the first. We pulled up beside a green oval beyond which rows of red brick buildings spread like ripples up towards the slopes of the downs. Mickey pulled out a map.

'We're here.' She pointed to a cross. 'This is where we have to go.' She stabbed another cross on one of the outer circles. 'You tell me which way.'

Easier said than done. We ended up in more than one dead end where parked vehicles made it difficult to turn. Children came out to watch Mickey's manoeuvres, dogs got in the way, barking furiously, and she nearly ran over a cat. We were late after all, which didn't improve Mickey's mood. She was admirably restrained though, only snapping at me once.

The house was unremarkable in every way.

'I'll see what I can do. Perhaps we can come back at a more convenient time. You have had it with other agents, haven't you?'

They were discomfited. 'Well, yes' he said.

'Thank you for contacting us. I'll be in touch.' We shook their hands. At the front gate I turned and waved to the kids watching us from behind their net curtains.

'Let's have a drink,' suggested Mickey. 'There's a great pub a bit further on near the university. Excellent beers.'

'Weren't you a bit rough with them?' I asked, as we savoured the local ale. She was right, it was very tasty, if you like that kind of thing.

'Not at all. I'd seen it advertised weeks ago. You see, Dany, it has no "wow" factor.'

'What do you mean?'

'When you walk into a place and say "wow!" It can be anything. Patrick's had a wow factor, lots of originality. There has to be something you fall in love with.'

'Can you imagine anyone falling in love with that ordinary semi?'

'The kids are cute.'

'We're not selling the kids. Come on, let's go and eat.'

She was very careful with me for the rest of the evening. Since we didn't seem to have a lot to say to each other she suggested going to the cinema at the other end of town, to see a new film in German, a language we both understood. Our first day thus ended harmoniously.

I stayed up late reading. I was restless, missing Ellie, chewing over the events of the day. I had to restrain myself from phoning Ellie at half-past midnight to say I loved her. When I did finally sleep I had a dream in which Lady Bestwood discovered the "wow factor" when she met Roz, and the two of them set up home in the ordinary semi, which had a swimming pool in acres of ground. The scene changed to a mansion on the edge of a park. Tracey, who was running round in the sitting room playing with a dog so tiny it looked like a mouse, stepped on the animal, changed into Raymond and shrieked "Oh no!"

I remember no more.

# Chapter 6

'I'm going to have another look at Lady Loxley's estate,' announced Mickey the next morning. 'I'll drop you off at the office. I need some more information. Make sure you don't let anyone go without their name, address and phone number.'

'Yes, ma'am!' I almost saluted.

This time it was more enjoyable. A crowd of university students arrived. They weren't so much younger than I was, but they were more like high spirited children.

'We'd like a big apartment, all five of us together, with a view over towards France, because Sandrine, this is Sandrine, is French and she gets a bit homesick. It would be good if we could have a room each, it would be easier when we have our boyfriends to stay' said one.

'Not that we all have boyfriends' objected another.

'Not yet' replied the first. 'Some of us are more choosy than others'

'And some of us are not looking for boyfriends.' The girl who spoke was a tough looking little butch. She looked me up and down appraisingly.

'Et moi, je voudrai simplement un peu de calme' was Sandrine's contribution.

The fifth hadn't yet spoken. She appeared withdrawn.

'Have you any particular requirements?' I asked her.

She shook her head. The little butch put her arm around her.

'She's going through a bad time. We're looking after her. She'll be happy wherever we end up as long as we're together.'

The others nodded. It would be nice to have friends like that to support you when you're down, I thought. I'd never wanted to belong to a group though, not since childhood when I was the leader of a gang in London.

'Let's see what we've got.'

There were several houses due to become vacant at the end of August when the present tenants left, after the expiration of a six month lease.

'Isn't it a bit early to be looking for something for September?' I asked.

'We want to have first choice. It's the beginning of the summer term already, we can't leave it or we'll all be scattered.'

'Well, I only have houses for that number, none with a view. Look!'

They gathered round the computer. I was sure Mickey wouldn't have wanted them to do that. 'I'll print out any you're interested in.'

Their comments, their giggles, their happiness in being together was enviable, even for a loner like me. Baby Butch stood behind me, her hand on my shoulder, one finger on the nape of my neck. An experienced touch, which sent a shiver down my spine. They were disappointed – a terraced house in a back street was not what they had planned.

Suddenly there was a simultaneous intake of breath, even from the girl going through a bad time.

'Wow'

Ah yes, the "wow" factor!

A mellow country house five miles from the University. Five bedrooms, a garden, an owner more than happy to let to students. In fact the present tenants were from the Art college.

'And there's a dishwasher, and a television with a satellite dish. It's just fantastic.'

'It's not on a bus route,' I pointed out.

'That's O.K.' It was the same young woman doing most of the talking. 'Sandrine is bringing her car over next year. I'm getting Dad's old one, well, it's not that old, it'll keep going for a few years, and Robbie has her motorbike.'

No need to ask who Robbie was.

'Can we have it? Please, we've got to. It's got our name on it.'

'I'll have to contact the owners. They're working abroad. I'll need references for all of you.'

'No problem.'

'Don't you want to see it first?'

They all shook their heads.

'It's not what you said you wanted.'

'It's perfect' they chorused.

'What's your name?' I asked the spokesperson.

'Des.'

Since my fingers were still on the keyboard and I was obviously expecting her to continue, she continued reluctantly 'Des O'Flynn.'

'Address? Is Des your full name by the way?'

She looked round at the others, who were all looking at her, then back at me.

'Do I have to give you my full proper name?'

'Yes,' I lied, remembering Jiminy Cricket.

'O.K. It's Desdemona Portia O'Flynn, York House, University of Sussex.'

Judging by the amazed expression on her friends faces this was news to them.

'My parents are mad about Shakespeare. They liked the name Desdemona then decided they'd better join it to a happier one. Nobody ever calls me anything but Des.' She glared defiantly at Robbie, who was trying hard not to laugh.

In order to avoid any other unwanted revelation, I passed round a paper so that each could write her name. I took the opportunity to chat to Sandrine in her own language. I'd missed speaking French.

Des handed me the paper back.

'You'll ring the landlady immediately, won't you?'

'Sometime today. Bring me those references.'

They all left together as they had arrived, except for Robbie who said she had some shopping to do, so she'd see them later. Predictable.

'You never told me your name,' she said, sitting in the chair facing my desk.

'You didn't give me a chance. I'm Dany.'

'Pleased to meet you, Dany.' Her handshake was firm, lingering.

'Nice little business you have here.'

'It's not mine. I'm only the assistant. It belongs to Michaela, who isn't one of us, in case you were wondering.'

'Why don't you come up to the campus, some time?'

'Why should I?'

'We're an interesting group.'

'Robbie, I'm 29 years old. I have other things to do with my time.' Not strictly true. I had been wondering what I was, in fact, going to do when I was off duty. There was no shortage of clubs, for almost the first time in my life I had plenty of money, so I could go out on the town almost every night if I wanted, which I didn't. My libido had been at a low level since last summer.

'For goodness sake!' I'm 22, so what? There's a great band playing a gig the day after tomorrow. Why don't you come out? I'll be there.'

'If this is a proposition, I'm not interested.' I'd been more attracted by the lawyer the day before. As a friend, you understand. The older woman, a substitute for Ellie?

'Don't worry, you're not my type' was her dry comment. 'Can't you just think in terms of having fun?'

I wasn't sure what was meant by "having fun". I was pondering this when Mickey walked in. Something about the attitude of the pair of us must have indicated wasting time, because she asked immediately 'I'm Michaela, can I help you?'

Robbie returned her gaze coolly. 'Thank you, I'm just leaving. Dany has given me all the information I need.'

'Was she genuine or just wanting to know who we were?' Through the window she observed Robbie's swaggering departure.

'She came in with her friends.' I pushed the list of the names towards her. 'They want to rent Honeysuckle Place.'

'Desdemona Portia O'Flynn, I don't believe it!'

'They'll all bring references. Should I ring the owners?'

'E-mail them. You'd better tell them all these kids are students. I don't expect they'll mind as they let to students already.

I asked, 'Had a good morning?'

'Very interesting. Look, I have to contact people about a meeting on May Eve. Change of venue, so I'll be busy in my office, not to be disturbed. You can take care of all calls and make appointments, O.K?'

'Don't forget Ray.'

'What?'

'Ray was most insistent that you let him know about 1st May. I'll tell him personally, if you like, I guess it's time I fetched us some sandwiches.'

'Absolutely not! I mean, yes for the sandwiches, no for the message. I'll e-mail him, don't worry. Please be quick.'

'I don't get a proper lunch break, then?'

'Not today if you don't mind. You can have the afternoon

off tomorrow instead. You don't mind too much do you? I haven't much time, it's May Eve the day after tomorrow. I'll be out all night then, by the way.'

Ray wasn't behind the counter. Perhaps it was his day off, or perhaps he had lost yet another job. If I had the afternoon free the next day, I might call round at his great-grandmother's for tea. I really didn't want to go back indoors. At the end of each side street I passed, the sea beckoned. Sailing boats drifted past on their way to nowhere in particular. Some day soon the weather was bound to change, bringing rain and cold. I wanted a week, not an afternoon, to take advantage of this un-English spring.

Mickey ate her ciabatta in the back room, I ate my baguette near the open door, flicking through a programme of local events I had picked up at the deli. There was going to be a festival, starting the following weekend, lasting most of the month. Concerts, plays, films, events, here, there and everywhere. Artists opening up their homes to sell their products, dozens of them, all in separate leaflets with maps of where to go.

Maybe we had only just sunk into the public's consciousness, because things began to take off that afternoon. Between two and five thirty the phones never stopped ringing. I answered calls as briefly as I could making appointments, taking details. As soon as I put the receiver down I had to pick it up again. Mickey's line was switched to answer phone, messages which would have to wait until the following day. Officially we closed at half past five, but since Mickey showed no sign of emerging from behind her frosted glass door by six o'clock, I checked the e-mails, then rang the owners of Honeysuckle Place, contrary to the boss's orders. A man with a seductive Irish voice told me he and his wife would be delighted to have the five girls as tenants, particularly Desdemona Portia O'Flynn. They were in no hurry for references, the present incumbents, who were in their final year, wanted to stay until the very last minute, enjoying a well-earned rest.

By six-thirty I was bored and tired. Ellie would probably be home from work by now. I might just try her. My hand had just reached out for the telephone when Mickey bounced back in, her mood exuberant.

'I think that's all sorted' she declared. 'Let's go home. I've plenty to do there.' Then, as an afterthought, 'Unless of course you have plans to stay in town.'

Plans? I had no plans whatsoever. I didn't want to admit it, though.

'As a matter of fact I have. I'll probably be back late.'

'Fine. You don't have to tell me when you'll be home. I'm not your mother. You have your own key, your own apartment, you can come and go as you please.'

'With whoever I please?'

She frowned. 'That's another matter. I have to be careful about who comes and goes. Some time you'll understand why.'

Oh, I do understand already, I thought. Trading in narcotics is a dangerous business.

We left together, she in one direction, me in the opposite. I had no idea where I was going. When in doubt, go to the beach I decided.

Bar tables spilled out on to the shingle. There were crowds of young people having a good time, relaxing with friends. They all had friends, lots of friends, it would seem, moving round from group to group, laughing, teasing, almost as if everyone knew everyone else. Or maybe that was just the way it seemed because I, myself, knew no-one and was intensely lonely. I didn't want to sit amongst them, a solitary figure inspiring pity, like the sad drinkers I had seen in every pub I'd worked in, unnoticed or ignored except by those who saw them as prey to be exploited. I felt uncomfortable in my smart clothes, which shouted "sharp business person" before I even opened my mouth. Keep on walking Dany, I told myself. Keep on walking until you have worked up enough appetite to demolish some food. So I walked, wishing I was wearing my trainers, instead of the smart leather shoes which began to rub my heels. If I didn't stop soon I'd have dreadful blisters, I realised. However, with a grim determination I continued. I passed more bars, with more happy people. I started to limp. Self-punishment had gone on long enough. I turned up into a quiet road where there was an equally quiet looking pub. I flopped into a comfortable armchair next to the door, unable for the moment to take the extra few steps to the bar. I leaned back, closed my eyes.

'May I bring you a drink? You look completely done in.'

Annoyed at the intrusion, I glared up at him. He was smiling encouragingly. He was in his forties, I guessed, Southern looking, Mediterranean, Greek maybe, black hair, black eyes, tanned, good looking, clothed in good denims. I liked his face at once. You know how you take to some people on sight, you feel you actually know them although you've never seen them before in your life? This life some would say, in another you could have been intimate. Not that I believed that, then or now, I simply felt at home with this man.

'That's very kind. A pint of beer would sort me out.'

I was pleased that when he brought my glass over he didn't immediately bring his own. No assumptions. A simple act of kindness. We were the only two customers. He had been reading a newspaper, the barperson, a mere boy, studying some kind of textbook.

'Would you care to join me?' I wasn't usually so formal, it must have been my suit speaking.

'I'd be delighted.' He left the paper on the bar. 'I'm Craigie Richardson.'

'Danielle Divito. Dany.'

'You were limping badly, Dany. Have you hurt your foot?'

'It's only my shoes.'

'Could I have a look?'

Was this nice man going to turn out to be a foot fetishist?

'It's alright.' I tucked my feet under the table.

'Let me have a look. Trust me, I'm a doctor.'

What could I do but obey? The backs of both my heels were red-raw. The barperson was despatched to find anti-septic and sticking plaster for the dressing. Dr. Richardson had most gentle hands as well as a charming bedside manner.

'Where were you walking to? I repeat "were", because you shouldn't walk any further tonight.'

'Nowhere in particular.' I was still marvelling how extra-ordinary it was that I should hobble into a place where there was a doctor waiting. 'I was just walking, you know, an evening stroll.'

'You should have stopped strolling a long way back.' A kindly reproof, which invited further revelations.

'I didn't quite know what else to do with myself' I confided. 'Tonight' I added, 'I was at a loose end tonight.' In case he thought this aimless wandering was a regular occurrence.

'Have you had supper?'

I was about to say yes, when he answered for me 'Of course you haven't. Would you like to eat with us?'

I didn't refuse quickly enough. He whipped out a mobile phone. Whilst dialling he asked 'Do you like Indian food?'

I nodded.

'Hello, I'm on my way. Would you order some chicken Korma.' He looked questioningly at me. I nodded again. 'Some chicken Korma as well as the usual. I'm bringing an extra guest. Nobody you know. See you later. You too. Ciao.' He put the phone away. 'Take your time finishing your drink. We only live in the next street. I don't have the car with me, but I think you'll be able to make that distance without too much discomfort. No further, though. I'll drive you back to wherever you live. Or stay. You don't look like one of the city homeless.'

It was the most agreeable kind of bullying. 'Do you often invite strangers home?' I asked.

'Never have done before. I don't often talk to strangers

either. There's something about you, Dany, inspires confidence.'

I was hearing this so often, I supposed it must be true.

His house was a classic white villa. This would fetch a good price, if he ever wanted to sell it. Once inside, I could see he wouldn't. I didn't know how long he had lived there but it was full of beautiful paintings and sculptures, all looking as if they belonged here and nowhere else. His wife too, suited the house in some indefinable way, as she suited him. It was an obvious match, two beautiful people making an exquisite pair. Actually neither of them was conventionally good looking, she less then he. Her brown hair was cut short and spiky, she had a turned up nose, a big mouth and wide set green eyes. She was like a little cat with her pointed chin, her delicate bones. She danced up to me, hugged me and said 'I'm Fran. Welcome to our home.' Come and sit in the courtyard. The food should be arriving any minute now.'

I was glad she didn't call it a "patio". It was most definitely a courtyard, surrounded by old flint walls, covered in climbing plants, many already in bloom. There was a kind of mosaic on the floor. It was hard to make out exactly what it represented as it was hidden by a table and chairs.

'We eat outside whenever we can. In winter we sit around the fire. I'd never have a house without a fireplace. On dark days it's a substitute for the sun.'

The doorbell rang.

'Oh good the food. Craigie will you set out the knives and forks?'

I had a most pleasant evening. Balm to my soul when it was most needed. Craigie's wife Francesca was a firefly, darting about in the dusk. It was her house, it had been her parents' house, her parents' collection of artefacts with additions of her own. They had offered it as a wedding gift to the happy couple. They had bought themselves a camper van, and for the last two years had been driving round the world, relishing the nomadic existence they'd always dreamed of, they claimed. Their retirement coincided with their daughter's marriage, Francesca being a late, unexpected, nevertheless much loved child.

She was a good deal younger than he, my age, I guessed. They told me their life stories, more or less, and I told them mine, less rather than more, selected passages, let us say. He had worked abroad, then in general practice in rural Sussex before joining a group practice in Hove. She had studied performance arts in London and was now concentrating on writing poetry. They met at a party, when she decided he was the man for her. It was not love at first sight in the same way for him, he said, since he was already in love, or thought he was, with another doctor, for whose sake he had moved to the city. When they met a second time, however, he was completely bedazzled, unable to believe he'd remained indifferent to her charm. There was a violent rupture with his partner which resulted in her moving to a practice in the North of England. The wedding took place as soon as the bans had been published. I swear there were stars in his eyes as he relived the moment when fatal passion struck. She leaned over the leftovers of vegetable Biryani to kiss him on the nose.

'You see Dany, when that happens, there's absolutely nothing you can do about it. I loved my partner, I was distraught when I told her. We both broke down in tears. She assumed it was sex, some pre-middle age crisis. It wasn't. I hadn't even touched Francesca when I was smitten. Do you understand?'

I did. How strange, to be so intimate so quickly. Could it be that they needed friends as much as I did? Was this going to be the beginning of a friendship?

Francesca disappeared into the kitchen to make what she described as "something to drink". She was gone a long time. Meanwhile Craigie and I exchanged anecdotes about countries we'd lived in, travelled through. I was about to suggest getting a taxi and forgetting about the drink when she came back with three cups.

'I'll have to go soon. I'm still trying to get used to a working day which starts in the morning.' An odd smell wafted from my drink. 'What is this?'

'A mixture of different herbs with particular properties. Calming, restorative. Not only will you sleep well, you'll wake up full of energy.'

'You didn't tell us exactly which agency you worked in, not that it's important.' Craigie was inhaling his brew as if examining the bouquet of a good wine.

'*Her Place*. It's new. Mickey's latest venture.'

For the first time since I'd met her, Francesca was sitting still.

'You know Mickey?'

I don't know why I should be surprised. It wasn't such a big town.

'Yes.' A somewhat laconic reply from someone who had been so free with information about herself until now.

'I'm living in her house.'

'Yes, Craigie will give you a lift back whenever you're ready.'

'I could get a taxi, or maybe walk.' I wasn't at all sure where I was but I felt I was probably close to home.

'No. Please. You shouldn't walk anywhere. Your heels will be O.K. tomorrow, but let them heal overnight. And wear some other shoes for a couple of days.'

'Mickey will give you some cream to rub in that will work like magic' Francesca assured me as she kissed me goodbye.

It wasn't far at all. I could easily have arrived back on foot under different circumstances. It was really only three blocks away.

'You'll remember where we live, won't you?' Craigie leaned out of the car window as I opened the gate. 'You can call on Francesca whenever you feel like it.'

'Sure. Thanks again.' I waved goodbye. It was all too much. I had to sleep on it, as they say.

# Chapter 7

'Sure, I know Francesca. Better than I know him. I'm not at all certain he's the man she should have married, but she wanted him and she got him.'

'They're very different. They seem to adore each other, though.'

'Of course he adores her. Always will.' There was something odd about the way she said this.

'You don't think she adores him?'

'So far so good. She's capricious. I'm just going on a visit. You open up and deal with whatever.' She jerked to a halt to let me out. 'Probably see you around lunchtime. You're beginning to get the hang of things aren't you? Everything you need is in the outer office, no need to look in the back room. It's locked anyway.'

I supposed she was right, I was beginning to get the hang of things. There were already potential customers looking hopefully in the window, even though it was exactly nine o'clock when I put the key in the lock. These were buyers, tenants, at this rate, if we didn't have any more vendors soon we'd run out of properties, I thought. Fortunately, at half-past eleven, when I at last had a moment to listen to the answer phone, I found about half a dozen offers of sale. As I was busy writing details, my peace was disturbed again. I looked up at the figure standing in front of me.

'Oh, hello. Welcome to *"Her Place"*. Surely you don't need to buy or rent an apartment, or are you planning to sell?'

'Oh no!' It was the response I had deliberately provoked. I'd now grown quite fond of his catch phrase.

'Oh no. Hello. No. I wanted to talk to Mickey.'

'I'm afraid Mickey is out on a visit. Can I help you?'

'Oh no, it's Mickey I have to speak to. When will she be back?'

'I'm not sure. Would you like to sit down and have a cup of coffee, Ray? Please do!' My manner was especially persuasive so as not to elicit the usual negative.

'Oh all right. It's nearly lunch time anyway, so perhaps she'll be here soon.'

'Quite possibly. Is it something urgent?'

'Yes it is a bit. Because Saturday is May 1st.'

'The beginning of the Festival.'

'Is it? I suppose it is, yes.'

'This urgency has nothing to do with the Festival, then?'

'The Festival? Oh no.'

'Some village carnival? Dancing round a pole, wearing ribbons. Pretty girl chosen as May Queen?' I was prodding as hard as I could.

He picked up his coffee. 'I don't think so. The thing is, I couldn't understand Mickey's e-mail. The directions how to get there. I don't want to get it wrong again. Then I deleted the message by accident. They have to be deleted but only when you're certain of the content.'

'Get where?'

'What?' He choked on his coffee. 'Sorry. Breathed in as I was drinking.'

'The directions to get where?'

'The Meeting Place.'

'What meeting?'

'The May Day meeting.'

We were going round in circles.

'What sort of meeting?'

He looked hard at me.

'You're not one of us, are you?'

'What do you mean, Ray? Who are "we"?'

It was just bad luck that Mickey returned at that moment. She was smiling until she caught sight of Ray, then her expression changed.

'I've told everybody they shouldn't come here. Don't you remember?'

'Yes, but I wanted to make sure I wouldn't make a

mistake. It's very important for me. I deleted your e-mail before I read it again.'

She glared at him. 'I'm giving you one more chance. If you mess this up, you're out.'

'Yes, yes, I understand. I won't, that's why I have to check with you.'

'Come into the back room.'

The phone rang as she slammed the door behind them. It was Jiminy Cricket.

'Good to speak to you again Danielle.'

'How can I help you Mr. Cricket?' Any lewd suggestion and I'd put down the receiver.

'Much as I'd love to chat and get to know you better, it was Michaela I needed to speak to.'

'She's busy I'm afraid. In private consultation, not to be disturbed. In her back room' I added, with heavy meaning. 'Could I give her a message?'

'Yes, I just wanted to remind her about our lunch date and to tell her we'll meet at English's at one o'clock. I've booked a table. It's one of her favourite restaurants, isn't it?'

'I believe so, I'm not too familiar with her gastronomic tastes' I lied. He was as irritating as ever.

'Perhaps next time you might accept an invitation?'

No way, I thought. However, he added 'Greta, my.......' there was a long moment of hesitation before he finished 'my protégée, would love to meet you.'

Now that could be interesting.

'Mickey's told me about Greta. I would like to meet her.'

'I'll organise it. What kind of food do you like?'

'Anything that Greta likes.'

'Fine. You'll tell Mickey to be at English's at one o'clock?'

'Without fail.'

'Ciao, Danielle. It's a pleasure to hear your beautiful voice.'

'See you soon Mr. Cricket.' Could I really stand him for a whole lunchtime, I wondered, after ringing off. Even for the sake of meeting his mysterious "protégée", his illegal immigrant, possibly his sex slave.

When Mickey had finished with Ray, he looked more anxious than before. He was clutching a sealed envelope, holding it close to his heart.

'Do not let that out of your possession. Do not let anyone else read, and above all, do not lose it.' She was addressing him as she might address a small child. "Is that clear?"

'Yes, yes. Trust me. It was just that I'm not familiar with my new computer yet. See you Friday evening, then.'

'Without fail.' She pushed him out.

'You had a call from Jiminy Cricket. Meet him at one o'clock at English's.'

'Oh damn!' She slapped her forehead. 'I'd forgotten. You wouldn't like to go instead?'

'No.'

'It'll just have to be a short break then. I have to be at a client's at 2. By the way, will you do Friday and Saturday on your own? You can have tomorrow off if you like.'

'I've made several appointments for one of us to take buyers out tomorrow.'

'O.K. You do that then. I'll stay here.'

'I don't know my way around, like you do.'

'Take the mini and the map.'

'I don't want to look stupid in front of customers.'

'I'll write out for you how to get there tonight if we look at your appointments list together. It'll be much more fun than sitting here all day, I can tell you.'

I guessed she was right. What would I do with a day off anyway?

I wasn't exactly bored all afternoon. I was too busy for that. A stream of women, young and old, came and went. At 5.30 I escorted the last one out and sat back to listen to the messages. I methodically rang everyone back so it was 7.30 when I looked up. I didn't take a taxi immediately, instead I headed for the nearest fish and chip shop and took my supper to the water's edge. Close by sat an Islamic family, the kids squealing with delight as they splashed each other, the father gingerly wading beside them, the mother and possibly grandmother, who knows, sat covered from head to foot in black. I had read somewhere that wealthy Arab women wear the latest couturier clothes and expensive jewellery beneath these all enveloping garments. The husband was young, handsome, the children adorable. What is the wife like, I wondered? Is she an almond eyed olive skinned beauty? There were no clues in the still, shapeless form, except the voice when she called out to her family. She sounded like a child herself.

'Sets your imagination going doesn't it? I had heard the pebbles scrunch behind me but had been too absorbed in my contemplation to look around. Robbie grinned down at me. I scrambled to my feet. I wasn't going to have her in this dominating position.

'Coming for a pint? Tell you what, I've got my bike over there, I'll take you for a ride.'

'I'm not dressed for it.' I wouldn't have accepted in any case, but unsuitable clothing was a good excuse, I didn't want to appear churlish.

'I suppose not. You don't always wear these suits do you?'

I resented her intimacy, which bordered on rudeness.

'None of your business.'

'Sorry. Come for a drink anyway.'

All of a sudden, I felt a lot happier. I hadn't been here for a week yet and already I was being recognised. I was very pleased to have company, just as I had been delighted to be invited home by Craigie to meet Francesca.

'O.K. A quick one. I'm pretty well wiped out. It's been an action packed day.'

There was a quiet bar in a nearby side street. A tiny place. The kind of old-fashioned pub that is hard to find these days.

I insisted on paying. Students were always poor, I knew that much.

'What are you studying?'

'Psychology and Spanish. I get to have a spell studying in Spain in my third year. My mother is Spanish, so it's an easy option. Actually I might be able to go to South America instead, which would be really cool. What about you? You're not exactly an English rose, are you?'

'Italian, German, Caribbean French, not a drop of English blood, but British through and through.' I was beginning to unwind. 'This job isn't my scene, it's a stopgap.

'I'm glad about that, you don't seem like the archetypical business woman.'

'What do I seem like then?'

She considered for a long moment, gazing at me searchingly. She had nice eyes, I realised.

'Hard to say. You're elusive. I know – a policewoman!'

'That is the most absurd idea. Absolutely ridiculous!' So ridiculous, I burst out laughing.

'I know. I wanted to make you laugh. You're too serious. I told you, you should just have some fun once in a while. Have you just split up with your girlfriend or something?'

'I'm not going to go into details of my private life with you. I've only just met you.'

She shrugged. 'Suit yourself.' She paused. 'How about you and I doing the clubs together?'

'Your glass is empty. I'll fetch us another beer.'

How about it? It didn't appeal to me. Not yet. I told her so when I returned from the bar.

'Then won't you come to the gig on campus I told you about?'

'Maybe.'

She fell silent. I told myself I was being quite objectionable. I had been relieved not to be on my own, had welcomed Robbie's overtures. She wasn't trying to pick me up, she'd said I wasn't her type, so what was my problem?

'I would enjoy going out on your bike, when I'm properly prepared.'

Her face lit up.

'What about Sunday? We're all going to look at the cottage. We've been in touch with the present tenants and they've invited us for tea. Would you like to come? Then we could have a ride around the countryside. Will you?'

The mention of the cottage reminded me of something. 'I've spoken to the owners. They are pleased to let to you, but you haven't brought me your references.'

'Tomorrow. Des will drop them in tomorrow. Will you come on Sunday? Please!'

'Thank you. Yes, I'd like that.'

'I'll come and pick you up. Where do you live?'

I hesitated, recalling the disapproving look on Mickey's face when she'd run into her in the shop. Also I wasn't sure I wanted her to know where to find me after office hours.

'Or we can meet somewhere else if you prefer to keep your hideaway secret.'

Her faint irony provoked me, so I gave her Mickey's address.

'I'll call by at half-past three Sunday afternoon. O.K.?'

It was O.K. A few bricks of the wall I had built around myself during the winter fell down and I felt a breath of fresh air. I smiled at her, a proper smile. She smiled back delighted.

'Hey! That's more like it. I'd better go, I have an essay to write. I came by your agency at half past five, hoping to ask you out for a drink when you'd finished work. But you didn't finish work for a long time, so I had to kick my heels for a couple of hours.'

'Are you stalking me?' In my new lighthearted mood I found that quite amusing.

'No. I've got what I want now. I've broken through the professional barrier.'

'Hmm. Don't be too confident. You've found a little gap that's all.'

'It's a start. Do you want me to give you a lift home?'

'I've told you, I'm not dressed for it.'

'See you Sunday, then. Next time the drinks are on me.'

The barman called me a taxi. My feet were still too sore to walk far. I asked him to drive slowly along the front. I had no desire to go indoors yet, but Mickey would be wanting to go through the list of visits and work out with me the easiest way to drive. Or so I thought. She was in her kitchen throwing things into a saucepan from the row of bottles lined up in front of her.

'Hi Dany! Look here are some maps of the city and surroundings. I can't help you now, I have to concentrate on this. Then I'll have some studying to do, which will probably keep me up nearly all night. I'm in a bit of a mess here. I must have done something wrong, it doesn't smell right. I'll have to start again. I do miss Aunt Miranda.' She sighed. 'You drop me in the morning and then be off. You'll cope all right, I'm sure. Goodnight, sleep well.'

Not much chance of that. I pinpointed six widely spread locations on the various maps. The schedule had been made on the assumption that the driver would know where she was going. Not that Mickey was much better than I was, judging on past experience. I took several sheets of paper to write myself instructions, praying that I wouldn't come across too many one-way systems. I tried to be methodical. At the end of the afternoon I left two apartments to inspect in the same estate as Patrick's house, planning to call by to see if the handsome lawyer was there. I realised that it would be about six o'clock by then so it was just possible she might be around after work. When I'd done as much as I could I went out on to my terrace with a cup of tea. A light was shining across the garden from the room which used to be Miranda's. It was strange that Mickey had picked on me to be her right-hand woman. I stayed for a good hour in the light of the waning moon. Mickey was still up when I went to bed. From time to time it seemed as though she was singing, or chanting, or something. I was on the point of closing my eyes when a large thing flew past my open window. An owl, I assumed. A very big owl. Then I fell asleep.

# Chapter 8

We were both bleary eyed in the morning. It took two cups of strong black coffee to jerk me awake. Mickey looked positively worn out. She was waiting for me in the garden.

'Did you get it right in the end?' I asked.

She sank into the passenger seat.

'What?'

'The mixture you were concocting.'

'Oh that. I hope so.'

'Did you find what you were looking for in your aunt's room? I noticed the light was on very late.'

'Eventually. Her papers need rearranging so that I can understand them. Her filing system was a mystery, if she had one. We all have our own special ways. It wouldn't do for an intruder to be able to put together the pieces.' She changed the subject.

'You're all set for the day?'

'More or less. I won't come back to the office, if you don't mind. I anticipate working until at least seven o'clock.'

'That's beyond the call of duty Dany. I'll pay you over-time.'

'For goodness sake, Mickey, don't be so silly.'

We drove the rest of the way in silence.

I was pleased with myself. I found my way with little diffi-culty, only getting lost once, and dealt with the clients pleasantly. At the end of the morning I was near Lewes, in a village which had corners of picture book prettiness. It also had a relatively new extension, called, quaintly, "The Green", which is where my customer, a professor at the University lived. It was an academics' corner, since it was within cycling distance of the campus, giving enough daily exercise to those intellectuals who were worried that their lifestyle might be bad for their health. This particular egghead was in his thirties, he told me. He told me much more than he needed, but I made a careful note. Apparently he was already a Professor of English with an international reputation. It could be that he was counting on his reputation as being the "wow" factor his home was sadly lacking. "Strictly functional" were the words I scribbled down. Later on I would turn it into "streamlined, classic simplicity, easy to maintain".

'I've met one of your students,' I remarked.

'I know.'

'You do? How's that?'

'I've just given her a reference for you. She's the reason I decided to contact you instead of all the other crooks.'

I stared at him coldly. 'If that's a compliment, it's not one I appreciate. I understand that all my colleagues are reputable, well qualified and honest.' I prayed that he wouldn't ask to see my own qualifications, or Mickey's if it came to that. 'You'd better be more careful what you say.'

'O.K. O.K. A badly chosen word.'

'A Professor of English shouldn't choose his words badly.'

Oh Dany, I thought, you sound so uptight. 'Anyway, I'm glad Des recommended us.'

I smiled at him.

'She's a wonderful girl. Very, very bright. One of the most intelligent students I've come across. We're lucky she chose us. She could have gone to Oxford or Cambridge.

There was a glint in his eye that told me it wasn't only her brain he was interested in.

'Tell you what. Today is my research day. Come and have a bite to eat at the local inn. It's very good. I'll treat you to one of their special ploughman's lunches.

The local inn was a few minutes walk away. Although it was only half-past twelve, the tables in the yard were already crowded. We found a shady bench where he invited me to sit down whilst he fetched the lunch. I stretched luxuriantly. Almost every tree around me was in blossom. The sound of the bees was louder than the talk.

'There we are.' He put down two plates containing a chunk of mature cheddar, a slice of stilton, half an apple, a helping of chutney and some fresh bread and butter. 'I'll just fetch the drinks. Bitter O.K?' He was gone rather a long time. My cheese began to sweat and my bread curled up at the edges.

'Sorry. I ran into one of my colleagues. Hard to avoid him in fact. He props up the bar every lunch time and most evenings. You know the type.'

'I do. I've spent most of my life the other side of a bar.'

He looked at me with new interest.

'Des told me they all liked you a lot.'

'I hardly know them. They've invited me to go with them to see this cottage you've given them a reference for.'

'I see. Tell them I took you to lunch, will you?' He gazed into the middle distance. 'When I was at Cambridge, we used to go regularly to my tutor's house. He wasn't much older than we were. He was happy to socialise with us. Des is one of my personal students, you know. I'm sort of responsible for her welfare, along with my forty-nine other personal students. She's supposed to come and see me to chat about her progress from time to time, but she never does. I've tried meeting her with a few others. They aren't interested. Strange isn't it? Did you go round to your tutor's house?'

What's a tutor? I asked myself.

'No,' was all I replied. 'You're a bit old for them, perhaps. They seemed like a bunch of schoolgirls to me.'

'I'm not out to seduce her,' he said, with dignity. 'Or any of them,' he added hastily. 'She has a fine mind. It's not often you meet a woman on the same wavelength. Would you put in a good word for me? Tell her my intentions are honourable. I've got some rare editions of Shakespeare that would interest her parents.'

'I don't want to be your go-between, Professor Bradshaw.'

'Richard, please. I'm giving a party to celebrate the publication of my latest book. I've had the official publication do in Cambridge of course, but I want to have a party here, in the garden. Would you like to come?'

'And bring Des? She's not a special friend of mine.'

'She likes you. She trusts you. If you say you're coming she might come too.'

'Shall I invite all her friends? She'll certainly come then.'

'They're not my students. I don't see why I should entertain them. Students can drink and eat an awful lot, you know.'

'Suit yourself. I pass on the invitation to all of them or none of them.'

He reluctantly agreed.

'When is the party?'

'A fortnight on Saturday. Noon onwards.'

'What is your book called?'

'The Influence of popular music on the English novel from 1960 to 1965.'

'Fascinating.'

He was piqued by my sarcasm. 'It is, actually. Look it up on the Internet. It's had excellent reviews. Consult my website. It's the reason the University has increased my salary so that I can buy a better house. They don't want to lose me. Do you mind if I smoke?'

He was defensive rather than arrogant. His hands trembled slightly.

'Would you like a cigarette?'

'No thanks. Go ahead.' I'd had enough bread and cheese. He had also pushed his plate away. He inhaled deeply, closed his eyes, leaned back, giving me the chance to scrutinise his features. He was unusual looking. His name was typically English, his looks quite different. A trace of Asian I would say. Smooth skin, black glossy hair. He opened his eyes suddenly before I could look away.

'Neither of us is what you might call racially pure. My mother was Chinese. What about yours?'

'French Afro-Caribbean German mix.'

He laughed and stretched out his hand across the table.

'Well Dany. Don't you think this should make us allies?'

**\*\*\*\***

I'd just turned the key in the ignition when my mobile rang. I switched off the engine.

'Dany? Mickey here.' Who else would it be? No-one had my mobile number.

'How are you doing?'

'Not bad. I'll report back later.'

'You said you wouldn't finish until late, so you won't come back to the office.'

'That's right. I'll talk to you when I get home.'

'I'll be busy. Keep everything in order and file it tomorrow. I probably won't see you until Sunday evening. I'll be in conference all weekend. Incommunicado. Mobile switched off.'

'Shouldn't I know where you are?'

'No. My apartment will be locked. Have a good weekend!'

'You too.'

'Ciao.' I immediately rang Roz's office. 'It's Dany, the estate agent.'

'Hello, Dany.' I'd forgotten how attractive her voice was. 'I've been hoping you'd call.'

'I'm going to be near Patrick's house on business. I was wondering if you'd be there, by any chance. If so, I'll pop in to have another look.'

'You don't need an excuse to "pop in". I'll be there. See you.'

I whooped with joy.

In anticipation of seeing Roz, I had brought jeans and a tee-shirt with me. I changed in the car. A splash of subtle cologne and I was ready.

'A cup of tea or a gin and tonic? As long as this place isn't sold I'm at home here. We can sit out at the back, it's lovely at this time of evening.' She kissed me on both cheeks, French style.

'A cup of tea is what I could do with right now.'

'Good. Me too. I've had a hard day. Some nasty divorce cases. Go through, I'll bring the tea.'

I was struck again by the prettiness of it all. It would certainly look good on the publicity. Truly a little gem, unfortunately in a setting which took away it's lustre.

'I'd be tempted to buy it myself.' Roz set down the tea things, 'if I didn't already have a home, I live very near the city centre. I fought hard for my home when my husband and I divorced ten years ago and I propose to stay there until I die. You must come and visit.'

Husband! The word gave me a slight shock. Ex-husband, though. She caught my expression. 'It was ostensibly over a lesbian affair which had become too serious. We should have parted years before, but we stayed together because of my son. He was fifteen when we made the break. He adored my girlfriend, fortunately. Or unfortunately. Another cup of tea?'

'Unfortunately?'

'She was much younger than me. I found them in bed together. Last year. I blamed her not him. She cried, swore she loved us both. I couldn't take it. He had a job in London, she moved there with him. I don't want to see her ever again. So what's your life story then?'

My mind was reeling. I'd had far too many confidences for one day – Richard Bradshaw's confession of attraction to Des, even if it was only for her mind, now this baring of her soul from a woman I'd only met once.

'My story? Not very interesting. I've knocked around here and there all over Europe. My girlfriend lives in London.'

'You and Michaela.....?'

'Just friends.'

'That's what I thought. So you're in Brighton during the week and back to base in London at the weekends.'

'More or less.'

'Pity. I'm having a party on Saturday. I think you'd enjoy it. Can't you persuade your girlfriend to come down here instead?'

A dyke's party would be just the thing to end my first week.

'As it happens, my girlfriend has to go to see her mother on Saturday. She'll stay overnight in.....' I hastily picked a town out of the air '- in Liverpool.'

'So you'll be free? You'll come?'

'Yes, if I'm not too tired. I'll have been working all day.'

'But it's the opening of the Festival. There'll be all kinds of things going on. Won't Michaela let you have a day off?'

'She's busy herself and it might be a good opportunity for business.'

'Sounds to me as if a party will be just what you need then.'

It most probably would, it most definitely would.

'Here's my home address. We'll start at seven.'

'Thanks. I'd better be off. Thank you for the tea. We'll do our best to find you a good customer and a good price.'

I felt it important to remind her about the ostensible reason why I was there.

'See you on Saturday then.'

'Most likely. Thanks.' I hurried away.

Mickey had a surprise for me. A compensation, I suppose, for the extra hours she'd asked me to put in, especially Saturday when it was quite clear that most people would be out enjoying themselves. She had taken time off from her mysterious preparations and had booked a table at a new Thai restaurant, considered she said, to be very good, for herself, me, Craigie and Francesca. It never occurred to her that I might have alternative plans, how could I?

'You like them, don't you? You'd enjoy meeting them again?'

Sure I would. It so happened that I had been considering going to the gay disco on the university campus, now I was less defensive towards Robbie. Already life here was presenting difficult choices. The disco would doubtless go on until late, and if I promised to stay sober Mickey would most likely let me take the mini, so with luck I might be able to have both.

Sitting opposite Craigie I thought about Mickey's assessment of them – "he would be passionately attached to Francesca for life, she might be more fickle". There was something in the way he looked at her, and he was looking at her most of the time, although she was beside him, that reminded me of the way very small children sometimes look at their mothers, with an ever present anxiety that she might go away. When he'd finished eating he took her hand. If he lost her, the damage would be irreparable. Imagining it, my own pain, scarcely suppressed, rose to the surface.

'Are you alright, Dany?' He had turned his attention to me. 'You're rather pale all of a sudden.'

'I'm fine.' I took a gulp of water.

'How about eating with me tomorrow? I'm being abandoned. Fran is off with Mickey, you know.'

'Is she?' This news jerked me back to the present.

'One of these "meetings". One day she'll tell me what she's getting from them. For the moment it's a mystery.'

She stroked his arm. 'I'm learning wisdom, darling. Ancient wisdom. It's a difficult and complicated process, isn't it Mickey.'

'Very.'

'If I tried to describe it now, I'd make it too simple. I will share it, I promise, when I'm ready.'

'But I never know where you are or exactly what you're doing. At least you could take your mobile phone.'

'Never!' This was Mickey at her sternest. 'It's most important that we shouldn't be disturbed.'

'You mustn't be jealous my love.'

'I'm not jealous, just very insecure. You don't seem to realise how desperately important you are to me.'

'But I do.' She glanced quickly at Mickey. 'Believe me I do.'

'Believe her, she does,' affirmed Mickey.

This is not what they should be saying, I thought. What Francesca should be saying is "You are desperately important to me too darling" and Mickey should be adding "Yes, she would die without you". Something of the sort, anyway. I was very uncomfortable.

'So you'll come to keep me company, tomorrow night Dany? Saturday night I'm off to stay with an old friend. If you're free, that is. I expect you have other plans for the weekend.'

'I have plans for Saturday and Sunday. I accept your invitation with pleasure.'

'Great. About 7.30. I'll collect you. How are your feet?'

'Better. So much so I feel like dancing on them. Could I take the mini to the University Campus, Mickey?'

'I'd rather you didn't. I don't want to attract the wrong attention to "*Her Place*".'

'What do you mean?'

'The logo printed all over it might provoke vandalism. Late at night they get up to all kinds of mischief out there. Take a taxi. I'll pay.'

Her refusal was humiliating.

'I'll pay for myself. Here is my share of the meal.' I put two twenty-pound notes on the table. 'If it's not enough, let me know.'

'But this is my treat. Don't be silly.'

'See you Sunday evening. Have a good weekend. I'll be ready at 7.30 tomorrow Craigie.'

'Dany! Please take back your money.'

She tried to thrust it into my hand. I slammed it back on the table.

'It's all *your* money in the first place!'

I stalked off, seething. I shouldn't have asked her for the car. I found a taxi immediately. The driver asked me if I wanted him to pick me up later. I declined. I wanted to leave myself free for whatever adventures might arise.

There was no adventure. The music was very loud and people already very drunk. I drank a couple of whiskies quickly then threw myself onto the dance floor. I didn't see Robbie. I didn't look for her. What I was trying to do was wear myself out so that I would eventually be too tired to relive the agony and ecstasy of the previous year, wipe out memories stirred up by Craigie's dangerous attachment to his wife. I hadn't danced like this for a long time. I had another whisky, refusing other substances offered to me, and whirled and jumped and stamped until the bitter end. When I came to a halt, a circle of young things gathered around me and applauded. "For heaven's sake, Dany, you're a young thing too", I told myself. Stabbed the air with my fist in a victory salute, "Yes".

I should have asked my taxi man to come back. Every company I phoned promised at least half an hour wait. 'You'd be better off taking a bus,' someone suggested. 'Look, there's one coming now. It's been great since they introduced the night service.' So I joined the revellers returning to the city. It was one o'clock, so maybe they were going on to a nightclub, though half of them looked entirely wiped out. They were a merry crew, everyone seeming to know everyone else. I leaned back in my seat, eyes closed, listening.

The bus reached Hove with me the only passenger on it. I recognised a few landmarks. When we passed the name of a road I knew was not too far from home I asked the driver to stop.

Since the light in Miranda's old room was still on, I assumed Mickey had not yet gone to bed. I found a note pinned to the door to my apartment. *"Take the mini. I'll have the BMW. Go when you like, do what you like after work. Have a good weekend. Lots of love."* I fell on my bed fully dressed and slept until my alarm clock rang at 8 o'clock the next morning.

# Chapter 9

I took the mini as instructed. The BMW had already gone.
The traffic was worse than usual, I was ten minutes late for
an appointment I had made at the office with an agitated
couple who seemed to have planned to inspect ten houses
during one day. They were looking at their watches as I
rounded the corner. 'This is a bad start,' the man com-
plained. I did what I could to please them. I showed them
two apartments and two houses, all of which matched what
they said were their requirements. They were dismissive of
them all, called them cheap rubbish, and accused me of
misrepresentation, since what they had seen on the descriptions wasn't anything like the reality. When I asked them to
be specific, they protested and walked out. I made myself
a strong coffee before listening to messages. I'd been able
to keep my temper, which was a miracle.

The rest of the day was much better. I worked over
lunch, fell into some kind of routine in the afternoon. I was
about to call it a day, when Tracey burst in. She looked
terrible. Black ringed eyes in a drawn white face.

'I can't deal with that lot, they're weird,' she accused me.

'What do you mean weird?'

'They've got odd ideas about bringing up children. They
let them run around naked most of the time. They sit
around naked themselves as well. They don't have very
nice bodies. And they let their animals sleep on the beds.
They said I should let them sleep with me if they wanted
to. And the children kept trying to get into bed with me as
well.'

'You haven't given it a chance. You haven't been there
even a week. You could discuss it with them, make your
point clear.'

'I've been there long enough to know I don't want to
stay. Discuss! They'd discuss all right. They sit round
discussing everything for hours.'

'You'll never get another deal like this. No rent, a lovely room.'

'I don't want a deal like this. You don't get anything for nothing in this life. I'd rather pay money than have to romp around with no clothes on and have big dogs come up licking my private parts. I've told them I'm leaving, they said no problem, as I wasn't liberated enough yet. If that's being liberated they can keep it, thank you very much. It's disgusting the way they carry on.'

'I've told you before, we don't have anything else for you.'

'Nothing's come in?'

'No.'

'Isn't there some empty property I could sleep in until I get myself sorted?'

'Absolutely not. That would be squatting. And how do you propose to "get yourself sorted?"'

'You're not going to help me then?'

'I can't. I'm an estate agent not a social worker.'

'Well, fuck you!' She nearly smashed into the door as she rushed out trying to hide her tears.

I wondered whether I should run after her, then decided not to. All I could have done for her would be to take her back to Mickey's, let her crash out on my bed for a night whilst I slept on the sofa. Would I have the heart to turn her out in the morning? Then where would she go? It was true, I wasn't a social worker, it wasn't my responsibility to provide for the homeless. There must be a hostel she could go to. I walked around the streets and the promenade before driving off, in the hopes that I might run into her. Buy her a meal, pay for a room at a hotel even. I had plenty of money, I could make sure she had a good night's sleep and ask Craigie's advice. He was a doctor, he would have come across plenty of Traceys. She was nowhere to be seen.

I went home to change, then drove to the Richardson's. I didn't want Craigie to have to give me a lift back.

I was early. I hadn't counted on getting there so quickly. I parked the car in the street and was about to sit listening to the radio when Craigie saw me and came hurrying out. He looked sweet in an apron.

'Come on in. The meal is almost ready. Settle yourself down with a glass of wine.'

The wine was good. I hadn't spent so long in France without learning a lot about it. The food was even better. I congratulated him on his cooking, very subtle flavours.

'I bet this didn't come out of a recipe book.'

'No. I like to invent. I've always liked to cook, even when I was a boy. When I came home in the school holidays I spent most of the time in the kitchen. Mum and Dad owned a rather exclusive little hotel you see. I can tell you the guests were delighted when I was on duty. The regulars found out when the school terms finished and booked in specially.'

'I'm surprised you didn't become a chef, not a doctor.'

'Cooking was my creative outlet. Medicine was my vocation.'

If I lived here permanently, I thought, I'd certainly register with you as my G.P. After spiced apple pie, a piece of ripe Stilton and a glass of port, he finally collapsed opposite me. We had moved indoors.

'What kind of music do you like, Dany?' He moved towards the CD player.

'Oh, anything. I like all sorts. Put on whatever you like.'

'I only want to provide a restful background. Nothing demanding. Here we are. This is Francesca's. I'm not terribly keen on it, but it's pleasant and unobtrusive. It's based on whales. You know the communications whales have with each other. They sing, apparently.'

It was bizarre. However, it was gentle and he kept it turned down.

'Another glass of port?'

'Better not. I do have to drive home, even if only round the corner.'

'You could stay here. I'm off duty tomorrow. We could make a night of it.'

What on earth did he mean? I made sure there were no misunderstandings.

'You do know I'm a lesbian?'

'Of course. I'm not asking you to sleep with me.'

'O.K. The problem is, *you* don't have to go to work, *I* do.'

'Oh come on, it isn't necessary to start dead on the dot of nine, is it? Mickey won't care. She won't know. She's not being fair to you. You open up when you want and close when you want. Nobody will come in tomorrow morning. They'll all be watching the festival procession.'

He was right. It wasn't fair. Nor did I want to return to the empty house. I wanted to stay and talk to this nice man. I didn't want to spend hours the following day in an empty office either, sorting through boring files.

'I'd appreciate it very much if you'd stay, Dany. I'm very uneasy about tonight. I probably sounded stupidly possessive or something yesterday evening, but I'm getting very worried about Fran.'

'Dinner was a bribe?'

'It must seem like that I suppose.' He sounded hurt. 'I only wanted to have the chance to give you a good meal. But you might find me boring and prefer to go home and read a good book.'

I couldn't help laughing. 'I hardly ever read. I don't find you boring. I will have another glass of port, although I'd rather have whisky, and to hell with the morning.'

He leapt up and hugged me.

'You don't mind. Irish whiskey? I have a bottle of Bush Mills.'

'I'm not prejudiced, unlike most other Scots.'

'You're Scottish?'

'Sort of. Yes and no. I was born in Edinburgh. But I'm a Londoner at heart. Could you change the music? I'm finding these wailing whales a bit tedious.'

'Let's forget the music.'

He poured a whiskey for us both.

'When I first laid eyes on you Dr. Richardson, I thought you were Greek.'

'Well spotted. I am. Greek Cypriot.'

'Richardson is a Greek Cypriot name, is it?'

'Anastasia and Philip Richardson aren't my real parents. They brought me up and I took their name. Anastasia is my mother's older sister. My parents were killed in a car crash. Let's start on you. I'm sure there was a lot you didn't tell us the other night. You were very guarded. Fran guessed you must be recovering from an unhappy love affair.'

'Did it show so clearly?'

'Not to me. Fran is highly intuitive.'

'I wish I were recovering. Have you any suggestions for mending a broken heart, doctor?'

'Unfortunately not. It's a very serious condition. But I can tell you it can be soothing to describe the circumstances.'

So I recounted my last summer's adventures in detail. How it was love at first sight with Anita, how extraordinary she was, how mysterious. How she had some kind of protector who finally allowed me to approach her, how she and the protector disappeared after a violent incident in the village when she had been taken hostage.

'You have no clue as to where they went?'

'Back to where they came from, I guess. Louisiana. It's a big state.'

It was true that talking about it all helped. A bit. He was silent for a while.

'Perhaps her disappearance was your salvation,' he said at last. 'If she'd stayed you would have had even more grief.'

It was his turn to bare his soul. His feelings for Francesca were so strong that it was painful. It was extraordinary that he couldn't feel sure of her. He had no reason to doubt her love, no reason to suspect that she would be unfaithful, yet there was always a fear of a loss which would prove fatal.

'I was perfectly happy, in a sane balanced relationship with a woman of whom I was extremely fond. I still feel guilty about her. Maybe I broke her heart too. I certainly betrayed her. Our breaking up was awful. I was going to ask her to marry me, then, wham, I'm struck by lightning.'

'But not the first time you met her. As soon as Anita walked into the room I was smitten.'

'No. It was strange. The first time I hardly noticed her, the second it was instant. Another whiskey?'

I shook my head. He helped himself.

'It's not just sex. Sex is a big part of it, not the most important part because when we're both completely physically satisfied, I still want something else. Oh God, Dany, it's as if I want to devour that woman, swallow her up where no-one else can get at her.' He took a large gulp. 'I'm getting drunk or else I couldn't talk about this. I couldn't talk about it to anybody else except you. You might have some sympathy. Is it all right? Just stop me if you don't want to listen.'

'Go on. Please go on.'

'Are you sure you don't want another drink? I could make you one of Fran's teas if you don't want alcohol.'

I pulled a face. 'Anything but that! Another small whiskey then. With plenty of water.'

Given permission to talk he hardly stopped. An almost uninterrupted monologue for hours. I didn't mind, I was transfixed. His life for the last two years had been a constant torment. When he was working he was able to detach himself, to become absorbed in his patients, devote himself to his first passion, medicine. At home his obsession with his wife dominated his existence. He was two men – the competent doctor and the jealous husband. This was not the ideal couple I'd imagined when I first met them.

'I hate jealousy. It's corrosive I've seen it turn love into black hatred. So I struggle with it. I'm telling you Dany, my mind is a constant battleground between my good and evil selves. The worst is this association with Michaela.'

'Hang on a minute, Mickey isn't a dyke, you know, and from everything you've said Francesca certainly isn't either.'

'It's not that, it's all this secrecy. Mickey and she go off somewhere, they won't say where, they won't say what for. O.K. most of the time I'm excessively insecure but I would say that under these circumstances even the most normal of husbands might be suspicious don't you think? You heard her trying to reassure me yesterday evening. It's not enough. I shall drink until I fall unconscious tonight, which is not usual, believe me, but I have to do it otherwise I'll torture myself with visions of her sleeping with other men They've never said that these "meetings" or "conferences" or whatever, are for women only.'

He poured another whiskey. It might take quite a lot to knock him out.

'It's generally one night only. This time last year though, it was two nights and a whole day. Something to do with the importance of the first of May.'

'So I gathered.'

'You gathered? Do you know anything more about it? Has Mickey let you in on it?' His eagerness was pathetic.

'Afraid not. I met another person who is involved.'

'What kind of person?'

'A boy. Hardly a man. As you are Francesca's type, she certainly wouldn't be attracted to that idiot. I tried to winkle information out of him without success.'

'It least it proves there are men there too.'

'Have you tried asking her if you could go along?'

'Every time. She always says "Not yet".'

Mickey's answer to me.

'Why don't you follow her? Or have her followed? Look through her papers, her computer, for clues?'

'I'm ashamed to say I already have. Not followed her, looked through her papers. There was nothing. That's suspicious in itself, isn't it? If she's part of a regular group, following a course, she should have documentation, shouldn't she?'

'Don't ask me. I've never followed any courses.'

'She has a locked cabinet. I couldn't find the key. If I broke into it she'd leave me. She's already threatened to walk out immediately if I pry into her private affairs. If she caught me following her that would be the end.'

'She's not a very nice lady is she?'

'She's a wonderful lady. I don't deserve her, grumpy paranoid brute that I am.' Tears came into his eyes. If he'd reached the maudlin stage, I wanted to go to bed.

'I can't go on like this. I don't know what to do.'

Nor did I. Wear him out? Get him off the subject? Difficult. I had an inspiration.

'Craigie, do you know how to dance? Greek dances? Men's dances? I'll bet you do.'

'What are you talking about?'

'Dancing. Let's dance until we drop. Greek, Spanish, Scottish, Irish. Go wild!'

His bloodshot eyes gazed at me as if I was crazy, then he grinned.

'Yeah. Let's go for it!'

So for the second night running I let my body take over. We did Zorba the Greek stuff, then we pretended flamenco, a very particular version since we both wanted to strut as macho men, we reeled, we Highland flung and at last collapsed against each other on the sofa.

'It's a bit of a bother to go to bed.' murmured Craigie. 'Why don't we just stay here? It's a big sofa, room for two. It's very comfortable. Fran and I often sleep on it.'

I sat up straight.

'Craigie, we agreed.....'

He put his arm round me. 'Dear girl, do you think I'd be capable of any hanky-panky? I just thought a cuddle would be nice.'

I sank back. 'If Fran could see us now would she be very, very cross?'

'Who cares what Fran thinks?' were his last words before he blanked out.

A minor triumph, I concluded. And that was my last thought before I blanked out too.

# Chapter 10

I woke at 10 o'clock with a hangover and a wonderful feeling of irresponsibility. I crept out without disturbing the master of the house, who was likely to feel much worse than I did. There was no line of angry people waiting for me, it was obviously true that the public had better things to do. There were crowds already gathering in the town centre and I passed flocks of little children in surprising costumes. I remembered reading that the theme of the festival was "The Primitive" which accounted for the little faces made up to look like apes, monkeys and other jungle creatures. Sipping my coffee, I remembered Tracey. I still felt uneasy about her. The irresponsibility was replaced by guilt. I could have done something couldn't I? At least temporarily. But then, what good would that have done? Paying for a hotel for a night, two nights, a week, wouldn't solve her problem. Whatever it was. Lack of money was only the surface. I closed my eyes, hoping my headache would go away soon. When I'd looked in the drawers for an aspirin all I found were anonymous products of evil looking powder. Mickey was running a risk if she kept illegal substances openly. They probably weren't illegal, they certainly looked and smelled nasty. I did see one labelled "For headaches and migraine, take sparingly with water *never* with caffeine". I went for the caffeine instead. I hadn't had enough sleep. I should try to catnap. I began to drift.

'Why haven't you been to see me, young woman? I've had my teapot at the ready all week?'

Lady Bestwood's eyes were twinkling despite her accusatory tone.

'Oh, I'm so sorry! I didn't hear you come in.'

'Dozing at your post. You could be court-marshalled for that. The enemy's always waiting for his opportunity.'

'Are you my enemy?'

'No dear, I'm certainly not. I'm your ally.'

'I'm afraid we haven't had any interest in your apartment. It's early days. To tell you the truth we haven't printed up the details and Michaela hasn't had time to do the photos.'

'Can't you use a camera yourself?'

'I'm learning.'

'Then bring it round this afternoon. Actually, I have a very good camera. I can take my own pictures. I wanted your company, though.'

'I think it's our policy to take the photos ourselves. I don't know where Michaela's left her camera. It may well be in the back room which is always locked. It's private.'

'Ah! The strategic centre, eh? Top secret docs kept in there.'

'Apparently.'

'We could break in.'

'No we couldn't.'

'Never mind. Doesn't matter. It would have been fun. Spying is always fun. However, I didn't come in here for that. Not to pester you about my sale. I have an acquaintance of yours I picked up on the seafront. I feed the gulls every evening and yesterday evening I found a young person to feed as well.'

Feeding gulls was a completely unnecessary activity, I thought. Whereas feeding people was, on the contrary, vital. I had seen soup and sandwiches handed out to the homeless as a regular routine. I guessed who this particular needy young person was.

'Tracey?'

'Right, Tracey. I've put her in Ray's place, he's away for a couple of nights.'

'Wouldn't he mind?'

'Shouldn't think so. He often has the most peculiar friends staying there.'

'They are his friends, though. She's a stranger.'

'She's harmless, I can tell. I'm a good judge of character.'
She chuckled. 'She didn't want to accept, I expect she
thought I was a batty old bird who just wanted to bend her
ear all night. Instead she bent mine. At the end of it all, I
told her she ought to join the army.'

'If you don't mind me saying so, she doesn't look as
though she's got what it takes.'

'How do you know what it takes? Have you ever been in
Her Majesty's Armed Forces?'

'I have to admit I haven't.'

'Don't make assumptions, then. She has a lot of anger. A
lot of, what do they call it these days – attitude. She's spoil-
ing for a fight.'

'Maybe she'd be better off taking up boxing, or something.' This was turning into a ridiculous conversation.
'Why is she so angry?'

'Her parents. They abused her.'

'Ah, I guessed as much.'

'I don't mean physically abused. She's the eldest girl of
a family of seven. She's been used as a drudge. Her
parents are feckless. Always out at the pub. And they
gamble, so she tells me. If she's ever had any money she's
had to give it to them. She has two older brothers who are
as bad as her parents, don't lift a finger, and four younger
sisters.

Is this all true, I wondered? It wasn't a story that would
have convinced me, but Lady Bestwood had lapped it up.

'I reckon Ray could put her up until she signs on.'

'Does she agree about the army?'

'She was a bit shocked when I suggested it. She's considering it though.'

Heaven help us if there's a war, with soldiers like Tracey.

'I can see you're looking doubtful. I've seen many a girl
totally transformed by a life in the services.'

'I'm sure you're right, Lady Bestwood.'

'Davina. Davina is my name. Now are you coming to tea
this afternoon? Four o'clock. Today's a fun day dear, not a

working day. Where's your other half? She can take over can't she?'

'She's busy enjoying herself.'

She must be having a good time, I thought. At least it couldn't be worse than being stuck in an office.

'There you are. So should you be. Four o'clock. We'll take photos together and, I'll give you the disc for that Michaela person to use. I'm off. See you later.'

My goodness, she was sprightly for someone over a hundred years old. Perhaps she'd live to one hundred and thirty and beat some sort of record.

I couldn't face lunch. There was a water-dispensing machine Mickey had wisely installed, so I drank glass after glass until I felt human. No visitors, no messages. I put my feet up and had the nap interrupted earlier by Davina. I came to at quarter to four, checked the e-mails, wrote a note to put on the door saying "Closed until Monday morning", took a shower in the little washroom. Mickey had thought of everything, there was even a mirror with a good light above it, for renewing her makeup. Studying my face I decided that I didn't look too bad, signs of my dissipated nights had almost disappeared.

When I rounded the corner at the end of the street I saw the mini had two tickets slapped on the windscreen. A legitimate parking space with a well-exceeded time limit. "In for a penny, in for a pound" was my reaction. Mickey could afford it, I could afford it, so what did it matter how many tickets I collected? I waved to a warden busily writing in her pad a few blocks away. She waved back bemused by this unusually friendly action. Even as I watched she tore off her piece of paper and was fixing it under a windscreen wiper when the angry owner rushed out from a bar waving his arms and shouting abuse. I rang Davina's bell, I didn't want to witness an ugly scene which would spoil my holiday mood.

'Come in' said a voice I didn't recognise, a man's voice through the entry phone system, 'Whoever you are, come

and join the party. Come straight through and out the back.'
No complicated security system today, clearly. Out the back
was straight through Davina's living room where the long
windows opened on to the communal gardens. There were
trestle tables laden with cakes and jellies – jellies! I hadn't
eaten jelly for twenty years, and there were children, gangs
of children in the bizarre costumes I'd seen that morning.
There were adults in strange costumes too. A giraffe came
up to me and greeted me with 'Hi! You must be Danielle,
Davina's guest. I'm Jim.' He was speaking from the bottom
of the creature's neck, the head towered way above.

'Hello Jim. Call me Dany. I'm a bit disorientated. I
thought I was just invited for a cup of tea!'

'She didn't want to frighten you off. I've got a costume
you could borrow if you like. Come and have a look.'

He took my hand, guiding me in and out of the milling
throng, to the pavilion across the lawn. It was an Aladdin's
cave of shiny material and glitter.

'Props are my main thing, but I do certain types of
costumes too. Here, I think this leopard would be just you.
It's a reject from *'The Lion King'*. Do try it. I think it's just
your size.'

I looked again at the crowd. I couldn't spot a single
person in ordinary clothes. If I hadn't been in this lighthearted post-alcoholic state I would have been horrified
and furious with Davina for letting me in for this.

'You can change in my bedroom. Shout if you need
help.'

I didn't. The stretchy gold fabric with brown spots fitted
like a second skin, the animal's ears were on an attached
cap. Unlike the main living room splashed everywhere with
bright colours, the bedroom was simple, stark even.
Exceptionally tidy.

'You look fantastic darling,' drawled Jim from the doorway. 'You need a bit of face paint, though. May I? Come
into the dressing room, I'll make you up like the cutest big
cat you've ever seen.'

When he'd done with me, I was not only cute but totally unrecognisable, fortunately. Although I wasn't likely to meet anyone who knew me, I wanted to be incognito in that guise.

'Your bedroom is very elegant,' I remarked.

'It's Zen. Japanese. I spent a lot of time in Japan. It's a peaceful room for meditation. I don't spend the night there, of course. I call the other bedroom Ernest's room because the décor is purely his. He's pretty untidy, and he likes somewhat gross retro stuff, have a peep before you face the public.'

I'd only seen southern American bar rooms in the cinema, so I wasn't sure of the authenticity of Ernest's choice of juke box, stools and a bed that resembled a snooker table. Jeans and checked shirts were strewn around haphazardly.

'I generally only come in here when the lights are low, or it's completely dark. If I didn't adore him, I don't know if I could stand it. Anyway when I climb into that ridiculous bed, I soon forget about the décor. Ten years together and the passion hasn't diminished. Could be because we have to spend time apart when we both work abroad. Come on, grit your teeth and take the plunge.' He dragged me into the fray.

I'm not used to children. I don't really know how to deal with them. It must have been the leopard skin that changed it all. I shared cake with two minute lion cubs, I indulged in a bun fight with a wart hog and wrestled with a hippopotamus. Actually I'm not sure that he was a child he was so much stronger than I was. We were all tired out by running around and screaming when the entertainment began. First a clown, then a magician, and finally that good old favourite Punch and Judy. I yelled 'Behind you' with the rest, responding to the spirit of the show, putting aside my dislike of nasty little Mr. Punch. The kids loved it.

'Aren't you glad you came?' asked a chimpanzee with Davina's voice.

'I guess so.'

'We do this children's party every year after the festival parade. We have a much wilder do with loud music and fireworks after Brighton Pride, for the select few, of course.'

'Brighton Pride?'

'Brighton's Gay Pride, darling.' The giraffe had joined us. 'The lovely folk of the city are so proud of us that they want to be included, if only in name. You know, like Brighton Pier.' He put a leg across the chimpanzee's shoulders. 'Davina is always one of the stars of the show. You should see her top hat and tails routine. A Marlene in miniature.'

'And a few decades older.' She squeezed his hoof with her paw. 'I just love the boys, they're such fun, don't you think?'

The head poked out of the giraffe's neck, a bit like an alien, and kissed the top of the chimp's nose.

'Where is your other half? I haven't seen him all afternoon?'

'No, my love. He had a sudden call this morning from the director he'll be working with on the next production. Urgent discussion was necessary for the design, could he get there as soon as possible? So he dashed to Heathrow to see if he could get a standby ticket.'

'Goodness me. That man is hardly ever still. Where's he off to this time?'

'New Orleans. It's a mega musical about the history of the place. Money has poured in in sympathy for the flood victims. There'll be a free show for all the people whose homes were affected. As far as I can gather they are going to include the floods in the last act and end with a sort of resurrection finale. It's very complicated. Poor old Ernest has sweated blood over it. Dany, are you all right?'

I had collapsed onto the nearest chair, my heart thumping as if to burst. Every possible link with Anita still brought me out in a cold sweat. New Orleans, Louisiana. Ernest was on a plane to Louisiana.

'I'm O.K.' I gasped. I sounded as though I was suffocating.

'Lie down and put your feet higher than your head' commanded the giraffe, whilst the chimp rushed to find some water.

'No, she's panicking, hyperventilating. Do you have a brown paper bag?' A black bear hurried over, most concerned. 'Breathe deeply, breathe deeply.'

I was trying to calm down. I did as I was told, took deep breaths.

'I'm fine now. Thank you.'

'It's her costume. It's too tight. And she might be allergic to all that make up.'

A small crowd of adults were standing around me, making sympathetic noises.

'If you can walk I'll take you back to lie down. I'm so sorry.' Jim offered me his arm.

It was good to be still and quiet in his uncluttered space at the back of the Pavilion, facing away from the gardens. I had discarded the leopard suit in favour of a silk kimono and Jim had gently cleaned my face with cold cream. He left me for about half an hour or so before asking if I would like some tea or maybe a nip of brandy, or both.

'Or maybe an indigestion pill. I'm sure your stomach isn't used to all that jelly and cake.'

'A cup of tea is actually what I came for, and I haven't had one yet.'

'China or Indian?'

'Just tea.'

He pulled a face. 'We don't do "just tea". I take it by that you mean Indian.'

I heard him busy in the kitchen, whistling softly. It was very soothing.

Beside the bed was a lacquered table with two bamboo chairs. We sat together sipping our tea from china cups.

'Do you often have these funny turns?' asked Jim at last.

'I've been a bit wobbly from time to time since last summer. Something happened to me in France which caused a sort of nervous breakdown.'

'Perhaps the noise and the crowd were too much then.'

'No it wasn't that.' I was silent, stared at him, looked down at my tea then back at him. I liked him much better as a human being than as a giraffe. 'It was you talking about New Orleans. My breakdown was something to do with a person from there I think. Louisiana anyway.'

'Ah!' I didn't want to elaborate, nor did he ask any more questions.

'I'm supposed to be going to another party tonight.' I changed the subject.

'Would that be wise? Why don't you go home and rest?'

Going "home" didn't appeal to me in the least. I would only mooch around in that empty house.

'No. I'm absolutely recovered. Thank you.'

'If you're dressed to go out you can just stay here then until later. As it happens I'm going to a party too. We could take a taxi together if we're heading in the same direction. Where are you going?'

I repeated Roz's address.

'What an amazing coincidence! You're going to Roz's. That's where I'm going!'

'You are a friend of hers?'

'She's our solicitor darling. She's splendid. She always invites the most interesting people. Media people, theatre people.'

'Oh dear. Doesn't sound as though I'll fit in.' I began to get cold feet.

'If she's invited you it's because you will. That's really too marvellous. We'll go together.'

'Do you think I'm dressed for it?' I remembered I'd slept in my deliberately casual clothes. 'Won't it all be a bit flashy?'

'Not at all! You look beautiful.'

I was even less happy with my appearance when Jim was ready. He wore a purple satin shirt set off by a scarlet cummerbund. He saw my dismay.

'Sweetie, I could lend you something more exotic if you like, but believe me, you look just great in what you're wearing. I'll tell you what. I have a bandana which would match your shirt perfectly. It would give you a more rakish look. I suspect you can be quite rakish when you're in the mood.'

If only I was in the mood, I thought.

I took the mini, in spite of Jim's misgivings, since the police would be coming down especially hard that night on drivers with even a fraction over the limit.

'Don't worry,' I assured him. 'I'll be on water. I'm afraid if I leave the car any longer where it is it may be towed away.'

When he saw the accumulation of tickets, he agreed.

Roz lived in what looked like a small colonial villa hardly a hundred yards from the main shopping street. It had the kind of veranda that to my uninformed imagination suggested the Southern States of the U.S.A., and a walled garden crowded with elegant guests who outshone the spring flowers.

'I think I'll drop you off and go home,' I said to Jim.

'You'll do no such thing. I know Roz, if she invited you she really wants to see you. She'll be very disappointed.'

'She won't even notice my absence amongst this lot.'

'She will. She notices everything. She's a very sharp lawyer.'

Not sharp enough to notice what is right under her nose, her girlfriend getting off with her son, I thought.

'Really, I'm very tired all of a sudden. I'd be better with an early night.'

Too Late! The hostess herself had come out into the street to greet us.

'Jim, my love, you've brought the gorgeous Dany with you. Well done! I was afraid she'd duck out.'

'She nearly did. I told her you'd be heart broken.'

'You're right.' Her arm was round my shoulders. 'She's my breath of fresh air.'

I had been called many things in my time, never that. She could have said "She's my bit of rough", because that's what I felt like amongst all these sophisticates. The bandana wasn't enough to transform me into a star. I should have let him dress me up in order to fit in. But then why should I want to fit in? I didn't belong here, I was passing through, an outsider, a lone cowboy. I probably looked like one. I was conscious of surreptitious stares. Who is she? What is she doing here? I was especially interesting as Roz's arm was still round my shoulders. Jim was already engaged in animated conversation with a group of young men, one of whom was telling a story with much emphasis and many gestures bringing forth alternate bursts of laughter and gasps of horror from his listeners.

'Who's the handsome stranger, Roz?'

The speaker was a distinguished looking middle aged man, sensitive face, pale skin, wavy blond hair and very shrewd blue eyes.

'This is Dany,' Roz finally took her arm away. 'Talk to Simon for a bit Dany, I'll get you a drink. Champagne?'

'Water, water.'

'How very abstemious! Simon raised his eyebrows. 'I hope you allow yourself a little indulgence from time to time. You could fill my glass, Roz, darling. I'll drink Dany's share. Do you act?' He asked me.

'I'm an estate agent's assistant at the moment. I'm usually a barperson or a cook.'

'I don't care what your job is. Do you act? Have you ever done any acting?'

'No.' It was an extraordinary question which made me nervous again about by appearance.

'Pity. You would be great in my next production. I'm a director for an amateur theatre group. I'm always on the lookout for new talent. Do you fancy having a go at the stage?'

'No way!'

'A great pity,' he repeated, shaking his head. 'Never mind.'

'Simon, we wondered where you'd got to. I need your advice about a part I've been offered.'

The woman at his elbow was the closest I've seen to Marilyn Monroe in real life.

'Amelia, my protégée,' he smiled at her fondly. 'Amelia, meet Dany, whom I was trying to persuade to join the Brighton Players. Amelia has taken wing. She's left us amateurs far behind and flown to the West End.'

Not difficult if you look like that, was my private comment.

He read my thoughts. 'She's not only a pretty face, she's very talented. We got her through Drama School and she's never looked back.'

'He's been wonderful to me, Dany. He's an absolute poppet.' But her eyes were on me not him, on my body.

Roz arrived with water in a crystal tumbler. 'Your champagne is over on the table Simon. Your friends said I was to drag you back to them.'

'Don't go away, Dany. I haven't finished with you yet!' He strolled back to the band of what I assumed were would-be thespians. Amelia didn't go with him, which was surprising since he was the ostensible reason for her coming over to us.

'I can see it hasn't taken long for Amelia to find you,' remarked Roz, dryly.

'She came to fetch Simon.' I was embarrassed.

'Is that so, Amelia?' She was amused.

'I needed his advice. I can get it later. I'd rather talk to Dany now.'

'I bet you would! I'll leave her in your tender care. Don't worry Dany. She comes across like a femme fatale, but she's easily rebuffed. I'll come and help you out if you look as though you're in trouble.'

I was even more embarrassed. I wanted to tear off the "rakish" bandana, which appeared to be fascinating my glamorous companions.

'You look very dashing,' she said at last.

'I look stupid!' I ripped it off angrily.

'My you look handsome when you're cross!' She was giggling at the cliché.

I stuffed the offending object in my pocket. This

encounter could easily lead in directions I would regret. I tried to introduce a little more distance. 'Is it an interesting part you've been offered?'

She pulled a face. 'Not especially. That's why I want Simon's advice. He's acting as my agent for the moment. Roz is right, as usual, though. I came over because of you not him. You're the only person here I don't know. Roz and I had an affairette when she was still married. It didn't mean much but was good fun.'

Lights were beginning to come on in the garden as the sun went down and the air cooled.

There was a drift indoors.

'It's getting chilly, do you want to come up to my bedroom?'

'Your bedroom?' Had I heard right?

'Yes, I rent a room here. Roz has plenty of space now. It suits us both. I'm an easy tenant. Sometimes I'm away on tour, often I'm playing in London so I don't get home until late. I'm resting at the moment, which is why I'm free on a Saturday night. It won't last long. If I accept the role I'll be off, off all over the country for two months before we open in the West End. Are you coming?'

She was already leading the way.

I was still debating with myself whether to follow her or not, when the decision was made for me.

'Amelia has monopolised you for long enough. Come and circulate.' Roz gave her lodger a warning glance.

'Spoilsport!' Amelia sounded resigned.

I hate the word "circulate", almost as much as I hate the word "network". Who would be really interested in me in this high powered gathering? I was wrong. Well, it wasn't that I, Danielle Divito, was found to be fascinating in her own right, it was my job. It was extraordinary how many inhabitants of this city were selling or buying houses. I was pumped for information that I didn't have. "What is the state of the market? Is there likely to be a downturn? Which areas are best to invest in?"

'Excuse me,' I said to a couple who already owned five flats but were considering buying a few more, 'Excuse me, I'm feeling faint, I'll have to lie down for a bit.'

It was the truth, moreover. It was hot, I was hot. I shouldn't have come. I pushed my way to the front door. Again for the third time this evening, my moves were blocked.

'Come in here, it's quiet. We can have a glass of brandy together. It'll calm you down.'

Calming down was what I needed. My anger at allowing myself to be constantly manipulated was almost suffocating me. I felt like yelling "get out of my way, woman, leave me alone!" Instead I went with her into what I took to be a library there were so many books lining the walls.

She shut the door behind us.

'Dany, you must let go' she said.

'I let go last night, and the night before.' Whether she and I meant the same thing by "let go", wasn't clear. 'What I need to do now is catch up on my sleep.'

'Feel free.' She indicated a long sofa. 'There are a couple of blankets in a box in the corner, I keep them there for emergencies.'

'I have to go back to my apartment.'

'Why?'

Why indeed?

'I haven't been back since yesterday evening.'

'So?'

'I have to change my clothes.'

'I can lend you some.'

Everybody wanted to lend me clothes. Ironic since I now possessed more of my own than I ever had before.

'Maybe you should have suggested that as soon as I arrived, then I wouldn't have felt so out of place.'

'Out of place?' She frowned. 'Out of place! That's nonsense! People were queuing up to talk to you.'

I didn't try to explain. I was very tired. There had been a moment when events might have taken a different turn, if I'd been allowed to play with Amelia. At least she was interested in me for myself, my body, who cared? She wasn't going to pump me about real estate.

There was a tentative knock at the door. Roz sighed. The knock was repeated, somewhat louder.

'Roz, most of us are leaving.' It was Simon's voice.

She got up. 'Stay there, Dany. I assure you the couch is as comfortable as any bed.' She went out into the corridor, where I could hear the usual cries of 'Darling, a great party.' Jim flitted into the library. 'Take care sweetheart. Come and see me soon. Keep the bandana. I'll invite you over when Ernest gets back.'

'Please do. That would be nice.' I'd forgotten Ernest winging his way to New Orleans. The abrupt reminder made my heart race.

'You've gone pale again. I don't think you should drive home.'

'She won't. Not yet anyway. We're all going to leave her in peace.'

She opened an elaborately carved oak chest, pulled out a pile of woollen covers. I guessed I ought to do as she said. I let her tuck me in, reverting gratefully to childhood. She kissed me lightly on the lips before putting out the light.

# Chapter 11

I got up at first light, before the sun was up. I left the house quietly, and drove off. I was feeling great. I poured half a jar of invigorating salts into a bath, changed, and sauntered down to a café which served substantial breakfasts. I bought a paper, ordered a mug of tea, eggs, bacon, and sausage and two rounds of toast. An hour later, much fortified, I strode out as far as the marina. It being bad for my almost recovered blisters to walk too far without a rest, I decided to visit Davina on the way back. I hadn't had much chance to speak to her the previous day. It occurred to me also that I hadn't seen Tracey. Not that I would have recognised her in animal guise. I was curious to know if she was still there or whether she had run off.

The security system had been re-established as normal. It was Tracey who eventually let me in. She and Davina were in the latter's bedroom.

'Come in, Dany. I'm having a lie-in this morning, yesterday was a little bit energetic for me. This morning my body reminds me I'm not as young as I used to be.'

She was propped up against a pile of white pillows, wearing an embroidered cotton nightdress, an Indian shawl around her shoulders. Although the bed was of a normal size, her minute form was almost lost in it.

'Tracey's sitting here beside me. You can pull up that chair. The bergère chair in the corner. There! Isn't this cosy?'

'Are you feeling unwell Davina? Is there anything I can get?'

'She's got everything she needs. I'm looking after her.' Tracey's tone was hostile as ever.

'I'm pleased to see you Tracey, I missed you yesterday.'

'Yeah, well, I didn't stay long. I couldn't be doing with the costume Jim lent me.'

'What was it?'

'A dragonfly. It was the wings. I couldn't fold them up so they kept swiping kids in the face and knocking jellies on the floor.'

'She and I sneaked off in here, closed the curtains, watched DVDs and ate chocolates. Then we played cards. I'm going to teach her how to play chess later today, aren't I Tracey?'

'We'll see how you get on. We don't want you overtired again.'

Quite the little nurse, I thought.

'What did you get up to last night, then? If I were eighty years younger I'd have asked you to take me dancing.'

I smiled, Tracey glowered.

'I went to a party with Jim.'

'Oh, Roz's party. I was invited, I always am.'

The idea of Davina crushed in the chattering crowd was frightening.

'She's my lawyer, you know. Good woman. Did you sleep with her?'

'No, I didn't.' I was shocked.

'She's a good looker,' Davina mused. 'I never liked that girlfriend. Shifty. Sly. Don't know what Roz saw in her except sex. It's not enough, is it? And look what happened. You'd be much better for her.'

I gave a sidelong glance at Tracey. She was studying her fingernails. I cleared my throat uneasily. 'I'm glad Davina was able to help you out, Tracey,' trying to bring her back into the conversation and put an end to Davina's attempt at matchmaking.

'Yeah, it's a good thing there are some bighearted people in this world, not like some other selfish bitches.'

'Tracey dear, do watch your language' Davina admonished.

Ignoring her Tracey went on, 'Selfish bitches who would leave you in the street to die of cold or starve to death.'

'I ran after you. I was going to pay for a few nights at a hotel whilst we sorted something out. You'd disappeared.'

'Yeah, yeah, I don't think!' Her scornfulness made me flinch. 'I could have drowned myself for all you cared.'

There was no point in trying to argue with her. Davina's head was back against the pillows, her eyes closed.

'She should have a nap now. Visitors can be very tiring.' The implication was clear.

'I'll be going then.'

Davina opened her eyes. 'I'm so pleased you called in dear. Any time. Don't forget what I've been saying to you. If you're searching for a partner, you could do a lot worse than Roz.'

'Thanks for the advice.' I patted her hand gently. I would have kissed her, except that Tracey was standing over her like a guard dog.

'I'll let myself out.'

As I sauntered past the first day trippers clambering from their coaches, I wondered how Ray and Tracey would hit it off. She would probably terrify him into submission. Or he might bring out her protective side. Would she extract from him secrets he had sworn never to reveal? Unlike her, he would find lying difficult. I was pretty convinced that what she'd told Davina was fiction, with perhaps a dash of truth. I strolled along the pier and sat on a deckchair. I scanned the horizon. It was said that on a clear day you could see the Isle of Wight from there. Not clear enough today. Distant cargo ships were making their way to the docks between Hove and Shoreham, sailing boats began to drift out to deeper water, maybe crossing the Channel. I had an urge to cross the Channel myself – hop on a ferry at Newhaven, work my way down to the South, back to Les Fontaines. To see if she was there, to see if Anita had come back. I had friends there who'd sworn to let me know if she did. In my heart I knew she never would.

I rang Roz in the early afternoon. She sounded as if she'd only just got up. I arranged to meet her for a pasta the following week. I hadn't given her much of a chance. As long as she didn't want too much from me, I had so little to give until I could build up my resources, and that might take years.

Meanwhile I had a date. My escort arrived at 3.30 as arranged. 'Cool!' she said eyeing up the leather trousers I had bought years ago and didn't have the heart to throw away. 'The boots are great too. And if you ever want to get rid of the bomber jacket, I'll have it. Here, grab a helmet.'

She drove very carefully, which made me smile. I'd had a bike of my own once, an old one I'd bought from a friend. I rode it fast and dangerously, thrashing it to death. I killed it before it killed me. 'You don't have to slow down for my sake,' I yelled into her ear. 'I don't mind a bit of speed.' Whether she didn't hear me or didn't believe me, I don't know, since she continued as before. It struck me that possibly she wanted to prolong the journey, with my arms around her waist, my body against her back. It wasn't exactly thrilling, but the warmth of our closeness was very pleasant. It took almost an hour to reach Honeysuckle Place, by roundabout country lanes, not normally attractive to bikers. It was even more like something out of a travelogue than the computer picture showed; surrounded by trees in blossom – apple trees, I was informed – the downs with their sheep and lambs forming a backdrop. The present tenants were three art students – one in fashion and textiles, the other two painters. Their work was scattered everywhere inside the bedrooms and living room, only the kitchen had any clear space, not much of that. 'It's the degree show soon,' they explained. 'We've got to get all this finished. We'll have tea outside.' At the end of a garden was a honeysuckle hedge which gave the house its name. Protected by the hedge was a rustic table set around with benches roughly hewn from tree trunks. The nine of us carried the necessary cups, saucers and plates across the lawn.

'The garden takes quite a lot of time to look after, but they'll get somebody in to sort it out after we've left and before you come in, the fashion artist assured us. There was much conversation, exchange of information, stories told about the curiosity of local farmers, suspicious of what young people might be up to. I listened, feeling much more at home than I had the night before.

'Where's the nearest pub? Can we walk to it?' The question was from Des.

'If you're feeling energetic. There's a pub out of the back gate to the village. It's a bit of a climb to start with' she indicated a steep hill. 'By car, it's a couple of miles. It's too trendy though, that place. If you're taking a car it's better to go further on where there's a proper country inn.'

'What's the name of the nearest village?' I asked. As their estate agent I should know these details. It sounded familiar.

'Isn't that where your tutor lives Des?'

'What?' She had been deep in a discussion of the virtues of hemp, the cloth variety.

'Your tutor, Professor Bradshaw, doesn't he live in that village?'

'Tricky Dickey? I have no idea.'

'I think so. which reminds me, he's invited you to a party to celebrate his latest publication.'

'Oh yes?' She was evidently disinterested. I tried again.

'All of you. He's invited all of you.' I might as well include the artists.

'Are you going?' Robbie asked me.

'Yes,'

'Then we'll go too, won't we, Des?'

'I don't want him to get any ideas about me.' Des was doubtful.

He already has I thought.

'Oh yes, Des, please let's go. This would never happen in France, we'll be your chaperones.' Sandrine's eagerness did the trick.

We took a different route back. I held her more tightly, partly because she drove a little faster, partly because I wanted to anyway, my hands under her jacket.

'Thanks for the ride.' I dismounted, a little unsteadily.

'It was truly a pleasure. Let's do it again. How about next Sunday?'

'Give me a ring, or better still, call by the shop.'

Mickey's BMW was back. The kitchen light was on. I tapped lightly on the door. There was no response, although I could hear her moving around. I went upstairs and rang Ellie. She was out, so I left a message saying I'd had a good week and that I loved her.

'Dany, may I come in?'

It was the first time Mickey had come upstairs since my arrival.

'Of course. Let's have a nightcap together.'

I was shocked at her appearance. During the weekend she had grown paler, thinner, tenser. She waved aside my offer of a drink, slumped into the nearest armchair.

'How's things?'

'You mean at the office? Quiet.'

'No, you. How is it with you?'

'Oh, absolutely fine. An amazing social whirl.'

'You look good on it.'

Which is more than I can say for you, I thought. I said 'Yeah. And you?'

'I'm a bit stressed out. Could you manage on your own tomorrow morning whilst I have a lie in?'

I could have been, should have been, angry. However, since she looked on the verge of collapse, I felt sufficiently sorry for her to agree. We sat in silence, she staring into space, me with my eyes closed in the hope that she would leave, unless she was going to tell me at last what she was up to. After two or three minutes during which she said nothing, I couldn't bear it any longer.

'Did your meeting, conference, whatever it was, go well?'

She snapped out of her trance.

'In the end. It got off to a sticky start on Friday. Temperamental clashes. They were sorted out.'

'A few more steps on the path of wisdom, eh?'

'Actually, yes' she said coldly.

'Craigie will be glad to have Francesca in his arms again.'

'I keep telling her this dependence can't go on. She has to do something about it.'

'Indeed. It's driving him mad. It's a delicate matter, isn't it? She's tied him so tightly to her that if she cuts the ropes he'll fall in a heap.' It wasn't a very clever metaphor. I tried again. 'I mean he's totally obsessed.'

'Of course.'

'Why of course?'

'You wouldn't understand. There is a remedy, though. I'm sure. We just have to work on it.'

'We?'

'Fran and me.'

'Mickey, if you don't mind me saying so, it isn't really your business.'

'But it is, oh yes, it is. It's partly my fault. Actually she and

I tried to work on it a bit this afternoon when everyone else had gone home. It wasn't any good. She called me. He'd made a terrible scene about the fact that she hadn't told him there were going to be men present.'

There was no mistaking the accusation.

'Ah!'

'For goodness sake, Dany, why did you have to blurt out that Ray was involved? That's properly put the cat amongst the pigeons. Don't tell anyone anything about my affairs do you understand?'

'It came out by accident. I didn't tell him anything about your "affairs" as you call them. How could I? You keep them top secret, you and Fran. Even Ray's terrified into keeping his mouth shut, though he's so dumb if I wanted I could find out a lot. I don't want to, it's of no interest what-soever to me.' (A white lie!). It is of vital interest to Craigie. He's a good man whose wife is destroying him. Why does-n't she share the wisdom thing with him? Until she does he'll believe she's having sex not going to classes.'

'We don't go to classes. And having sex is one road to wisdom.'

Oh dear, oh dear! I stared at her.

'She can't share anything yet. How many times do I have to repeat that?'

'Having sex is one road to wisdom, eh? Then you do sleep around. It's not a conference it's an orgy! A drug crazed orgy.' I'd gone so far in provoking her that I may as well go further. 'You employ me, because you trust me, you said. All right, I would never, never betray a friend, but I'm not happy about living with a drug dealer. "*Her Place*" is just a cover, isn't it? You'll make your money, which you don't even need, you told me, by trading on wretched people.'

She had turned scarlet, opened her mouth then shut it again.

'If you want me to stay you'll have to be up front with me. I won't inform on you, but I have to know what I'm into here.'

She tried to speak, failed, swallowed, took a deep breath and found her voice.

'So that's what you imagine I'm doing, peddling narcotics?'

'Aren't you?'

'No! I swear by the Goddess I'm not. I've never touched drugs in my life.'

Swearing by some goddess didn't quite convince me.

'Then what is it all about? Don't try to fob me off with that wisdom crap.'

'Please don't insist, Dany. You're not ready.'

'I'm as ready as I'll ever be.'

'It's not illegal.'

'What's not illegal?'

There was a very long pause. Then her answer was scarcely audible.

'Wicca' she whispered.

'What?' The word was incomprehensible.

She cleared her throat, pronounced more loudly 'Wicca!'

'What on earth is that?'

'An ancient wisdom.'

I was beginning to get the picture: 'a religious cult!'

'No. Not exactly. We take from many religions. We're very powerful, Wicca is an Earth religion, centuries old.'

'Why all the secrecy? It's ridiculous to make such a fuss, if it's not a dangerous cult.'

'Some people are frightened of it. I told you it's very powerful.'

'In what way powerful?'

She shrugged. 'Influence. We have influence. Make people do things.'

'Brainwash them, you mean? Into giving you money to put in a Swiss bank account? Kidnap adolescents into a closed community?'

'Of course not. We don't live in communities. I live here don't I? Fran lives with Craigie, we are all individual priests or priestesses who get together when we choose to and have ceremonies.'

'Priests of what church? When were you ordained?'

'Don't be silly. I became a priestess when I chose to be. A priestess of the Goddess.'

This was becoming weirder and weirder. I'm pretty open-minded but this sounded like a load of rubbish.

'What Goddess?'

'The Goddess. The Earth Mother.'

'So you are a what did you call it, Wicca? A Wicca priestess?'

'Yes.' Another long pause. 'I am called by another more common name. I'm a witch.'

It was as if she'd kicked me in the stomach.

'Mickey, you're joking!'

'I'm perfectly serious. I'm a witch. Fran is a witch. Ray has just become a witch. It was his inauguration ceremony. May Day evening. It's a very important date for us.'

My mind was still in shock.

'Oh, my God, that's terrible.'

'You see! That's how everybody reacts to the word witch.'

'You cast spells?'

'Sometimes. Miranda had a book. A Book of Shadows. It has lots of spells in it.'

'So Miranda was a witch too. What about Samuel?'

'She became a witch after he died. She had special powers. Quite naturally. She was psychic.

'Do you have special powers?'

'No, unfortunately. I mean you don't have to. It helps. It would help me to be able to get in touch with her when I can't quite read her recipes. The right amount of each ingredient is crucial.'

'These spells in Miranda's book, you've tried them all?'

'Some little ones. Nothing much yet. Miranda used to be the organiser of covens all over Sussex. So I'm doing the same. It's not easy. Some of the older witches say I'm too young. They squabble with each other, you know. This last weekend was very trying. Especially as it was the first initiation ceremony I'd designed. I introduced some new invocations which were disapproved of by the old guard.'

'Where did all this go on?'

'In Lady Loxley's place. I realised that's how her mother knew Miranda. Dany, you won't tell Craigie, will you?' She implored.

Craigie! Fran was a witch! She'd put a spell on him! No, I didn't believe in the power of magic. It was superstition, wasn't it?

'She put a spell on him!'

'She and I mixed a potion. She put it into his glass when she met him the second time. She knew he was going to be at the party. She made sure she offered him the first drink. It was a bit bitter but he just thought the wine was off. It must have been too strong.' She looked so rueful I almost laughed. 'We're trying to find the antidote. The difficulty is, she doesn't want him to fall out of love with her, just to love her more normally. We've experimented with powders she's mixed with his food. They make it worse. Please, please, please don't tell him. Promise.'

'You're asking me to stand by whilst you evil sisters practise your black arts on an innocent victim?'

'We're not evil sisters and they aren't black arts. It's white magic, good magic.'

Hmm, debatable I thought. 'Alright,' I said. 'But you'd better unlock the spell pretty quickly as it will end in tears if not murder and mayhem.'

'Thank you, thank you. You won't mention Wicca to anyone at all? I mean some of us have come out recently, but I don't think it would be good for business.'

'No, it probably wouldn't. Don't worry, my lips are sealed.'

'And you will do tomorrow morning?'

'Sure if you'd do tomorrow afternoon, and all day Tuesday.'

'O.K. Goodnight Dany. I'm glad it's all in the open. I mean between you and me, if you're interested I can teach you some magic.'

'From what you've told me you don't have quite enough experience to be a teacher. Good night, Mickey.'

Shocking though I'd found them, in a way I was relieved

by these revelations. Lying in the dark, mulling them over, I regretted I had promised to keep quiet. I would love to laugh over it with Ellie, since I was more inclined to be entertained than scared. I wondered about Ray's "initiation". What had they inflicted on him? I would use my free time the following afternoon to call on his aunt. Was she a witch too? Is that why she had lived to such a great age? I would look at all our customers with new eyes from now on.

# Chapter 12

Monday morning was slow. The highlight was a Russian couple, exuding money, who wanted a cliff top residence, cost no object. Oh joy. I was able to use my Russian, rusty though it was, it was better than their English. They fell for an old lighthouse which had been converted many years previously.

I checked the name of the vendor's solicitor. Surprise, surprise! I dialled.

'Roz?'

'I'm her secretary. She's with a client. Can I help you?'

'This is Danielle Divito of "*Her Place*". I have a buyer for the lighthouse. The asking price.'

'More if necessary,' he emphasised. His wife nodded vigorously.

'Will you let Ms Browning know as soon as possible and would she ring me back. Thank you.'

'You'll e-mail? We want to know as soon as we get back home that it's O.K.'

'They strode out, tore up their parking ticket, zoomed off, taking full advantage of the vehicle's smart acceleration, leaving the space vacant for Mickey's taxi.

'Who were they? They looked loaded.'

'Russians. I think I can say that my ability to discuss in their own language clinched the sale of one of our most expensive and difficult to sell properties.'

This was a lie, they would have bought it anyway. I wanted to impress Mickey, and I did. She was over the moon.

When the telephone rang five minutes later I beat her to it.

'*Her Place*. Daniella speaking.'

'You don't have to tell me, I'd know that voice anywhere.'

Alas, not what I was expecting. It was Jiminy Cricket.

'Daniella, you haven't forgotten our lunch engagement this week?'

Oh yes, I had.

'Can you make it tomorrow? I'm afraid I'll have to be in town after that.'

'Er, I'm not sure.'

'I do hope so. Greta will be terribly disappointed if you can't.'

Oh, why not, I thought.

'Splendid. I'm so pleased. One o'clock? I'll pick you up at 12.45. I thought we'd eat Italian.'

'Fine. See you.'

'I'm so looking forward to it.' I cut off any further gushing.

The phone rang again. Mickey answered.

'No it's Michaela, Dany's off for the afternoon. About the sale of the lighthouse. Yes, we have a buyer. Russian. The asking price.' She turned to me. 'It's the woman who's responsible for Patrick's place. She seems to have a finger in every pie.'

Not a happy phrase, I thought sulkily.

It was beginning to rain hard. I dived into the nearest coffee bar, "The Sugar Twist". I hadn't been in before but I'd noticed it had a most interesting clientele. A girl's bar.

'You work at "*Her Place*" don't you? The woman who served me had the most elaborate tattoos covering her arms and shoulders. And piercing. Everywhere, probably. I've seen you coming and going. Why don't you chill out here in the evenings? You'd like it.'

I looked at a poster advertising a list of evening events.

'It's a great meeting place.'

Pick-up joint, she meant. I'd bear it in mind.

There were papers and magazines scattered around, Lesbian and Gay weeklies, and alternative city events bimonthlies. There was a noticeboard with adverts mainly for house or flat sharing. Cheap deals for compatible women. I briefly wondered if any would suit Tracey before concluding they would definitely not be her scene. I flicked through a guide to the festival. Maybe there was something I might like to see. Too much for me to take in. Too much to choose from. I studied the list again.

'Confusing isn't it? I'll tell you where to go if you're wanting a night out. Come with me to the opening night of Simon's production.'

She was leaning over my shoulder, her blond hair brushing my cheek, her perfume intoxicating.

'Do you mind if I join you? I often come here to chill out.'

Amelia slid into the chair opposite, flashed a devastating smile at the waitress. 'My usual, darling.'

The "usual" turned out to be a banana milk shake. So that's what gave her all those curves.

'It's generally quiet at this time of the day. It will be positively throbbing tonight.'

She sucked on her straw and looked into my eyes.

'Such a shame Roz confiscated you the other evening. She's very protective of vulnerable young women who she thinks I'll devour and then spit out the pieces. She doesn't want me to break any more hearts.'

Mine is already broken, I thought.

'Have you broken many?'

'Not a single one. You have to fall hook, line and sinker to suffer and nobody falls like that for me. Which is just as well. I'm a very shallow person.'

The remainder of her drink gurgled in the glass as she greedily sought every last drop. She sighed. 'It's probably a pity. I'd be a better actress if I were deep, but there we are, that's the way I am. Are you deep, Dany?'

'No, I'm shallow too. Love 'em and leave 'em.'

'Oh good. That means we can play together. I'd just

love to play with you. Would you love to play with me?'

The look I gave her was answer enough.

'Why don't you come to Simons's play then, and we'll go on to his first night party? He wants me to, but I usually find other people's first nights wearing. They're all on a high that has nothing to do with you. I can't bear it. If you're with me it will be fine. And Simon will be delighted. He took a fancy to you.'

'In that case, I'm not sure...'

'He doesn't want to sleep with you. He has the most charming long term partner, who is incredibly tolerant. We'll see the play, spend a little time at the party then back to my place. How about it?'

It was a tempting proposition. I didn't take too long to decide.

'O.K.'

She laughed. 'I usually get a more enthusiastic response to my invitations. I have a reputation for giving a girl a good time.'

'So I gathered.'

'See you 7 p.m. at the Clock Tower. Ciao!'

She took up her umbrella and bounced out.

'You paying for her milk shake?' asked the waitress.

'I suppose so, yes.'

'It's funny how she always finds a friendly butch to do that. She has an instinct.'

'She has sex-appeal.'

'Yeah!' She had a knowing grin as she picked up the money.

I spent the afternoon back home on my bed. I needed to rest, also to review the weekend, especially Mickey's revelation. On the one hand, it all seemed like childish nonsense, the kind of hocus-pocus you ought to grow out of in adolescence. I had never been attracted to magic, the real world was quite enough for me without worrying about the supernatural. On the other hand "witchcraft" was a word which evoked dark deeds, pacts with the devil.

There was absolutely nothing devilish about Mickey, nor Francesca. Mickey had denied any association with evil, with the "Black arts". They practised white magic she said. They used their powers for the good. If they got it right. Who knows what noxious powder they had produced to trap Craigie, nor what they were working on to counter-balance it. They could have poisoned the poor man. All those jars of plants Mickey had in the kitchen might not be harmless; nature produces some nasty berries, some terri-ble leaves, not to mention ghastly roots. I resolved there and then to refuse all drinks Mickey would offer. Fortunately she wasn't likely to cook for me, so I didn't have to worry about contaminated food. But Craigie in his innocence ate and drank whatever his wife placed before him. And what about Ray? What had they done to that poor idiot?

I turned my mind to Roz. I wanted to see her alone. I was looking forward to an intimate dinner in neutral surroundings. Get to know each other properly. I hoped that we wouldn't run into her later on the stairs. It was awkward that she and Amelia shared the same house. I couldn't stand jealousy, I suffered from it over Anita, I didn't want to inspire it in others. Did Roz and Amelia like threesomes? If so, they could count me out. I had been persuaded into it once with identical twins. It was weird and most unsatisfactory.

I took a shower, spent time choosing what to wear for a night out with a glamour queen. If she was so femme I would be a dashing butch. A dinner jacket would be going too far. Black linen, crisp white shirt, Italian boots were my final choice. A spicy cologne which had met with much approval in the past. I called a taxi.

I enjoyed the play. It was a comedy about an airline pilot who was having affairs with several air hostesses at once. The theatre was tiny, everyone in the audience knew almost everyone else as well as all the actors.

'O God, it's worse than I expected,' whispered Amelia as

we made our way down to the bar at the interval. Simon was nervously sipping his gin and tonic.

'Wonderful, darling,' Amelia breathed as she kissed him.

'It's terrible. We've had several changes of cast at the last minute. Thank you for coming, but I wish you hadn't.'

'It'll pick up in the second half' she consoled him.

'I thought the first half was all right,' I ventured.

'Dany, you're a treasure.' He put his arm round me.

The second half did turn out to be better, even I could see that.

'They'd been nervous at the beginning,' I suggested to Amelia.

'Oh yes. But they're not Simon's first choice. He's had to include some very inexperienced newcomers. Let's have a drink in the pub next door before we go on to the party.'

Going to a pub with Amelia was an interesting experience. Jaws dropped, beer mugs suspended half-way to mouths. She took no notice, she was used to it.

'She's the "wow factor", I thought. I was proud to be the sole focus of her attention, to buy her a tequila sunrise. Simon lived close by. When we arrived the cast and friends were milling around a table of canapés, talking excitedly. There was a moment's silence when we appeared, then the chatter resumed. One of the air hostesses, a glass in one hand, a plate in the other, made her way over to us.

'Amelia, how nice to see you here. Fancy tearing yourself away from West End glitter to watch our humble efforts.'

'I wouldn't have missed it. You were terrific darling. Your German accent was almost convincing. Did you have much coaching? Just a little word of advice – go easy on the w's. At times it was a bit like a caricature of a nazi officer in a war film, "Vee haf vays off making you talk!" I know it's a farce, but there's no need for the comedy to be heavy handed. It was only once or twice and I expect Simon will have given you a note about it.'

'No. Actually he complimented me on my accent.' She was tight lipped.

'Well there you are! As long as he's happy. Don't mind me, I'm just a perfectionist. Excuse me, I must congratulate Andy. He's come on so much since the early days.' With a gracious smile she moved off.

'Are you a friend of hers?' The woman drained her glass, put it down and began to gobble her food angrily.

'Not exactly. We've only just met.'

'Well let me warn you, she's an arrogant bitch. Thinks she's made it because she's had one or two lucky breaks, done a bit of telly. I expect it's all the casting couch.'

'The casting couch?'

'Yes, you know, sleeping with the right people. I mean she's not particularly talented. Do you act?'

'No.'

'I wish she would. Have some food, Dany.' I took a plate Simon was holding out. 'Come and say hello to my partner, Julius.'

Julius was one of the most distinguished people I have ever met. Tall, thin erect bearing, dark hair greying at the temples, fine features, gentle hazel eyes.

'Enchanté, my dear.' He kissed my hand.

'He was brought up by a governess from Marseille,' Simon informed me. 'Taught him some juicy swear words as well as la politesse. Isn't she adorable Julius?'

'Quite delicious. I hope we'll see more of you dear. I'm off to bed now. These parties give me a frightful headache.'

'I love that man to pieces.' Simon gazed fondly at the retreating back. 'He puts up with an awful lot. I'm very temperamental, sometimes deliberately provocative. He takes it all in his stride, bless him.'

An hour later Amelia declared herself ready to leave. I was on the point of exchanging phone numbers with a girl wearing tight hipsters and a lacy cropped top, but Amelia dragged me away.

'Darling, I've just saved you from a fate worse than death,' she informed me as we stood waiting for a taxi. 'She's poison and she's too young for you. She's only seventeen. She hates me. Most of them do. Jealousy. They're all stage struck but none of them has what it takes.'

She sat so close to me in the taxi that another two passengers could have fitted in beside us.

'You smell gorgeous.' She said. 'You've got great muscles. Do you work out regularly?'

'Never.'

'You're lucky. To keep a body like that I'd have to exercise two hours a day.' Her hand was on my thigh.

We didn't meet Roz. Amelia said she usually went to bed early during the week.

'Fortunately my room is the other side of the house from her bedroom and she sleeps soundly, so she won't hear us whatever we get up to. She doesn't mind if I bring anyone back as long as I don't wake her.'

'Do you often bring people back?' I asked as soon as her door was safely closed.

'Very rarely, as it happens. Sit down, I'll put some soft, low music on.'

She did precisely that, then leaned back on her bed and said 'Undress me.'

I tiptoed down the stairs three hours later. I'd had more meaningful sex, more passionate, and nothing could ever equal my love making with Anita, but I had to admit that Amelia was in the top class for invention. Sheer pleasure, experienced over and over again. "Have you ever tried this?" she had asked a dozen times or more. I'm happy to report that I was able to show her a few routes to ecstasy taught to me by girlfriends of different cultures.

At home there was a note where I couldn't fail to see it.

*"Remember, Dany, never tell. Betrayal could bring dire consequences. I had a very tedious afternoon. Forget it, better tomorrow. See you, Mickey."*

I screwed it up and threw it in my wastepaper basket. I didn't need threats to keep me in order.

# Chapter 13

It was still pouring with rain the next morning, so I went to the library to kill time until lunch with Jiminy Cricket and his girlfriend. I looked up Wicca, as well as witchcraft. I discovered that Wicca was an old religion modernised and revised in 1939. The worship of the Great Goddess, practised by her priests and priestesses through sacred magic. Pretty much what Mickey had said. Apart from the Great Goddess, lots of other ancient deities were mentioned, and sacred days when rituals might be organised. Magic should always be used as a form for good by Wiccans, white magic, green magic. References to Witchcraft were much more sinister, especially the persecution of so-called witches for a presumed association with the devil. I remembered ceremonies I had witnessed in Martinique where I had spent time with my mother's family. Voodoo, witch-doctors, evil eye, sacrificing of animals, divination. One of my many cousins was convinced that her nasty skin condition, doubtless caused by an allergy, was the result of a spell. The suspect was an ex-lover on whom she in her turn, cast a counterspell. She was horrified when his car ran off the road for no apparent reason and smashed into a tree. She spent two whole days and nights praying in the local church until he came out of his coma.

Jiminy was on time. Greta was not what I had imagined. She was slim, delicate, with rich chestnut hair tied back in loose curls. Altogether too refined, too sensitive for Mr. Cricket, I decided. A simple, chic trouser suit, gold earrings, a golden chain bracelet and a ring with an enormous stone which I assumed was a real emerald. None of us spoke apart from the conventional greetings until we reached the restaurant.

Jiminy asked Greta in slow, simple English what she would like, she pointed to the appropriate item on the menu. She turned to me. 'Very nice to meet you, Dany' she enunciated carefully. Her accent was odd, but then, I'd never met an Albanian before. 'I've heard a lot about you.'

What exactly had she heard, I wondered. Jiminy knew nothing about me, except what Mickey might have told him, but she didn't know that much either.

'You have the advantage,' I said. She frowned. She probably hadn't understood. 'I haven't heard much about you. Tell me about yourself.'

She glanced at Jiminy, blushing slightly, then shrugged. 'My name is Greta. I come from Greece.'

'I thought you came from Albania.'

Another glance at Jiminy. 'No, Greece.'

'Sorry.' I wished I could speak Greek. 'A bona fide European citizen then.'

'Yes. But I've lost my passport, all my papers. Jiminy is trying to sort it for me. He's most kind.'

The food arrived. It was actually quite good. I congratulated the waiter, who was a real Italian, not a boy from London pretending to be one. We ate in silence. Why was I there? What did they want from me?

'Greta really needs friends' Jiminy announced. 'It would be so good if you could call on her from time to time when I'm not here. Take her out.'

Spy on her, did he mean?

'You would like a nice friend like Dany, wouldn't you darling?'

'Of course' said as if she could take it or leave it.

'You wouldn't mind escorting a beautiful woman, would you Dany? I'd pay for you both to go to the theatre, to concerts, eat at the best restaurants.'

'Suppose I wanted more than your money, Mr. Cricket?'

'What do you mean?'

'Spending the evening with a beautiful woman can be rather exciting, can't it? Both for the escort and the woman herself. The escort might prefer payment in kind.'

I wanted to needle him, test his intentions. If he agreed, I would leave immediately.

He looked questioningly at his mistress, ex-prostitute. 'Greta did you understand what she said?'

She shook her head. I was sure she did, whilst pretending not to.

He pursed his lips. 'Dany, that wasn't the deal I was proposing.'

'What kind of a deal is it then, Mr. Cricket?'

'Discreet friendship.' For the first time he seemed sincere. He stroked Greta's fingers. 'She's been hurt, abused. She needs to heal.'

Mickey had said he wasn't so bad underneath that offensively smooth exterior. There was a real person hidden within the shell of Jiminy Cricket. He too was vulnerable like the rest of us. As he kissed Greta's palm there was, on the contrary, a glint in the depth of her eyes which disturbed me. She glanced towards me then modestly lowered her eyelids.

'Give me Greta's phone number. I can't agree a regular commitment, I have too many other preoccupations. I'll take her out when I can.' I turned to her. 'Do you speak any other languages besides Greek?'

She frowned.

'French? Italian? German?'

She looked blank. I turned back to him.

'Is she Greek or Albanian?'

'Dany, don't probe.'

It was hardly probing, I thought, to ascertain whether she was an illegal immigrant or not.

'I'd like to know whom I have on my hands.'

'A sweet and lovely woman who needs all the support she can get.'

He gave me a lift back to the office. I was willing to relieve Mickey for the afternoon, especially as it was raining again. She wasn't in. There was a message on the door stating she was out on visits so the office would be closed for the rest of the afternoon. I would call in on Davina. There were few people around on the seafront, the pale grey sea merged into a concrete sky, the horizon line invisible. No winds. A handful of small yachts drifting past the end of the pier. A miserable spectacle altogether.

'Who is it?' There was no mistaking Tracey's voice on the intercom.

'Dany.'

No answer. She was obviously debating with herself whether to let me in.

'Tracey, I'd like to have a chat with Davina.'

Another pause. I guessed Davina was asking her who it was.

'Don't stay too long.' She reluctantly pressed the buzzer.

Davina was still in bed. Beside her was an array of untouched food. Her cheeks were more sunken than I remembered. I was concerned.

'Hello Dany.' Her voice, too, was more feeble. 'Dreary weather isn't it? Sit down dear.'

'Am I interrupting your lunch?'

'Good gracious no. I have no appetite. Later on I'll have some ice cream. Tracey's bought me a tiny tub of chocolate ripple. You can clear away that other stuff, Tracey. Give it to the seagulls.'

'You said you might eat it later on.' "It" was a congealed hamburger with cold frozen peas and a pile of mashed potatoes.

'No, no. Dany might like it.'

'No thank you. I've just eaten.'

'Take it away and bring three dishes of ice cream.' She was becoming imperious.

'I don't want any ice cream,' Tracey snapped.

'Nor do I.' I hastily added.

'Then I'll wait until later when I'm watching T.V. Tracey, you've been a positive saint keeping me company. You can have a break now Dany's here. She'll see to my needs, won't you dear?'

'I don't want a break.'

'Well you need one. Off you go. Get some fresh air. Take my umbrella and don't forget the gulls. There's some money in my purse over there. Help yourself. Buy yourself something nice. Whatever you fancy.'

'I don't want anything.'

'Take some money anyway. Just in case a pretty top or something attracts your attention. Cheer you up. I always used to buy a hat when I was low. I had so many. Gave them away. Just have two now, one for summer and one for winter. Go on, you silly girl. And bring me a chocolate éclair. And a meringue. You know where to buy them. Don't slam the door.'

The last advice was unheeded. Several doors crashed shut as Tracey left the building.

'Now come closer. Sit on the bed. She's a good girl but far too attentive. Treats me as if I'll peg out if she turns her back. If she weren't here I'd be up and about. She called the doctor, which was a mistake. He fusses too much. They all fuss too much. I've lasted this long, I'm not going to conk out yet. Now how are you? Have you and Roz got it together?'

'I haven't seen Roz since her party. I went to the theatre with Amelia.'

'Ah!' Her eyes twinkled. 'I see. She's good for a one night stand, so I hear. Don't get too involved, though. She's very shallow.'

'I know. She knows. It's fine. I'm fine. How is Ray?'

'Strange. He's always been dozy, now he's somewhere else completely. I hope he's not smoking those things.'

'I shouldn't think so. He doesn't look the type.' I wasn't willing to give away more, even to set an anxious old woman's mind at rest. 'Perhaps he's met a girl at these meetings he goes to, fallen in love.'

'Perhaps. He certainly hasn't fallen in love with Tracey.' She chuckled. 'She told me as soon as he walked into his room and found her sitting there, he shouted out "Oh no!" and ran out again. He came straight down to me for an explanation. Actually, I've never seen him so upset. He kept insisting he couldn't have another person in his private space. When I pointed out lots of his friends had shared this space already, so he could put up with a poor girl for a week or two, he shouted "oh no, oh no." at me as well. I'm not sure where he is at the moment.' She shifted uncomfortably. 'I'm beginning to think I did the wrong thing.' She waited for a response.

'Perhaps she should have moved out until you'd asked him whether he minded.'

'He's always been easy going. He's changed for the worse.' There was an anxious tremble in her voice, when she said 'I hope he hasn't run away. Gone off with a bad lot. I do love him. I'm sorry to have upset him so much. I don't know what to do. And Tracey. I can't kick her out now. I suppose she could sleep on my couch until we can sort her out properly.'

Who she imagined could sort Tracey out I wasn't sure. Not me. I might be able to help with Ray, though. I patted Davina's shoulder.

'I'll see if I can find out where he might be. I'm afraid Tracey's your problem. See you later.'

Mickey was back from her visit.

'We have to find some solution, and soon. Tracey is nothing but a load of trouble.'

'You've met her then?'

'I've heard about her. Ray was in here yesterday evening.'

'I guessed as much.'

'He's terrified she'll find out about him. Tell his grand-mother.'

'Davina wouldn't mind.' I said this with more confidence than I felt.

'This is a fine mess you've got us into.'

The accusation was unfair. It wasn't my fault Tracey had turned down the only good deal on our books, not my fault that Davina had picked her up. I opened my mouth to protest, but Mickey didn't allow me to speak.

'Ray says he didn't leave anything incriminating where she could have found it. A few objects which hopefully wouldn't be significant to her. A rusty cauldron and a battered broom he bought at a car boot sale, things like that. He says she frightens him. He doesn't want to go back home until she's gone.'

'Where did he spend last night?'

'With one of our circle. Will you make sure she disappears as soon as possible?'

'Why doesn't he make her disappear himself? Waive his wand over her, abracadabra and she's gone. He's a bone fide witch now, isn't he?'

My sarcasm made her furious. 'Don't say things like that, especially in public.'

I looked around for the public. The shop was empty.

'Don't dare to belittle what we do, what we believe! You're being absolutely stupid.'

Two shapes hovered outside the window, pushed the door open. Two women. Stunning chic clothes. Meticulously cut hair, discreet make up, identical designer jeans.

'I wonder if you could help us?' Upper class accent.

'Of course. I'm Michaela. Please sit down and tell me what you want.'

No, tell *me* what you want, I thought.

'Danielle, would you mind dealing with the urgent business we were discussing? See if you can find suitable alternative accommodation for the person in question?'

'Sure.' Pity. The clones were as interested in me as I was in them.

'Let me know as soon as it's sorted. Now, ladies are you looking to buy or sell? A house or apartment? Ciao, Danielle. See you later.'

Leaning on a lamppost at the corner of the street was a familiar figure.

'I just came by in case you were around. I've finished a long and difficult piece of work, so I'm having a break before I have to go back this evening to get on with revision. Will you take me for tea? I'm very partial to lemon drizzle cake. We could walk to the teashop. My bike will be safe on the lower promenade.'

Why not? I was becoming quite fond of Robbie.

We bumped into Tracey who had been buying Davina's order of cakes.

'Hi, Tracey. Will you join us? We're about to have tea.' I guessed Robbie wouldn't be too pleased but I couldn't help that.

'You've got to be joking!' was her polite answer. 'Don't think you can get round me like that. Find me a proper place to live, that's what you've got to do.'

'Tracey, I haven't got to do anything for you.'

'No you haven't have you? And you don't want to. You want to make money out of people, that's all. If I were a rich kid, you'd bend over backwards to find me a place.'

Fortunately for me there were so many excited customers around tucking into their cream teas, that only Robbie and I heard her unjust accusations. Robbie intervened.

'Sit down anyway. I'm Robbie, hello Tracey.'

Tracey sat. 'Are you a friend of hers, Robbie?'

'Yes. She's a good friend and a kind person, so there must be a misunderstanding.'

'No there isn't. She could fix me up, I'm sure she could, but she can't be bothered.'

Robbie looked enquiringly at me.

'I found Tracey a really nice room, rent free. She wouldn't stay there.'

'They were stark, raving mad that lot. I expect she's found you somewhere nice if you're a friend of hers.'

'I'm a student, I live on the University Campus.'

'Oh, a student. Well you're all right then aren't you? Don't have to worry do you?'

Robbie raised her eyebrows. 'I do a bit.'

'I've got to go. Davina's waiting. Her grandson's a right weirdo, by the way. He's got some very funny things in his room.'

'I gather he doesn't feel he can share with you.'

'He'll have to do what his granny tells him. I'll see you, I expect, more's the pity.'

As she made for the door Robbie called her back.

'Tracey what do you know about student life?'

'Not a lot. You all take drugs, get drunk and have a good time at the taxpayers expense.'

'Sounds like good fun, do you think?'

'I don't do drugs, and I don't drink.'

'Have you ever been out to the campus?'

'No.'

'I live in a residence on the edge of the downs. We see badgers. It's great. At the moment there are empty rooms because some of us prefer to go home to revise. Courses have finished. You could stay with us.'

'How much would it cost?'

'Nothing to you.'

I kicked her under the table to signal my reservations. She moved her foot away.

'Just for a week or so. Give Dany a chance. How about it?'

Tracey was as dumfounded as I was.

'Completely free?'

'That's right. Why don't you take that stuff to Davina whoever she is, collect your belongings and I'll meet you at the pier in about an hour. If you haven't got much stuff we can put it in the pannier of my bike and I'll give you a ride.'

The mention of the bike seemed to clinch it. She agreed.


# Chapter 14

So that was settled for the time being. I reported back to Mickey.

She was obviously preoccupied, nervous. I changed my tune.

'Anything wrong?'

The usual pause before she answered.

'Fran's run away. Left Craigie. She couldn't take it any more.'

I was stunned. Then angry. Very angry.

'How could she do that?'

'He was intolerable. Ever since he knew there were men at our meetings. Kept her awake all night, crying and begging her to tell him the truth.'

'Which is just what she should do. If she doesn't I will.'

'You can't! You promised.

'Has he been violent?'

'No. He wouldn't hurt her. He won't leave her alone, that's all. Except to go to work. She packed a bag and hopped it when he went off to the surgery.'

'Where is she?'

'I'm not telling you.'

I wanted to shake her.

'You know when he finds her gone he'll smash the place up? Then he'll drive round to you, and he'll create mayhem until you give him an answer.'

'He wouldn't do that!'

'He would, he would! You two are unbearably stupid.'

'We didn't mean it to happen this way.' Her voice trembled. She was about to burst into tears when more clients arrived, a middle-aged couple with an elderly mother. They had an appointment.

'Hello, I'm Danielle. You probably spoke to Michaela. I'm her partner. I'll show you the properties we have in mind as Michaela has other urgent business to attend to. Would you let me have the details, Michaela?'

Her hands were shaking as she passed me the paper.

Michaela was out when I returned leaving no explanatory note. Alone staring at the computer I felt my anger rising again. If only Fran had come clean with her husband. To keep silent was to taunt him beyond endurance.

The phone rang. It was Craigie. In the middle of evening surgery.

'Hello Dany. Could I speak to Michaela?'

'She's not here.'

'I've tried her at home. She's not there either and her mobile is switched off.' I'd never heard him so tense.

'I wondered if she knew where Fran was. I've tried calling her several times and there's no response. I was in a helluva state when I left home. I wanted to say sorry. I don't suppose you know where she is by any chance? Her mobile is switched off too, but then it often is when she's meditating. I suppose she could be meditating, to calm down. We had the most dreadful row.'

'I don't know where she is, nor where Mickey is. What time do you finish?'

'Usually round about 7ish.'

'If I were you, I'd leave it alone until then. She's probably gone out shopping. Isn't that what women usually do to change their mood?'

'She doesn't like shopping. There's a lot going on for the festival. Perhaps she's gone to an exhibition, or an afternoon concert or something.' He was clutching at straws.

'You're right. It's most likely that.'

'If you hear anything ring me. Just to say everything is O.K. I'd better go. See you.'

It was six o'clock. I locked up and went straight home. Both cars were in the drive. The door to Mickey's flat was locked. I walked around the outside peering in the windows, tapping on the glass. I stood listening, straining to catch sounds from within. There was nothing. I went upstairs to make a cup of tea, take a shower. I was relaxing in my bathrobe, gazing out of my small bedroom window, when I saw Mickey emerge from the shrubbery. She had a book in one hand, a rod in her other and a glass box under her arm. I scooted down the stairs to waylay her in the entrance hall.

'We have to talk.'

Too exhausted to protest, she ushered me into her living room.

'You've been to that place, haven't you, in the middle of

the maze? What is it some kind of chapel?'

'You might call it that. Miranda's altar is there. She used it regularly before she was ill, then she set up an altar in her own room.'

'What were you doing? Is Fran there?'

I don't know where Fran is. I was trying to find out how to get in touch with Miranda's spirit. Her ashes are in there. And Samuel's. It wasn't any use. So I tried to cast a spell to bring her back. It might work. There's a formula in Miranda's book.'

'Is this her book?' I stretched out my hand towards it. She whipped it away.

'Don't touch it!'

'What's in the box?'

'Crystals.'

'And what's that?' pointing to her rod.

'A wand of course.'

'Of course! You'll tell me you have a broomstick next.'

'I do. I use it for all kinds of things – sweeping away evil influences, bad vibes, symbolic cleaning. It's not just for cleaning.'

'It's for flying I suppose.'

'Don't be silly. It symbolises the union of male and female, the joining of the phallic stick to the feminine brush. It's used in fertility rites.'

Exactly how it was used in such rites I didn't wish to know.

'So you were in this chapel, sweeping and chanting spells. Did it work?'

'No. I'm beginning to feel very guilty.'

'I should hope so.'

'It was bad magic we used on Craigie. We shouldn't administer love potions without the subject's consent.'

'Like you shouldn't give drugs without being a doctor.'

'It wasn't drugs, it was pure herbs. We did say a spell over it, to make sure. That's probably what made it so strong.'

We stared at each other helplessly.

'You must surely have some idea where to find Fran,' I said at last. Didn't she give you a clue?'

'No. She said it was better that way. She has friends all over the place. She might even have left the country.'

Her phone rang. It was just seven o'clock. Mickey didn't move.

'Answer it. It might be Fran.' She shook her head. It rang a few more times then clicked on to the answering service. She waited for a while then played the message back.

'Mickey, there's still no reply from Fran. I've been delayed. I have to make an urgent home visit. Please, if you have any news, ring my mobile.'

'If you don't ring him back, I will. I've told you what will happen if he gets back to an empty house and no word of explanation.'

She bit her lip. 'We'll have to make something up.'

'Will we? Why should we do that? Tell it how it is.'

'We'll have to make something up. Invite him over for a drink. I think I've got the right antidote.'

'I am not, most definitely not going to allow you to give the man any more poison.'

'This is truly harmless. And the other wasn't poison. He's blooming with health. And then when he's not so much in love, he won't care.'

'You want to make him fall completely out of love with his wife?'

'Not completely. Just less.'

'And you believe you can do "just less"?

'I'll try.'

She picked up the phone, dialled Craigie's mobile number.

'Hi Craigie. Just picked up your message. The thing is, Fran tried to get through to you, but couldn't for some reason. Strange. Anyway she asked me to try, and to tell you not to worry. She had a call after you'd left, from…' she hesitated for a second, 'her aunt. One of her aunts. Her favourite uncle has been rushed into hospital with a heart attack. He may not live long. Fran's always adored him. She left immediately.'

There was a pause.

'She doesn't know. He might get over it, but they said it was bad.'

Pause.

'Northumberland. A remote farm.'

Pause.

'I'm afraid she didn't have time to give me the number or the address. I expect she'll call you when she can. She may be at the hospital most of the time.'

Pause.

'Well, I think she said heart attack. It could have been a stroke. She was upset. Why don't you come round here for a drink and a bite to eat when you've finished work.'

Pause.

'If she can't get you at home, she'll ring your mobile, won't she? You can't sit moping all night in case she rings. She may not. I'll send out for a Chinese take away O.K? Dany will join us, I'm sure. Bye.'

'That was about as convincing as the old story about having to go to your grandmother's funeral.'

She looked annoyed. 'I thought it was rather good for spur of the moment stuff. Besides, it would be much easier for him to be with us then on his own. We'll have a restful evening, calm him down. You'll see.'

Craigie arrived half an hour later. He burst in without knocking or ringing the bell. He was in a towering rage.

'She's with her lover, isn't she? Tell me the truth.'

Mickey backed way. He grabbed her. 'Who is he?' He shook her violently. 'Who is he?' Then he flung her aside, sank into an armchair, put his hands over his face and groaned, loud, heart rending groans from the depth of his being. We were petrified. At last he ended with a shuddering sigh, took his hands away, raised his bloodshot eyes to mine.

'I've had it, Dany.'

'I'll get you a drink', Mickey sprang into action.

'A bottle of whisky and a dozen sleeping pills are what I need. Put an end to it all.'

I went to sit beside him. Took his hand. 'Craigie, I swear to you, it's not what you think.'

He jerked his hand away. 'You're in on it too? You know where she is, who she's with? I trusted you!'

'I don't know, Mickey doesn't know. I found out something very recently that I'm going to tell you, though.'

At that moment Mickey returned with a cup.

'This will make you feel better.'

'What is it?'

'Calming herbs. You know, the sort Francesca gives you sometimes.'

He sniffed it suspiciously, then pushed it away. 'I said I'd rather have whisky.'

'I don't have any. Honestly this will do you good.'

'Dany, you have some whisky?'

'Some. Not a full bottle.'

'Get it for me.'

I had three quarters of a bottle. I sometimes had a nip before I went to sleep. Not often, but I liked to keep it to hand.

'Have one with me.'

I poured us both a large measure. Then, without more ado, I announced 'Francesca is a witch. Mickey is a witch.'

'You can say that again.' He took a gulp.

'I will. It's not an idle description for women who have annoyed you. They are both witches. They practice witchcraft. When they go away it is to covens with other witches.'

'Wiccans, we are practitioners of Wicca.' Mickey's eyes were wide with fear. She had to speak nevertheless. 'Magic, good magic. It's innocent. Harmless. Power for the good. Nothing to do with the devil. We were going to tell you when you were ready.'

'They gave you a love potion.'

The truth was out.

He looked from me to Mickey and back to me. He could see from my face I wasn't lying.

'Oh my god!' He began to laugh hysterically. Neither Mickey nor I dared to move until he lay back in his chair with deep shuddering breaths.

'I'm a scientist, I don't believe in magic' he said. 'Do you believe in magic, Dany?' 'I don't know,' I said cautiously, in answer to his question.

'You don't know whether I fell in love with Fran because of some witches' brew?'

I shrugged my shoulders.

He turned his attention to Mickey.

'You led my wife into this childish rubbish.'

Mickey's fear turned to anger.

'How dare you call the most ancient religion childish rubbish. I didn't lead her into anything. She found her own way. And she wasn't your wife. She only became your wife through magic.

'Don't you give me that. Whatever neurotic, obsessive condition I have has nothing to do with your potions.'

'Then how do you account for the fact that you took no notice of her whatsoever when you first met, then when she'd given you the drink you couldn't keep your eyes nor your hands off her?'

He had no answer to that. Instead he sighed and went quiet, sunk into himself as if we weren't with him.

I broke the silence. 'Mickey, what are you going to do?'

'I could ask Marie Rose.'

'Who is Marie Rose?'

'She's a clairvoyant. The police use her sometimes.' This last sentence was said with some defiance, looking at Craigie, who showed no sign of even having heard her. 'She's very good. She was one of Miranda's best friends.'

'Well give her a call.'

'She doesn't like being phoned in the evenings.'

'Mickey do it!'

She reluctantly picked up the phone, dialled.

'Hello, Marie Rose, it's Michaela. I hope I'm not disturbing you.'

Then she listened for a long time without saying anything except 'Oh dear,' or 'Really, what a shame.' At last she managed to briefly explain her case, before listening again, this time occasionally agreeing 'I know,' or 'Yes, I understand.'

Craigie appeared to have fallen asleep.

Mickey replaced the receiver. 'You always have to listen to her telling you how her children are doing, her grandchildren, her animals and her garden. She told me she's more or less retired, she's not as alert as she used to be, makes mistakes. Because it's me she'll have a go.'

Craigie woke up. 'More hocus pocus.'

'Have you any other suggestions?'

'The police.'

Mickey was alarmed. 'Not the police. I'm sure she isn't in any danger. She'd hate you to contact the police. She'd never forgive you. Marie Rose needs some of Fran's possessions. Some clothes, some jewellery, personal things. Would you collect some and bring them here? It's a great favour that she's willing to work on it immediately.'

'Shall I come with you?' I wanted to talk to him alone. 'I'll drive you if you like.'

'All right. I don't suppose I should drive anyway.'

We took his car. As soon as he'd settled into the passenger seat, he let out a heartfelt groan.

'Doing all this is ridiculous. Absolutely ridiculous. If only I'd known. If only she'd told me. Why didn't you tell me?'

'I wanted to. I was about to. They were working on an antidote to make you less in love. They realised they'd overdone it.'

'They realised they'd overdone it! You sound as if you too are convinced I'm the victim of some fatal aphrodisiac. You're not are you? Surely, surely Dany, you're too sensible for that?'

'You're a doctor. You know how drugs can alter states of

mind. They've been playing around with all kinds of plants. Maybe they used hallucinogenic fungus or something.' It was a shot in the dark. 'Some fruits and roots can have very odd effects, can't they?'

We pulled up outside his house.

'Yes, but not that kind. Whatever's wrong with me is to do with my psyche, not their machinations.'

We went into the house, looked for the most meaningful bits and pieces, put them in a bag and got back into the car. Craigie was close to tears as he clutched his precious parcel.

'She's a silly, spoilt child, but I do love her so,' he muttered. 'Please god let her be all right.'

He was desperate to go with Mickey to see Marie Rose, she was insistent she must go alone.

'I'm not going to hand over Fran's belongings,' he growled.

'You have to. And you have to stay here and wait. Or go home.'

'He'll stay here with me, won't you?' I squeezed his hand. 'Come upstairs to my apartment, Craigie, it might be a long night.'

So I made him some tea, and we talked. About love, what else? It's an inexhaustible subject. We began with our first loves, his at the age of six, mine a little later. We discussed whether you can call it "love" at that early age and decided we could. Then we compared our first experience of sex, his rather young, mine when I went to stay with my uncle in Berlin. I'd played around with the boys in my gang before, but I never counted that. We drank lots more tea until the sky turned from black to a beautiful blue and then to the white of dawn.

Mickey returned as the sun rose. She ran up my stairs in a state of high excitement.

'She saw something' she panted. 'I'm ravenous. Do you have anything to eat Dany ?'

I fished a packet of biscuits out of the cupboard. She tore open the wrapper, devoured them, greedily one after another.

'Water, she saw water.'

We stared at her, waiting for more. She finished the last biscuit, smiled at us triumphantly.

'She was holding Fran's necklace and she saw water.'

She would, wouldn't she, I thought, considering where pearls come from.

'What else? What else did she see?' Craigie's voice was strained with tension.

'Boats, yachts. And fishing boats. And buildings.'

'Sounds like any seaside place in the world.' I was disappointed. I had hoped for more.

'No, she said it wasn't far.'

'The marina! Was it the marina?' She had at last ignited a spark of excitement in the abandoned husband.

'She said it could be.'

The marina covered a big area. There were yachts of all sizes, a hotel, shops, apartments. Marie Rose's revelation didn't seem to me to be at all helpful.

'She thought that Fran was possibly on a boat. Not moving, a boat moored somewhere, probably in the marina. Do you have a boat?'

Craigie shook his head.

'Do you know anyone with a boat?'

He shook his head again. Mickey thought for a while.

'I do. Fran does. A member of our coven keeps his yacht down there.'

Craigie leapt to his feet. 'Let's go!'

'No. I have to contact him. We can't just go. Anyway, I'm not sure which one it is.'

The light died out of Craigie's eyes. He sat down again, head in hands. I sat beside him.

'Dany, get some breakfast and take care of the shop will you? I might be busy all morning. Craigie, you'll just have to wait. I'll do my very best to get in touch with Fran, tell her it's O.K. for her to come back. It is, isn't it? You're not going to create a scene if she walks through the door?'

'I'll give her a big hug and take her to bed.'

'Don't rush things. Softly, softly. I'm making no promises. You'll have to be patient.'

'If you see her, tell her I'm desperately sorry for giving her such a hard time.'

'I will. I hope you mean it.' She disappeared, leaving us wondering exactly who was in the wrong here.

# Chapter 15

I went on duty at nine o'clock, as instructed. I took a moment to call Craigie, at morning surgery. I crossed my fingers that in the state he was he didn't make any terrible misdiagnoses. He was managing to stay lucid. He rang me back in between patients to reassure me that doctors are trained to do without a certain amount of sleep, so he could get through one more day without collapsing. Naturally he'd hoped I was ringing with news of Fran.

I was staring at the computer when I had a visitor who cheered me up no end. I hadn't looked up when he opened the door, as I usually did, so the familiar voice made me jump.

'Hi! I came to say thank you.'

'Ray! How wonderful. So you haven't left home for ever.'

'Oh no. I just kept out of the way until that woman had gone. You managed to get rid of her.'

'She was awful, truly awful. Anyway, I can't have another person in my room. It's not possible.'

I studied his appearance with interest, looking for changes his initiation might have brought about. He was disappointingly the same as ever.

'Of course not. You have a secret life your granny knows nothing about.'

He shifted uneasily. 'Oh no! Nothing like that.'

'Oh yes! I know all about it.'

He looked over his shoulder before whispering 'You do?'

'I do. You were initiated as a…. Wicca priest on May Day. In other words you are a fully fledged witch. Congratulations!'

He looked over both shoulders this time and put his finger to his lips.

'Who told you that?' He was still whispering.

'You can speak normally. No-one is listening.'

'But Mickey said we weren't….'

'It was Mickey who told me.' I cut in. 'How does it feel? Do you have the force?' I couldn't help being flippant.

He glared at me. 'I have a lot to learn.'

'I wanted to ask you a favour. Don't bring people to look at Granny's apartment, will you?'

'You're asking me to ignore my contractual obligations to sell your great-grandmother's flat? That is unethical.'

'She doesn't really want to sell it.'

'Then she must say so. Withdraw it from the market.' Oh Dany, to think that a few weeks ago you were totally ignorant of these matters. A market was a place in a street where you went to buy vegetables.

'She won't. She thinks I could do with the money. She loves it here. She can't stand her daughter, my grandmother. I can't stand her either. She'll kill great-granny off. She's too old to move. I'll take care of her.'

'Her apartment is very desirable. Worth an awful lot of money, did you know that? You'd be rich.'

'I don't care. I don't want to be rich. Money is useless. It's wisdom that counts.'

I wasn't sure that Mickey would agree with him. As far as she was concerned money and wisdom could go hand in hand. I could see his point, though. A move would be disastrous for Davina. I was touched by his concern.

'You don't have to try very hard do you? I mean, if you can find your clients something else to make them happy, that will be alright, won't it?'

'Davina will ask me why I haven't brought anyone round.'

136

'She won't. She doesn't want to be bothered. She's tired. She'll be relieved in her heart of hearts, I know she will.'

He paused, then lowered his voice again. 'I'm experimenting with herbs to prolong her life.'

This was bad news.

'What do you mean, "experimenting"?'

'I have a comprehensive guide to herbal medicines. I can't get all the herbs yet, I'm sending off for some through the Internet. I'll try them out myself first. And I'm composing a few incantations to say over them.'

At least incantations wouldn't harm her.

'You'd better be very careful. If you get it wrong and she died, you'd be had up for murder, for sure. You have everything to gain.'

'Of course I will. I'm not an idiot?'

Oh no?

'I'll see what I can do to go slow on the sale. Give Davina my love.' I caught sight of a smart, young woman looking at our advertisements. 'See you.'

At one o'clock I tried Mickey's mobile for the third time. It was still switched off. It was lunchtime. Would Roz be free for lunch I wondered? We had agreed to have a meal out together some time that week, so that, at least, was a good excuse to contact her. As I stretched out my hand to do so Amelia walked through the door. She hitched up her already short skirt to sit opposite me, legs crossed like Sharon Stone in 'Fatal attraction'.

'I've missed you,' she said. 'Come to the Sugar Twist with me. Buy me a banana split in return for services rendered?' Future services rendered? Was she what used to be called a vamp? I gave in. I'd leave Roz until later. The woman serving raised her eyebrows seeing us together again. I ordered a banana milkshake, a coffee, a sandwich, and a piece of cake. I'd keep the sandwich to myself, share the cake with Amelia.

'When are you coming round again?'

The waitress grinned as she put down the food. She winked at me. I didn't wink back.

'I don't know. I'm a bit busy the rest of the week.'

She placed her chin on her hand, gave me what I imagine she considered to be a melting look.

'Somebody better in bed than me.' This was said loudly enough to give rise to guffaws from a couple at the next table. Amelia acknowledged her audience with a delicate fluttering of her eyelids. What role was she rehearsing now, I wondered? I would play the game.

'I have yet to find that out.'

She pouted. Not many women can do that, at least, not attractively. It takes practice and a certain sort of mouth.

'You'd better give me another chance. You haven't sampled my whole repertoire.'

The couple at the next table blushed this time and asked for their bill.

'Seriously, I'm going to be in London soon. It's definite that I'm taking the role.

'Listen Amelia, I'll give you a ring. I have too many things on at the moment, I don't quite know where I am.'

'Don't leave it too long, darling, or I'll be off to the West End busy with fame and fortune.'

'And the casting couch?'

'I don't know what you mean. I succeed on talent,' was her haughty reply. 'Don't ring me, I'll ring you, maybe.' And she was gone.

The waitress shook her head in disbelief as she served me another coffee.

'Fancy letting her go like that!'

A grunt was my only response.

Mickey had not returned to the office at 2 p.m. I tried her mobile again. No response. I tried Craigie. No response either. I rang the surgery. An answering service telling me the surgery was closed giving me a number for emergencies. I rang Roz. Her secretary said she would be busy with a client all afternoon. A steady stream of would-be buyers poured through, a would-be vendor phoned to find out what had happened to Mickey who had promised to inspect her property at 3 o'clock that afternoon. I looked at the agenda. Nothing else today, fortunately. The next phone call was completely unexpected.

'Danielle? This is Richard.'

'Oh, hello.' Richard? Who was Richard?

'Richard Bradshaw.' Ah, yes. Tricky Dickey. 'I'm reminding you about my publication party. I've brought it forward. So many students go home after their exams. Next Sunday, four o'clock onwards. I'm sending a proper invitation to your shop. You will come won't you? I've asked Des, who won't commit herself. They'll all be off soon to the four corners of the earth, wherever they go for the summer vacation. I'd like to keep in touch with her. I'd like to meet her parents, if possible.'

'Isn't that a bit premature?'

'To talk about Shakespeare. Actually I've written several articles about *Othello* that I would be happy to discuss with them. So you'll be there? With Des, and if necessary, her gang of followers.'

'I'll do my best.'

'Thanks, Dany. Oh by the way, you haven't brought anyone to see my house.'

'Sorry. There's been no interest in it. See you.'

The phone rang as soon as I had replaced the receiver. I grabbed it hopefully.

'Good afternoon Danielle, I'm not interrupting anything?'

I gritted my teeth. 'Actually I'm waiting for a very important call, Mr. Cricket.'

'I won't keep you long. How would you like to take Greta to the circus tomorrow evening?'

'I don't like circuses. They're cruel to animals.'

'No animals in this one. It's Chinese acrobats.'

'I've read about those. They're cruel to children. Anyhow, I'm busy. I don't want to talk now.'

'I'll ring you later then. There are other shows you might enjoy. I have to be back in London by tomorrow lunchtime.'

'You'll have to find somebody else to chaperone your mistress. Goodbye, Mr. Cricket.' I hung up.

I was very tired. I lay back, closed my eyes. It was all too much. My life was spinning out of control. I was being pushed and pulled in so many directions, none of them my choice. All I was trying to do was get over my obsession with Anita and now I was at the beck and call of a sleazy businessman, a university professor and a witch. It was all the witch's fault. No, it was my fault not hers. I had become weak, easily led, I who was a natural leader. Before Anita. She had started it. Suppressed my willpower. Had she been a witch? Had the sinister carer who dictated all her actions been a witch too?

I looked at my watch. Time for evening surgery. I'd ring Craigie, find out how he was doing. This time the receptionist answered.

'I'm afraid Dr. Richardson isn't in this evening. Is it urgent? Do you want an appointment with another doctor?'

'It was Dr. Richardson I specifically needed to speak to. Thank you. I'll ring him at home.'

'Excuse me, are you a relative?'

I went cold. 'No a friend. A close friend. Why?'

'We're trying to get in touch with his wife. Do you happen to know where she might be?'

'I'm trying to get in touch with her too. She's gone away without leaving her number. You've tried her mobile?'

'There's no response.'

'Has something happened to Dr. Richardson'

'I'm afraid he's had an accident.'

'What kind of an accident?' I was shaking.

'A car crash.' She pre-empted my next question.

'He's in hospital. No-one else is injured. He's probably going to be all right.'

'Probably?'

'He has some broken ribs and he's unconscious. If you manage to reach his wife, let her know.'

He was under observation in Accident and Emergency.

At first they refused information, as I wasn't family. However, since I claimed to be a cousin, I was the nearest they could find to next of kin and they eventually gave in.

'What happened?' I asked his nurse.

'He swerved to avoid a big dog that suddenly ran out into the road. There were several witnesses apparently. Crashed into a tree. He was driving very fast.' She was clearly upset. 'He's such a lovely man.'

I was torn between sitting and waiting, and going home to see if by any chance Mickey was there. Her mobile was still switched off.

'Call us in a couple of hours' the nurse advised.

I was in a taxi half way to Hove when Mickey finally got in touch.

'I've found her. I'm with her.'

'You are? Then tell her to prepare for a shock. Craigie is in hospital. He had a car accident. Either you tell her or hand her the phone.'

I heard her say 'Bad news, Fran,' then Fran took over.

'Dany, what? What is it?'

'Craigie had an accident. He's in hospital. They've been desperately trying to get in touch with you.'

There was the complete silence of utter disbelief.

'Wherever you are, get to A and E as soon as possible. He's unconscious. He swerved off the road trying to avoid a dog. He was in a helluva state' I added accusingly.

She gave a kind of a gasp and a sigh, nothing more. The phone went dead.

I was in my apartment, trying to watch television to pass the time before there was any further contact. The first call was a young person started on some kind of sales pitch. I was so rude to her that she probably spent the rest of the evening in tears. So I was pretty brusque to Mickey. 'Yes?' I snapped.

'We're at the hospital.'

'Good.'

'He's still unconscious. They're trying to wake him every

hour or so. They've given him an X-ray. As far as they can tell there's no very serious injury. If he doesn't respond by tomorrow afternoon, they'll send him to another hospital. I'm coming home. Fran is staying.'

'I'm glad to hear it. I'm going to bed. Don't disturb me. I'm taking the morning off. Sleep well.'

## Chapter 16

When I opened my eyes the next day it was already mid-day. I'd never slept so long in my life. I felt awful. I rang the hospital.

'Are you a relative?'

'A cousin.'

'Would you like to speak to his wife? She's with him.'

'No. Just tell me how he is.'

'He's comfortable.'

What the hell did that mean?

'Is he conscious?'

'Yes.'

'May I visit him?'

'Perhaps not yet. He's confused. When he's awake, which isn't often. I'll put you through to his wife.'

'It's O.K. Don't disturb her.'

That's fine, I told myself. They're together, if his broken ribs don't hurt too much they'll fall into each other's arms, kiss and make up. It wasn't my business, anyway, passing stranger that I was. I was here to work, that was all, so work was what I had better do. I walked to the office thinking the air and exercise would chase away the cobwebs, as they say. There were plenty of these, spiders must have been busy in my head all night.

It was a grey day, uniform uninteresting grey washed across sea and sky. Cold too. My spring jacket was inadequate, so I proceeded at a brisk pace, almost a trot, which gave me a thumping headache. I slowed down, decided to have a rest at the café on the Brighton/Hove boundary. As I sat down I saw a woman I was sure was Greta, leaving with a man who certainly wasn't Jiminy Cricket. They were having some kind of argument, both of them gesticulating. He gave her a push which sent her staggering. I couldn't hear what they were saying but the sound of the words, the rhythm, sounded like English. I was ready to run after them, defend her if he became violent. However, they appeared to calm down. I didn't like the look of him, he had a mean face. I was intrigued. If Jiminy rang again I'd agree to take his mistress out the following evening.

I was feeling a little more human when I arrived at "*Her Place*". Mickey was alone.

'Dany, I've been trying to get back to you.'

'I don't walk the streets with my mobile switched on when I'm off duty. Unlike most other people.'

'Craigies's come round.'

'So the nurse told me.'

'I'd love you to hold the fort whilst I go to the hospital to give Fran a break. She has not left his bedside for a minute.'

'Become the devoted little spouse, has she?'

'Don't be horrible! She's been worried sick.'

I wasn't impressed. My opinion of Fran as selfish and manipulative was fixed forever. Worried sick. I'd rather she'd been scared witless by the possible consequences of her actions. What had she been planning to do whilst her husband went mad looking for her? It was a question I put to Mickey.

'She was going to go on a trip to Fécamp. With the yacht's owner and his wife. They were all ready to set sail. I had to do a lot of preliminary detective work to find out which was his yacht. It was rather exciting.

I was disgusted that she sounded so pleased with herself, as if it had all been a game.

'Well done!' I said sarcastically. 'Saved in the nick of time for the happy ending. I expect they're now holding hands, all past misdemeanours forgiven.'

She looked down, toyed with her pen.

'Actually, he's conscious but won't speak. To anyone, except in monosyllables to medical staff. They don't know whether it's total mental confusion or what. He isn't speaking to Fran at all, even to say yes or no.'

'Does he recognise her?'

'She doesn't know. She's worried he's lost his memory.'

That might be a very good thing, I thought, start again from scratch. Wipe the slate clean, start the marriage on a completely different footing.

'Will you take over then for the rest of the afternoon?'

No-one came in. Jiminy Cricket called.

'Danielle, have you thought about tomorrow night?'

'I don't want to go to the circus even if there are no animals.'

'What about comedy? There's an alternative show at a nice little cabaret theatre in the Lanes.'

I could do with a laugh, I thought.

'Sounds possible.'

'Good girl. I'm in London, I had to go back this morning, unexpectedly. I'll book you a couple of tickets to collect at the Box Office. I believe they start at 9. If you pick Greta up at 6.30 you could eat first. You may prefer to eat afterwards. Naturally I'll give her enough money for meals, tickets taxis and so on. Thank you so much Danielle. You're a sweetheart.'

'It's a pleasure Mr. Cricket.'

I rang Roz. Miracle of miracles, she wasn't with a client. She was delighted to hear from me, she said. She was meeting Jim that evening driving out of town to a country pub. Would I join them? I agreed to be picked up from "Her Place" at 7 p.m.

Mickey didn't come in again. I resolved to persuade her to employ a third person. We appeared to be doing well enough to need two people in the office at all times. There would surely be a bright student needing a vacation job until the end of the summer. She should be sympathetic to that, after all, she was a student doing a part time job when I first met her. How she had changed since then! Where was the rugby playing, beer swigging, jeans and tee shirt Mickey of the past? Was it wealth or Wicca that had brought about the transformation? Aunt Miranda had much to answer for. I supposed that with all her concentration on learning magic, she hadn't the time for love. Or sex. My musings were interrupted by Jim who bounded in with the energy of a young animal.

'Darling how marvellous that you're coming out with us tonight! Roz is waiting round the corner. I'm so pleased. I was beginning to believe that we'd frightened you off! I was chatting about you to Davina. She's very fond of you. You remind her of a lost love.'

'I know. Great to see you too, Jim.'

Jim reminded me of Ernest, and Ernest reminded me of Anita.

'How is Ernest?' I closed down the files, locked the drawers.

'Busy, busy busy. It's a mega production. And the director is a nightmare. Do you always work this late, sweetheart? It's beyond the call of duty.'

'It's an emergency. My partner has had to visit a friend in hospital.' I shut down the computer. 'Let's go.'

Roz was an excellent driver. Her car was extremely comfortable, the upholstery real leather. One of her extravagances now she was doing well, financially secure. Jim sat in the back, exclaiming every so often about the beauty of the Sussex countryside. I was happy to say little, enjoying the closeness of a woman I was increasingly drawn to. Every so often I glanced at her handsome profile, a gesture which was not lost on our other companion, who prodded me in the back knowingly.

Our destination was a small village not far from Eastbourne. An old inn with a reputation that earned it a place in most good food guides. The table was reserved. Roz had managed to warn them we would be three, not two.

'I'd already chosen a menu' she said. 'They assured me there would be enough for all of us. I hope you like jugged hare. We're starting with lobster bisque, but if you don't like that you can have cold vichyssoise instead.'

'Lobster bisque is fine. I haven't had jugged hare before but it sounds good.' I was glad I'd brought my cheque book as well as cash. It looked as though I would need it.

Whilst Roz was in the Ladies' room, I asked Jim if this was a special occasion. They didn't make a habit of dining together like this, did they?

'It's her birthday,' he replied. 'She likes to celebrate them quietly. She gives non birthday parties, but prefers an intimate meal on the day itself. It's often been with me and Ernest. We've looked after her a bit during her bad moments.'

'Should I mention it?'

'Yes, she won't mind. I wouldn't ask her how old she is, though. She's a bit touchy about that.'

When she returned I ordered a glass of champagne each.

'Please accept this from me. Happy Birthday, Roz.'

She blushed. 'We weren't going to tell.'

He spread his hands in a gesture of helplessness. 'She asked. You know me, I cannot tell a lie.'

He raised his glass. 'Happy Birthday, darling.'

We all had such a good time together we decided at the end of the evening that the three of us ought to make a habit of eating together.

I took the back seat on the way home. I was replete and sleepy.

'Any idea when Ernest will be back?'

'No, he'll be out there as long as it takes, if that's too long I might nip over and join him for a long weekend.'

Roz laughed at the idea of "nipping over" to New Orleans. I woke out of my dozy state, heart thumping.

'You're going over to New Orleans?'

'I might. Hello, darling, I thought you were asleep.'

Roz was turning into the road which ran along by Beachy

Head. 'I love coming this way when it's a fine night. It's very romantic.'

It was a very fine night indeed. All traces of cloud had disappeared, the stars had come out in abundance.

She stopped the car.

'It's still my birthday. It's not midnight yet. Let's go for a walk.'

We each took one of Roz's arms. It felt good. We came across a bench, sat down, gazed over the channel, Jim's arms round Roz's shoulder, mine round her waist. She took our free hands in both of hers. Before releasing us, she kissed my hand, then Jim's.

Back in the car, I returned to Jim's possible visit to New Orleans.

'Might you go soon?'

'I have a project to get on with. A musical scheduled to open in the autumn. If I work extra hard in the next couple of weeks, I'll be able to take a few days off. Why?'

'If you had time you might try to find something out for me. It would be a long shot. You never know.' I tried to sound casual, whilst a voice in my head was repeating, Anita, Anita, Anita.'

'I'll let you know. It might never happen. He might be back before I can get away. Life is full of imponderables, isn't it?'

*****

Mickey was still up. She wasn't alone, Fran was huddled in the sofa. I was shocked, she was limp, as if all her usual energy had drained out of her.

'What happened? Craigie isn't dead is he?'

It was Mickey who answered.

'No. He'll be all right. The doctor said so. He still won't talk. He hasn't lost the power of speech, but he won't talk. He understands, he responds to the doctors and nurses. He answers "yes" and "no", he knows who he is, who we are. He won't look at me, or Fran.'

'He looked at me once, only once.' Fran's voice was

scarcely audible. 'He hates me. The doctor told me to go home and rest. His eyes were closed when we came away.' She burst into tears. Mickey moved beside her, rocked her like a baby.

'She couldn't go home. She can stay here as long as she likes.'

'I want to be beside him.' Fran sobbed into her friend's neck. 'I didn't want to leave him. They made me. I want to keep saying how sorry I am until he believes me, until I know he still loves me.'

'Perhaps what's important is for him to believe *you* still love *him*.' Her tears left me unmoved. 'You were the one who ran away. Mickey says you were about to go on a jaunt to France. No wonder he smashed the car. He was probably trying to end it all.' She annoyed me so much I felt like putting the knife in.

The sobs redoubled.

'You've no right to say that!' Mickey accused. 'Witnesses saw him swerve to avoid a dog.'

'They also say he was driving too fast, I expect. Sooner or later it would have happened. Get on with your spells, you two. Wave your wands, dance in the garden, whatever. It won't work, he won't get off his bed and kiss you as though nothing had happened.'

I turned on my heel, slammed her door, marched upstairs.

# Chapter 17

Mickey and I spent the day together in the office. She was wary of me. She was so chastened she would have accepted any proposition I made. So I seized the opportunity and broached the subject of a third helper.

'Er. I don't think it's a very good idea,' she said, with a sidelong glance, not wanting confrontation, but determined to resist.

'Why?'

'You know why. I can only work with people in whom I have absolute trust.'

'What about a fellow Wiccan?'

'No.'

'Well, let me find you a student. They'll all be needing jobs for the next few months.'

'Definitely not.'

So I had to resort to blackmail.

'Then I'm leaving.'

We eyeballed each other.

'Mickey, for goodness sake, you react as though student was a dirty word. Put an ad in the job centre, if you'd rather.'

'You want to get that leather dyke in here, don't you?'

'No. But she has good, honest, trustworthy friends.' I was sticking my neck out there. It was Des I had in mind. My instinct was she'd do fine.

Mickey reflected.

'It's true it's been a bit awkward sometimes. We could do with a permanent presence. 'Let me ask around.'

'If you like'

I needed air. I went out for a walk. When I returned Mickey said 'Jiminy Cricket phoned. He's booked a table at a little bistro near the theatre. They start serving at seven. Greta will meet you there. He said he hoped you'd enjoy the show. He wondered if I'd like to take Greta out occasionally, but I assured him I had too many other things to do. And that girl Des called. Wanted to know if you were going to her tutor's party. Call her on this number if you are.' She pushed a piece of paper in my direction.

'Hi. Is Des there? This is Dany.'

There was along wait whilst several people searched for Des, calling her name. Eventually she was found.

'Dany. Good to hear you. Are you going to Tricky Dickey's party? Turn the music down, will you!' she yelled to someone in the background.

'Yes. It could be fun.'

'It will if we go to liven things up. Why don't you come out to the campus and we'll all go together. I've got the car, although I suppose you'd rather go with Robbie on her bike?'

'Ciao, see you tomorrow morning.' Mickey stood up.

'Ciao. Hang on a minute, Des, I need to ask Mickey something before she goes.' Her hand was on the door. 'How is Craigie?'

'The same.'

'Thanks. See you.'

With Mickey gone, I turned my full attention to Des.

'I don't know what transport I would like. How many of you will be going?'

'Oh, about ten or so. Maybe more. We all need to chill out a bit.'

'How's Tracey?'

'That girl Robbie's taken under her wing? She's being difficult. We'd like to be friends. She won't. She just mooches around miserably. We keep inviting her to supper so she won't have to spend money on food. She comes, eats as much as she can. We all feel very sorry for her. There's only so much you can do though, isn't there?'

I couldn't help but agree.

'So will you come out to the campus at four o'clock?'

'Right.'

I looked at my watch. Six forty-five. I'd just make it to the restaurant by seven o'clock.

I was two or three minutes late. Greta was already seated at a table near the window. All the other tables were full, in spite of the early hour.

'Dany, good to see you.'

Her accent was thicker, her speech more halting than I remembered. She was as beautiful though. Meeting her again, I was sure it was she I had seen on the seafront, with the unpleasant man.

'Good to see you too. Have you ordered?'

'No. I'm not very hungry.'

The menu could be described as hearty, even stodgy.

You'd have to be very hungry to eat most of it. Fortunately there were salads. Of the more inventive sort.

'Wine?' she asked. 'Jiminy has given me money.'

'In that case we'll have the best.' I grinned. I had noticed an already empty brandy glass beside her. The best cost five times as much as our meal. Strange that they should offer such fine wines with such solid food. It must be the latest fashion. Greta pushed her plate away having eaten very little. She drank the wine greedily rather than appreciatively.

'I saw you the other day,' I remarked casually.

She put down her glass. 'You did?'

'Yes. Near the Hove Lawns. You were with a man who treated you rather badly, I thought. I was on the point of coming to your rescue, when he changed his attitude.' I watched her reaction.

There was a hint of dismay in her eyes, then blankness.

'You are wrong.'

'Really? Do you suppose you have a sister who's been brought over here as well? Whoever it was looked just like you.'

'Strange. Not me. I not go out.' Her English had suddenly declined. She held out her glass for more wine. 'Sometime, I shop, if I need. Alone. Never, never with man.'

What a very odd accent she had. I'd met many Greeks, none of them sounded like her.

She pulled out a packet of cigarettes. 'We go outside? You smoke?'

'I don't but we'll go outside. There's an hour before this show starts. We can walk, or go and sit in the Pavilion Gardens.'

'Yes. We sit in the gardens.'

It was going to be a difficult evening if she was going to play the game of being an inarticulate foreigner. Which I was sure she wasn't. She had plenty of words when she was with her seedy companion. We sat on the grass, which turned out to be slightly damp, leaving us with uncomfortable wet patches for the rest of the evening. We watched children playing, lovers kissing, homeless vagrants snoring beside their devoted dogs.

'Are you happy Greta?'

'Happy? Yes. Jiminy is good to me. I miss my home, my family, my country, but Jiminy is kind.'

Oh good, she had regained some fluency.

'Tell me about your home, your family in Greece. They are in Greece, aren't they?'

She ignored the question.

'I have many brothers and sisters.'

'How many?' I would test her powers of invention. She would be lying, I was certain.

'There are nine of us. Five boys four girls. My father is a....' she hesitated 'a fieldworker and my mother she is a fieldworker too.'

'Field workers? You mean farmers?'

'No not farmers. They work in the fields for farmers when they can. Anything. They pick anything in season.'

'Your brothers and sisters? Do they work?'

'Yes. Everyone works in the fields. I worked in the fields until I came to Britain.'

'You are rather delicate and refined for a fieldworker. Aren't peasants sturdy?'

'I was a field worker. We were all fieldworkers.'

'Tell me how you were brought to this country.'

'I don't want to talk about it.'

'You've confided in Jiminy.'

'Not everything. It was horrible.'

The situation Mickey had reported was indeed horrible – drugged, turned into a prostitute, running away, constant fear of pursuit by Eastern European Mafia. So why was I so sceptical, so cool towards a woman who should have deserved my deepest sympathy? Intuition. Everything about her was slightly off key.

'Next time we go out together we could go to a Greek restaurant. There are several of them around. I don't suppose they are what you're used to – just inferior mous-saka and a bottle of ouzo, but you might feel at home and you'd be able to speak Greek.'

She looked down. 'But I'm not Greek. I'm Albanian.'

'Yes, I thought you were, but you insisted you were Greek.'

'It makes things simpler for the moment. I don't speak Greek. Albanian is a completely different language. A Greek wouldn't understand me and I wouldn't understand him. I have to be very careful. It was Jiminy said I should pretend to be Greek. Not as many problems.'

'Different problems, maybe.'

She looked up. Again there was a hint of something I couldn't quite fathom in her expression. Mockery?

'Where are you from Dany?'

'London.'

'Your family rich?'

'No. Not poor, not rich.' I was disinclined to go into the story of my life. Why did she want to know, anyway? She was simply trying to change the subject.

'You have boy friend?'

'Surely Jiminy explained that's not my scene.'

'He said you like women. That doesn't mean you don't like men, does it? I like men. Most men. I sleep with them.' The omission of "want to" was significant. She lit another cigarette. 'Jiminy is a kind man. He is a clumsy lover. I have been with many men, never with a good lover.' Her hand on my thigh left no doubt as to the underlying message.

'We'd better go. We don't want to waste Jiminy's tickets.'

She removed the hand, rose to her feet in one elegant movement whereas others might scramble. She certainly had class, however she had acquired it.

For two hours I hardly laughed once, whereas all those around me were splitting their sides. Strangely enough, Greta, who, as a foreigner, ought to have understood none of the references, the innuendo, giggled helplessly at obscure jokes. As we had an after show drink in the theatre bar I remarked on this curious fact.

'It was their faces, their gestures,' she explained, 'Not what they said.'

I wasn't convinced. Half the time the performers had deadpan expressions, relying on connivance with the audience. Her mirth had been triggered by a word, an inflection. She had momentarily lost her poise, her spontaneous guffaws reminiscent of some of the coarser bar girls I'd worked with. Strongly reminiscent in an uncanny way. Toying with her chardonnay she was now the epitome of the expensive courtesan.

'You were with a family when Jiminy met you?' She had been too evasive.

'Yes.'

'Friends of his?'

'Yes.'

'Where did they live?'

'Islington.'

'How did you get there, how did they find you?'

'I knocked on their door. That's all. They took me in. They were very kind. Dany, please. No more.'

'O.K. Let's go.' I ordered a taxi.

It didn't seem as though Mickey was home when I got back, so I went straight upstairs, listened for messages. I sat on my little terrace puzzling over the lovely Greta. The way she laughed, turned her head, had struck a chord, as if I had met her before. I hadn't, I would have remembered someone so beautiful. She was lying through her teeth, but then, nobody tells the truth all the time, lies are sometimes absolutely necessary. What was she up to, where was she actually from?

I was half undressed, ready for bed when I had another call.

'Not too late for you darling, is it? How are you?'

'Fine Jim, fine. How are you?'

'Utterly exhausted sweetie. But I wanted to tell you that I've been talking to my beloved, who is going to be across the ocean for a good while yet, so I've booked a flight for the end of next week. I'm probably up in London most of the time until then, so pop in tomorrow, if you can, whilst I'm still around, then you can tell me exactly what it is you want me to find out.'

Everything else went out of my head, to be replaced by a startlingly clear vision of Anita, sitting in the moonlight, stretching her arms out to me.

'I'll be over in the morning.'

'Not too early darling, I'll be working all night. How about lunch? I'll prepare us a little something at, say 12.30?'

He wasn't the only one who didn't sleep. I tossed and turned and eventually got up to walk through the deserted streets towards the sea. There wasn't another soul at the end of the promenade. Half a mile along there would be clubbers wandering the streets, the dancing finished but the night not yet over. I felt very old.

# Chapter 18

'Meet our new assistant,' Mickey announced.

Oh no, oh no, oh no! He smiled at me nervously.

'He's been here all morning and he's already learnt a lot.'

She must be out of her mind, I thought. If anyone could ruin a business, he could. He was sweet, he needed a job, he was a member of her coven, but I was convinced he would be completely incompetent.

'Hello, Ray. This is nothing personal, but I understood we were a team of women. Are you going to appear in drag, or what?'

'We can't discriminate, it's against the law.'

'He's not even gay. Are you?' I frowned at him, expecting the usual catch phrase.

'Well, I don't know. I mean maybe, maybe not.'

As there was no one else in the shop I was brutally direct.

'Do you hoist your flag for men or women?'

He looked utterly confused.

'Leave him alone, Dany. We're not allowed to discriminate against heterosexuals.'

We are allowed to discriminate against incompetent idiots, I thought.

'I'm giving him a week's trial.'

At least she wasn't signing him up for life.

'Is he our Man Friday?' I asked. 'If so he could nip round to the deli where he used to work to buy us some lunch. All right, Ray?'

Having despatched him with orders which I was sure he would forget, I gave Mickey a piece of my mind, for hiring a buffoon doomed to failure.

'Don't underestimate him,' she retorted. 'He was pickng up information surprisingly quickly. We've compromised, right, as good partners should. You wanted an assistant, I've given in. You have to accept my choice. If it all goes pear shaped it will be my responsibility, not yours O.K.?'

What could I say? Actually, I was prepared to believe Ray wouldn't necessarily spell disaster. What we would need him to do wasn't that difficult. He had an endearing quality, a boyish charm which could appeal to customers, especially those persuaded that all estate agents were sharks. He was more like a minnow than a shark.

I took him out to inspect a property in the middle of a big estate on the outer reaches of Hove. It was obvious that Mickey was glad to be rid of him for a while, boring though it was being on her own inside.

'Do you drive Ray?'

'Yes of course. You can't get to our meetings unless you drive. They tend to be in out of the way places.'

'So I gather. You were ordained, or whatever it was, in the grounds of a house we're supposed to be selling. Do you wear a special costume for these ceremonies by the way?'

'I don't like your tone of voice. It's no good asking me anything Dany. I won't answer. You don't take us seriously, and that's a pity.'

I was rather ashamed. Why shouldn't he believe what he wanted? It was none of my business anyway, unless he tried putting a spell on me.

'How's Davina?' We'd almost reached our destination. I stopped to check the map.

'She's tired actually. She was worn out by an interview she gave yesterday to a medical student doing research into aging. She's quite a phenomenon, you know. Not many people of her age are in such good shape. Not that there are many of her age still alive, in good shape or not. She's 105 you know.'

We stopped outside a shabby semi where a middle aged woman waited anxiously. We measured up, took photos and got out a contract. I took Ray aside. 'What do you think she should ask?'

He reflected for a moment or two before coming up with exactly the sum I had in mind. I was astonished.

'May I drive back? I'd love a mini.'

'Be careful. It's a company car.'

He drove well. He was au fait with the price of property and he hadn't said "Oh no" once. Mickey was right, he was not to be underestimated.

'Why did you say you didn't know whether you were straight or gay?'

'I don't. I have feelings for both boys and girls. Not very strong ones, though. Actually, I've never been in love. Except with granny, I'm in love with her. I prefer older women.'

'And men?'

'I like boys of my own age. But I'm not a very sexual person. I'm underdeveloped or something.'

I regretted the remark I had made about hoisting his flag.

'You haven't met the right one, that's all.'

'Is it? It doesn't matter. I'm going to concentrate on Wicca. I want to become very, very wise. Like Julius.'

'Julius?' The name rang a bell. 'Who's Julius?'

'The wisest of us all. He's wonderful. Very encouraging. Very discreet.'

'Is he the head priest or something? The chief witch? I thought Mickey was the organiser.'

'Oh no. There isn't a head priest. He's just the best. We all know it. Mickey organises covens, yes, because Miranda used to. Miranda was wise too, she and Julius were good friends. He's supporting Mickey. There's quite a lot of jealousy. If Julius says "lay off" they lay off.'

'Lay off doesn't sound like the vocabulary of wisdom.'

'You know what I mean. Julius is the person I admire most in the whole wide world.' Pause. 'He's gay.'

The bell rang again.

'So I wouldn't mind if I were gay. But I'm just not sure.'

'Does Julius have a partner?'

He realised he'd said too much.

'I'm not telling you.'

'Come on, you've told me a lot already. I could find out. How many gay Julius's are there in this city, do you think?'

He didn't have to reveal more. The door in my mind had opened. Julius, Simon's courteous partner.

We had taken longer than we need have done over the visit. Mickey made no comment. As she closed down her files for the night she said casually 'Do you want to visit Craigie this evening?'

Visiting Craigie, was what I realised I most wanted to do.

'Is he talking?'

'No. Maybe he will to you. I told you, he's going home tomorrow.'

'So you want me to perform the miracle of reconciliation? You're the one with the magic wand.'

Ray blushed and looked away.

'Don't be sarcastic.' She kept her temper in front of her underling. 'Do you want to go or don't you?

'I'll go now.'

There wasn't exactly a miracle, however, there was recognition and warmth.

'Dany, I've missed you.' He held out his hand.

'I've missed you too. I didn't want to intrude.'

'Intrude!' He said bitterly. 'There's nothing between Fran and me any more. There was so much, too much, now nothing. I don't want to go back to her house. That's what it will feel like, her house, not my home any more. I'm going to arrange to stay with a friend. I'm running away like she ran away. When Fran arrives tomorrow, I'll be gone. Oh Dany, what a tragedy!' His eyes filled with tears.

'Are you going to divorce her?'

'I can't think about it. I can't think straight about her. I've watched her sleeping in the chair by my bed. I'm in total confusion. The only words I spoke to her were "Go way". She wouldn't. She sat there for hours on end staring at me, every so often saying "Craigie I love you".

He lay back, exhausted.

'Will you have your mobile with you? May I phone you?'

'Text me. I'm getting a new mobile and I'll let you have the number. I don't want any contact with Mickey or Fran.'

'I understand.'

'Do you? I wish I did.' He made an effort to smile. 'Thank you for coming to see me, Dany. Tell them you couldn't get a word out of me, will you? Promise?'

I promised with a heavy heart. More lies. I pressed his hand and left.

Mickey was waiting. 'How did it go?'

'Not a word, except hello and goodbye.'

'You mean he wouldn't even talk to you.'

'Why should he talk to me if he doesn't talk to Fran or you. There's nothing special about me.'

'There is. You're his buddy! Did you try to make him listen to reason?'

'I don't know what reason is under these circumstances. That's it, finished. I'm having nothing more to do with it.' I changed the subject.

She stalked into her kitchen and slammed the door.

\*\*\*\*

It was fortunate that I had a stream of customers all the next morning because otherwise I would hardly have been able to contain myself until the lunch with Jim. Yet it was ridiculous to be excited. I had the flimsiest information for him, it was an unlikely basis for research.

At 12.30 I fairly flew round the corner. He had prepared an oriental salad. We ate surrounded by grotesque objects of various shapes and sizes.

'The really big props can only be made in our workshops' he said. 'I'll have several helpers. There's no expense spared in this production. They're paying me so much, you wouldn't believe it. Now dear, what's your problem?'

He dashed my hopes almost immediately. 'My love, all we have to go on is that she's from Louisiana. Not even New Orleans. It's a big state. I'll do my utmost sweetheart, I'll even get a detective on the job if you like. It would be like being in a crime novel. It would keep me busy whilst Ernest is in conference. Would you like some jasmine tea?'

I refused. As he was itching to get his packing done for the week in London, I crossed the lawns and tapped on Davina's window. She had seen me coming, she liked to keep her eye on the gardens, watching the birds.

'Am I disturbing you? Is it time for your afternoon nap?'

'Afternoon nap! What an idea. I'm not a baby. Of course you're not disturbing me. I'm always pleased to see you Dany. Sit down. Would you like a chocolate? Ray bought me this big box and champagne to celebrate his new job. Fancy him working with you!'

'Yes, fancy!'

'At last he might have found a career.'

'Yes, he might.' Call that a career, I said to myself.

'How about you? What have you been up to? A bit of sex, I hope. You're far too young to remain celibate.'

'I haven't been in the mood.'

'What's the matter? Unrequited love? Object unobtainable, eh?'

'Sort of. Let's say I'm going through a phase.'

'I hear you had a lovely night out on Roz's birthday. I

hardly ever go out, but I do keep up with the gossip. Jim says you've asked him to search for a mysterious woman in New Orleans. Who is she? Do tell. I love a good romance. Is she beautiful? How did you lose her? Was she married? Did her husband create a scene, take her back to Louisiana? Come along, Dany spill the beans!'

There was no getting out of it. I'd have to spill some of the beans, if not all of them.

'She was beautiful, the most beautiful creature I've ever seen. She seemed not quite human, She lived in the woods. She had a man who looked after her, controlled everything she did. He took her way. That's all.'

She was dissatisfied. 'Have you any photos of her?'

Photos? Photos of Anita? None. I didn't have a camera. No photo could ever capture Anita. There had been moments when I thought she was some kind of mirage.

'Hmm. Don't let it happen again. When you have your princess hold her tight, you hear me? And marry her! I'd love to go to a Lesbian wedding before I die. I went to Ernest and Jim's, it was a hoot. Outrageous camp. Reception on the lawn. The cake was extremely rude made by this fantastic chocolate shop. They insisted I had the choicest bit, they know how fond I am of chocolate. I felt rather embarrassed eating it, I tell you, with all the guests cheering. It was the very tip, you understand, the rest was carved up and passed round. It felt a bit like cannibalism. The boys made jokes about it reminding me of my husband. We didn't do anything like that, dear, it was all straightforward between us. I think you and Roz would make a good couple. I can see you in a white suit, her in a lace dress. We'd organise the reception for you.'

I had to put an end to this.

'Yeah, right. I'm sorry, I have to get back to the office. Take care of yourself.' She was indeed looking tired.'

'I'll try. People keep coming to interview me. The older I get, the more interesting they find me. Strange isn't it.'

'You'll beat all the records.' I kissed her forehead.

# Chapter 19

Saturday evening I was invited to a soirée at Simon's which turned out to be a kind of farewell to Amelia party. Not only would she be staying in London from now on, but also he was handing her on to a new agent, with wider contacts. His arm linked through hers, he said wistfully, 'I'm an amateur. I've taken her as far as I can, used up all my influence. She must go forth now and shine!'

Shine was the appropriate word. She had glitter on her cheeks, her eyelids, she was wearing a very short, very low cut dress of some material that looked a bit like gold wrapping paper, and jewellery on her wrists, her ankles, her neck and in her hair. She greeted me with a certain coolness, not used to being turned down, I supposed.

There were only a dozen guests, the woman who'd been so bitchy notably absent. I was disappointed that Roz wasn't amongst them. I asked Simon whether she would be coming later.

'No, she's away for the weekend. Come and sit down with me for a bit.' He led me into a comfortable room where he sank into an armchair.

'Amelia used to be such a sweetie. She came to join us when she was a schoolgirl, a young teenager. She has looks and talent. Unfortunately her personality might stand in her way, if she's not careful. Too much success too soon will completely turn her head. Partly my fault, I shouldn't have been so enthusiastic. Julius warned me.'

The mention of Julius had made me lose interest in Amelia. Was he the Julius Ray had mentioned? If so, was Simon in on it all? Was he a witch too?

'I like Julius,' I said.

'Have you met him?'

'Last time I was here, after your show.'

'Oh yes. Wasn't it awful? It didn't get any better. I'd hoped it would improve during the week's run. It got worse. I should never have used some of the cast.'

I broke in hastily. He seemed ready to give me a breakdown of the shortcomings of his actors.

'We didn't talk much.'

'No dear, you wouldn't. He is incredibly courteous, but you won't get much more out of him than "Pleased to meet you. Forgive me, I can't stay".

'Is he here?'

'If by "here" you mean at the party, no. He's not awfully fond of Amelia. He's not fond of parties either. He's upstairs, reading or something.'

What could the "something" be I wondered?

''He doesn't mind all this noise?' Someone had put a disc on and voices were raised to be heard above the music.

'No. He goes into his own world. He doesn't interfere with me, I don't interfere with him. Perfect partnership.

'What is his world?'

'How do you mean?'

'What are his interests?'

He gave me a strange look. 'Oh, you know, science, history, religion. He doesn't talk to me about it. Would you like to meet him properly?' He's not averse to having real conversations with interesting people. Wait here. I'll go and ask him if you can go up for a chat.

He left me alone for ten minutes. I didn't return to the other room, where Amelia was holding court. I tried to recall Julius's face, only his eyes were clear. Shrewd eyes.

'You're honoured. He remembered meeting you. Go up the stairs, first room on the right. Don't bother to knock.'

It was quiet on the upper landing. The door of the room on the right was slightly ajar. I coughed and pushed it open.

Julius had laid down his book. We were in a sort of bed sitting room, a small library with a large divan. At first glance I saw nothing comparable with Mickey's jars of herbs and potions, nor were there any obvious occult symbols.

'How gratifying that you not only remember me but also would like us to meet again. Please sit down.' His eyes were truly extraordinary. Unnerving. I felt sure he could see into my head, my heart, my soul. Now I was here, what did I want to say to him? I had a sudden crisis of confidence. What if I was wrong? There was another gay Julius in Brighton somewhere. I had to take the chance.

'I had a strong feeling that you were a very wise man.' I was hardly getting straight to the point.

He smiled. 'Very flattering.'

I struggled for the next sentence. It couldn't be "Are you a witch?"

'I believe we may have friends in common.'

'Oh yes?'

'I work with Michaela, you perhaps have come across her through her Great Aunt Miranda, who was a well-known figure.'

'Yes, she was. I do know Michaela.'

'And Ray, a young man who works with me. He's a fan of yours.'

'Is he?' He raised his eyebrows.

'He admires you tremendously, models himself on you.'

His lips twitched. 'Does he really?'

'You know who I mean?'

'Yes.'

We stared at each other in silence. He was not going to be the one to break it.

'Are you, are you a…….Wiccan?'

'Of course. That is my link with Michaela and Ray. But you already know that, don't you. It's your reason for being here, in this room.' He was matter-of-fact.

'Ray was discreet. He only talked about Julius who was wise and gay. He wouldn't give any more details.'

'Good man.' He chuckled. 'Michaela was worried about him, but I'm sure we're right to accept him amongst us. He's very young still.'

'Does Simon, is Simon……..?'

'Simon isn't a Wiccan. His father was a Church of England vicar, so he inclines to that faith rather than any other.'

'Do you cast spells?'

'Not usually. Why? Do you want to put a hex on someone?'

'The opposite I think. I don't know. I don't believe in spells, anyhow. You know Fran?'

'I do. You want me to smooth relations between her and her husband? There's no spell for that. Mickey's already asked me. It's a sad business. An unfortunate misunderstanding of what we do and how we maintain our relationship with the rest of the world.'

'I'm one of Fran's husband's best friends.' Curiously, although I'd only known Craigie for a short time, I felt my statement to be true. 'Can't you possibly help him? It's not fair, it's not his fault.'

'Danielle, the only help I can give is to talk to him. No magic. However, no one knows where he is, do they? Do you?'

'No. I can get in touch with him though.'

'Then you are the key player in the game. I'll be here.'

Our conversation was at an end.

I texted Craigie later that night. He texted back his new mobile number, his old one would be defunct from then on. I dialled the new one, relieved when I heard his voice. I told him there was a man I wanted him to meet. He was dubious. He needed more time. He would call me during the following week, when he hoped to feel fit to see Fran.

****

Fortunately for Professor Bradshaw, Sunday was one of those spring days which is more like summer. Hot. Too hot almost. Shorts and tee shirts weather. I didn't have a suitable wardrobe yet, so Mickey lent me clothes which were somewhat too girlie for me, but passable. Robbie gave a whistle of admiration, and said she was glad I was getting in touch with my feminine side.

'Cut it out!' I growled, climbing on the back of her bike. The other four piled into Des's old heap. There was one

Mr. Universe look-a-like with them, who I assumed was the hunk Des was pursuing.

Richard's garden was of a decent size. There were a few stringly bushes around the edge, a patch of grass masquerading as a lawn, and that was it. Patio doors opened into his kitchen where he was dispensing drinks. An elderly woman was handing round bits to the guests mainly congregated around the table indoors, partly to avoid the heat of the sun, as there was little shade except the shadow of the house itself. It was a genteel affair, voices were low and from somewhere, soft, dreamy music was playing.

'This doesn't look much fun,' Des whispered to me. 'My God, that's Busy Lizzie, our romantic novel tutor tottering around with the biscuits. She'll fall over in a minute. She's too old to be drinking. She should have retired long ago. She must be sixty-five. Poor Tricky Dickey! No wonder he wanted me to come and liven things up.'

She was into the kitchen to grab a glass of punch before I could warn her that "livening things up" wasn't exactly what Richard had in mind. Her gang followed suit. I watched Richard stiffen when he caught sight of the hunk, who made short work of the first glassful, and the second, before eyeing up the assembled company. His attention was attracted by an immaculate woman who could have stepped straight from the pages of Vogue. Black dress clinging to a perfect form, big straw hat with artificial poppies, she was standing in front of the only decent shrub, which had glossy dark green and yellow striped leaves, setting her off perfectly. If she were a permanent fitting Richard would sell his property to the first comer for twice the asking price.

'Oh shit!' exclaimed Des. 'That's done it. I've had it now.'

'Do you know her?' I asked.

'She's the critical theory tutor. Doesn't teach us until the final year. Everybody wants to sleep with her. All the men I mean.'

And probably some of the women, I thought.

'You mean she's a university lecturer?' I was amazed. 'She's more like a model or a film star.'

'Isn't she? She's frightfully clever. She's written four books already and she's not very old.'

'I can see that.'

'The last one was about descriptions of the sexual act in lesbian novels.'

'You're kidding! You mean she's a lesbian?'

'I don't think so. She just wanted to write about it. Rumour has it she's bisexual, though. That is an even greater turn on for the men.'

'What's her name?'

'Dr. O'Grady. Blanche O'Grady, La Belle Blanche.'

I guessed she was about my age. Four books!

'Have you read this lesbian sex book?'

'I tried. We all tried. It's very difficult, very boring and difficult. She keeps talking about French and French feminists I've never heard of.'

I had been thinking I might borrow it from the library, Des's judgement changed my mind. La Belle Blanche was flirting outrageously with the hunk, who was lapping it up. Richard took his chance to approach Des.

'So pleased you could come, Des.'

She turned to him. 'Yeah, thanks for inviting us.' She glanced back at the hunk to check whether he was still fixated on La Belle Blanche. 'Nice place you've got here,' she added politely.

'I don't like it. It's not me, it was just a temporary solution.'

'I must say I prefer old, myself. I've always lived in old, so I'm used to it. My dad and mum have an Elizabethan cottage. Shakespeare, you know. But of course you know.'

'Yes. I'm looking forward to reading your Shakespeare paper, by the way. You have such amazing insights.'

I moved off to leave his field clear. Not exactly a wonderful chat up line, I thought, but the poor guy was nervous. Suitably fortified by quick consumption of alcohol, the rest of the gang had dispersed amongst their elders, who appeared to welcome the invasion of the young. Perhaps they had needed to be livened up after all. As usual, I was on the fringe. If I'd had my own transport I could have gone home. There was a wooden bench in the far corner next to a cornfield. I would sit for a while, then ask Richard if I could phone for a taxi. Robbie was engaged in an animated discussion with two young men, so I guessed she wouldn't want to leave yet. I sank down on to the bench, closed my eyes, luxuriating in the warmth of the sun. I was grateful for Mickey's skimpy tank top and flimsy short trousers. My mind wandered to the beaches in Martinique, where I'd been happy and lazy for a year or so, to the woman I'd lived with, a passionate dark beauty whose temperament was in the end too much for me. I remembered her small, high breasts and her beautiful round buttocks, her full lips.......

'I love the heat don't you? I can't stand too much sun, but heat is blissful.'

She sat down beside me, took her hat off, revealing her deep red hair. Green eyes, pale skin, astonishingly without a single freckle. Her voice had a soft Irish lilt.

'I'm Blanche O'Grady. Who are you?'

'Danielle Divito.'

'Are you one of our students? I haven't seen you around the campus. I would remember you.'

She smiled. Her lipstick was very red.

'No. I'm a friend of Des.'

'Des?'

'Desdemona Portia O'Flynn. One of Professor Bradshaw's personal students.'

'You're not serious?'

'I am.'

'Good gracious! Poor girl.'

Was the sympathy because of the name or because of Richard? I never knew, as she brought the subject immediately back to me.

'So what do you do?'

It was a question I hated.

'This and that.'

'How mysterious! What sort of this and that?' She moved closer to me. Across the garden I could see the hunk with Sandrine, whereas Des and Richard had disappeared. She touched my bare shoulder. 'You're very brown.'

'All over and all year round. It's in my blood as well as my skin.'

'I see. What else is in your blood?'

Lust, I thought. If her chemical reaction to me was as strong as mine to her, we'd better find a bed soon. However, she was an intellectual, so maybe I should proceed cautiously.

'I hear you've written a book about lesbian sex.'

'I've written a book about lesbian sex in novels. Who told you that?'

'Des. She's tried to read it and finds it too difficult. Are you interested in lesbian sex in real life as well as in novels?'

'Real life? Now what do we mean by that?'

If she was going to play those sorts of games, I would give up, take a cold shower, call that taxi.

'I think you need to clarify your statement, Danielle. Leave generalisations aside. Attend to the particular.'

Her green eyes stared unblinkingly into my brown ones, challenging.

'Would you like to go to bed with me?'

'That's better. Yes I would. Come home with me.'

She had a racy little sports car. She drove me to the mansion where she lived, led me down to a basement flat. Huge rooms, sparsely furnished. Her bed was enormous. Was she into orgies? Mixed orgies?

'Undress me, Danielle.'

I took each garment off slowly, running my finger lightly across her arms, her breasts, teasing her pink nipples. Then, she undressed me, trailing her fingers down my back until she reached the base of my spine when she dug her nails in. I laid her down and parted her thighs. We stroked, licked, sucked, scratched, bit, experienced climax after climax until we lay sweaty and exhausted. It was by now totally dark. She got up to light a candle. I saw red marks of my nails on her white skin. I was overwhelmed by a feeling of tenderness. I stretched out my arms and she came to lie her head on my shoulder.

'Let's sleep now,' she said.

I woke up once to find the candle had gone out. There was no light at all. I went back to sleep pressed against her long back.

She left for work early leaving me a pot of coffee and a note thanking me for a fantastic night, telling me to be sure to slam the door hard behind me and giving her phone number at the university, should I need it. She would be in meetings all day but there was voice mail. Since I'd confessed I was to be found at "*Her Place*", she would pop in when she had a free afternoon. She was tired of her basement and she was hoping for promotion. Her bedroom was untidy, clothes strewn on every surface. She had an extensive collection of erotic underwear draped on handles and hooks. And the pictures on her walls! Blanche was a dyke, through and through, forget the bi-sexual story. Stroking her finger down my inner thigh in the waning candlelight she'd admitted to having slept around with men when she was an undergraduate, and having had an affair with her supervisor whilst writing her doctoral thesis, but that was before she discovered women. There were two photos propped against a mirror on her dressing table. One of a serious bespectacled girl in a cap and gown, clutching some kind of diploma, labelled "Before", the other of the seductress I'd encountered, labelled "After".

Next to her main bedroom was a much smaller one, obviously serving as a study. It was rather airless and the only light came from a small window placed too high up to be able to look out. On her desk, which covered half the floor, lay heaps of papers, half open books, a computer displaying her e-mails. There was a divan against the back wall. No pictures here, just shelves of books. It was very unpleasant. How she could work in such a claustrophobic environment I couldn't imagine. I couldn't wait to get out, blinking in the sudden brightness as I climbed her steps. It was half past eight, so I took my time ambling along the promenade, considering my good fortune in coming across two such sexy women. Amelia had been a vamp, Blanche, well Blanche was an absolute knockout. Was it because she was an intellectual, that her skill exceeded that of the bimbo? No, it couldn't be that. It must have been the magnetic attraction, pheromones, or what you will, that draws two particular individuals towards each other. It's to do with flesh and blood, not intellect.

A young man jogged past me, grinned and said 'My, you look happy!'

Happy, yes, satisfied, not quite. I wanted to leave a message for Blanche when she came out of her meeting. 'Blanche, come back to bed, I'm waiting.' My libido, stirred again into a half awake state by Amelia, was now flexing its muscles proclaiming, 'Hey, I'm here. Feed me!' How soon could I see her again? My pride prevented me from taking the first step. I had to be certain that she wanted me as much as I wanted her. She was the kind of woman who might have a great one night stand, then wave bye-bye in the morning. There was a spring in my step and I was humming a sentimental love song as I entered the office where Ray and Mickey were already busy in silent contemplation of the order of the day.

I took my place quietly. My phone rang. Already ! It was only five past nine.

'Danielle? How are you?'

'Very well, Mr. Cricket. How are you?'

'Worried about Greta. She's been moody recently.'

'Time of the month, perhaps?'

'No. She's on the pill.'

'We have a busy day's work ahead, Mr. Cricket. I can't help you. Has she seen a doctor?'

'She won't'

'Too bad.'

'I don't want to leave her alone.'

'Then don't.'

'I can stay down here until Wednesday night, after that I have to be away for a week.'

'Really, I'm sorry there is absolutely nothing I can do. She might have recovered by Wednesday.'

I put my hand over the mouthpiece and hissed at Mickey. 'Get him off my back. This is your fault.'

'I beg your pardon, Danielle. What did you say?'

'Nothing. I reminded Michaela about a responsibility of hers.'

'Not, it's not,' she hissed back.

'You couldn't move in with her for the week?'

'No way, Jiminy.' I saw Ray's eyebrows raised at the juxtaposition of the first and second names. 'Apart from the fact that I have my own home, my own friends, I'm out at work all day.'

'If you know anyone who might....'

'I'll bear it in mind. Have a nice day!'

Mickey took Ray out, I stayed in which turned out to be the right way round. At ten o'clock Robbie turned up.

'You look remarkably lively,' she said. 'I expected you'd be worn out.'

'Why would you expect this?'

'We all saw you leave with La Belle Blanche.'

'She wanted me to help with her research.'

'Yeah! Come on, Dany, is she as good as she looks?'

'I have no idea what you're talking about. Did you have a reason for coming to see me, apart from salacious gossip?'

'Gossip first. What a party! Sandrine went off with the hunk. How they got back to the campus I don't know, because Des didn't take them. She spent the night with

Tricky Dickey. I gave a lift to that old woman who teaches Romantic Literature. She's quite a goer. Lecturers' parties beat student parties any day.'

'Excuse me, I have to go through these papers. Now we're over the gossip, what else is there?'

'Tracey.'

'Ah.' I had feared that chicken would come home to roost again. 'Being a nuisance, is she?'

'That's putting it mildly. She's a pain in the backside. Nothing suits her. She found a little job helping in the bar. She couldn't hack it. She got the orders and the change all wrong. We invite her to eat with us, she thinks our food is good for rabbits and horses. I have never In my life met such an inverted snob. We don't ask for undying gratitude for what we're doing for her, just a word of thanks now and then. Anyhow, she's been sleeping in Samantha's room and Samantha is coming back on Wednesday to sit her exams.

'She'll be homeless again?'

'Exactly. Any suggestions?'

'When precisely will she have to get out?'

'Wednesday night.'

'I'll work on it.'

'Please do. Sure you haven't anything more to say about La Belle Blanche?'

'Sure.'

'Well all I can say is, more power to your elbow as it were.'

'Adios, Robbie. Have a nice day.'

In between taking down vendor details and making appointments, I considered the only solution to the Tracey problem, temporary though it may be. Who knows if she played her cards right (which was highly unlikely) a more permanent solution might develop. Jiminy Cricket needed a mistress sitter for Greta, Tracey needed a place to stay, put the two together and, hey presto, it's all sorted.

I outlined my plan to Mickey at lunchtime. She stared at me uncomprehendingly, then was overwhelmed by uncontrollable mirth. When she'd caught her breath again, she said 'That's the most stupid suggestion I've ever heard. What do you think, Ray?'

'Er, I don't know this Greta person but I wouldn't wish Tracey on my worst enemy.'

'Right,' I said, 'it's over to you then. See what you can come up with.' I concentrated on my keyboard.

At the end of the afternoon neither Mickey nor Ray had mentioned Tracey or Greta again.

'So, any inspired thoughts?'

'About what?' Mickey took out her car key.

'Tracey. Greta. Either or both.'

'Not yet. Do you want a lift?'

'Kind of you to ask. Yes, please.'

'You weren't home last night,' she accused as I fastened the seat belt.

'Observant of you to notice.'

'I wanted to talk to you.'

'So sorry. So did someone else, want to talk to me, that is.'

'I hear you went to see Julius.'

'I was invited to a soirée at his house. I didn't deliberately set out to see him. Is there anything wrong with that?'

'You aren't one of us, that's what's wrong. Meddling in Wiccan affairs.'

'Did he object?'

'No he didn't, but I do. And Fran does. He's our friend, not yours. Our associate, my associate from way back.'

'Sorry.'

'You may well be. Don't ever, ever do such a thing again.'

Sometimes she sounded like the head girl she possibly had been.

'No, Mickey.'

'Promise on your honour.' She screeched into her driveway.

'Don't be childish,' was my lofty reply.

In my kitchen, out of earshot, I called Craigie. He was mellowing. He asked how Fran was doing.

'My friends advise me to finish with her. A selfish little bitch, is what they actually said.'

'Have you told them about the potion?'

'No. That's not what it's about.' There was a long pause. 'I'd like to call round at the weekend, see her, if she'll keep calm. The moment she gets hysterical, I'm off.'

I hesitated a second or two before putting the crucial question.

'Are you still in love with her? She says you hate her.'

'Dany, I wish I knew. Tell her I'll come by Saturday afternoon at four o'clock, if possible.'

'This man I'd like you to meet, could I arrange something before then?'

'Why?'

'Craigie, I truly believe he'll be helpful.'

'Is he a family counsellor or something? A psychotherapist?'

'No. He's....' What was he ? 'He's a scholar. A wise man.'

'A scholar! What have I got to do with a scholar?'

'He's a nice person. You'd like him. He knows Fran. He understands her.'

'He'd have to be a genius to do that.'

'Could I take you to his house at two o'clock on Saturday? Please.'

'O.K.'

'See you one forty-five Saturday at the Clock Tower. Are your ribs better?'

'They're healing. Takes time. See you.' End of conversation. I called Julius immediately. He would be at home on Saturday afternoon.

****

I was restless. I had left a note of my home number on Blanche's kitchen table, in a prominent position. What time did she get in from work? When she found it, would she call me? There are few things more agitating than spending a whole evening by the phone waiting for the call that doesn't happen. I sat on my terrace feeling lonely, because basically I was alone. The elation of the morning gave way to gloomy introspection. What was wrong with me that I was always on the move, from country to country, job to job, woman to woman?

I went out, wandered along the front, in the opposite direction from Blanche's apartment, sat on the beach, threw stones into the water, had a beer, made my way back, listened for messages. There were none. I went to bed with a crime novel. Trying to keep up with the complications of the plot was so tiring I soon drifted into a series of unpleasant dreams, inspired by the numerous descriptions of mutilated corpses in the few chapters I'd read.

****

Tuesday was grey – grey sky, grey sea and grey moral. I waited until Ray had been sent off on a mission with a customer who was dying to spend his enormous city bonus, before broaching the subject of Craigie.

'Craigie called me last night.'

She froze.

'He called *you!*'

'Yes. He wants to collect some clothes at the weekend. Four o'clock. If Fran makes any kind of scene, he'll leave.'

'Where is he?'

'I don't know.'

'What's his phone number?'

'I don't know. He didn't give it.' Lies fall off your tongue so easily these days, Dany!

She stood up, eyes blazing.

'I'm going over to Fran's. I won't be back. You and Ray can manage.'

Ray was beside himself with excitement. His client had driven straight back to London, having made an offer on a Regency house.

'Honestly, Dany, it's awesome. Huge and beautiful, belonged to some Duke or other. The price is unbelievable. The offer is only slightly below the asking price and he'll come up if necessary. He just loved it. And he only wants it for weekends. During the week he lives in the Barbican. He must earn an absolute mint of money.

'Shall I tackle the vendors, or should I wait for Mickey?'

'Go ahead, but calm down first.

He took a deep breath before dialling. He forced his normally light voice down a note or two, to add weight. He was brisk, firm. The upshot was that the offer was accepted. After all it was a sum which few could afford. Ray rushed out from behind his desk, threw his arms around me, kissed me on both cheeks.

'Dany, I've done it! I've done it! Yes!'

He called the client's mobile with the good news before tackling the paperwork. I watched in admiration. For one so young, so apparently inadequate, it was miraculous. It was probably connected with his initiation as a Wiccan priest. The goddess had imbued him with new force.

'Any ideas about what to do with Tracey?' I asked when he sat back from his labours.

'Oh no! She went right out of my mind.'

I dialled Jiminy Cricket.

'I have a possible Greta sitter for you. I'll organise for her to come round for an interview. How about this evening?'

'Marvellous. I'm gradually bringing Greta round to having someone with her for the week. Naturally if she and this person don't take to each other I won't force the issue. I'll be waiting.'

I dialled Robbie. 'Can you bring Trace over to our office this evening?'

'I'll be glad to Since we've told her she really has to get out, she's been worse than ever. What shall I tell her? I can't tie her up and deliver her like a parcel.'

'She can have a week in a fab apartment, no expense spared as much spending money as she likes. All she has to do is be a companion to an attractive foreign woman.'

'Hey, forget Tracey, I'll take the job myself. Then Tracey can have my room.'

'The attractive foreigner has a jealous lover. She's his previous floozy.'

'I get the picture. See you later. Hopefully.'

Her persuasive methods, whatever they were, must have been excellent. Tracey was duly transported from campus to office, dishevelled, disgruntled, complaining about Robbie's driving.

'These students are rubbish' she declared as she strode in. 'They help you when it suits them, when it doesn't they don't give a damn that you'll be turned on to the streets.'

'She's all yours. Nice to have known you Tracey.' Robbie was off, ignoring Trace's two fingers stuck in the air. Not much hope of her meeting the approval of either master or mistress, I thought gloomily. I might as well go on with what I'd started.

'What kind of funny business is this, then? What are you trying to get me into?'

'You'll see.' I called a taxi.

She never stopped complaining the whole way, until we reached Greta's building. She went quiet at that point, impressed by the grandeur.

'You could have combed your hair,' I said as I pressed the bell.

'I haven't got a comb.'

She looked awful, Jiminy reeled back in horror, then flashed me a reproachful glance.

'This is Tracey.'

'How do you do Tracey.' He didn't hold out his hand, noting her dirty fingernails. 'I'm Jiminy Cricket and this is my friend Greta.'

'You're who?' Her jaw dropped. I nudged her.

Greta stepped forward. Until then she had been lurking in the background.

'How do you do, Tracey?' She smiled. 'I'm, Greta. Perhaps we can be friends.'

# Chapter 20

Who would have thought it? Greta took one look at Tracey and deemed she was O.K. The feeling wasn't mutual. Tracey was suspicious, ungracious, ready to run away from such an unknown situation. She kept repeating "I dunno, I dunno", until Greta invited her to look at the spare bedroom.

'We speak alone,' she declared, taking Tracey's arm.

'You talk funny English.' Was Tracey's rude response. Nevertheless, she allowed herself to be led off, and the door was firmly closed behind them.

'A drink, Dany,' offered Jiminy. 'Champagne? There's some opened. We drink nothing else in the evening.'

There wasn't a sound from the spare bedroom down the corridor.

'I'm not entirely happy about that young woman. She's not very co-operative. She's extremely unkempt.'

'She'll probably scrub up well. Greta seems to like her.'

'Yes.' He toyed with his glass. 'She does. She's being increasingly difficult and demanding.' He stared into the bubbles. 'She could be seeing another man.'

'What gives you that idea?' I asked.

'Nothing specific. Instinct. More than instinct. She was bruised once when I came back after a couple of days in London. Said she slipped on the beach.'

The other man certainly seemed rough, I thought. 'If she said she slipped, she slipped.'

'Hmm. It was disturbing, most disturbing. This girl you've brought, this Tracey person, is she into drugs?'

I shrugged. 'Maybe, maybe not. I don't think she can afford it. Are you? Is Greta?'

'That's indiscreet of you, Dany.'

'It was indiscreet of you to ask about Tracey.'

He poured himself another glass, offered me one, which I refused. 'They've been gone a long time.'

'They're getting to know each other.'

'The point is, I have to be very careful. In my position I am susceptible to blackmail.'

'You're worried Tracey could blackmail you?'

'I have taken every precaution. Greta doesn't know my London address, nor my home phone number. It would be disastrous if my wife found out. She's the daughter of the managing director of my company. I'm his right hand man, his blue-eyed boy. He only has one child, his precious darling.'

'I get the picture.'

'I have an awful lot to lose.'

'It's up to you. Send Tracey packing. I've no-one else up my sleeve, though.'

His mistress and her proposed companion emerged from the spare room. Tracey was grinning from ear to ear, an expression I'd never seen before. She was holding Greta's hand.

'Tracey will be my new friend,' Greta announced. 'She very nice, Jiminy. I like very much. You like me, Tracey?'

'O yeah. I like you Greta.'

'Thank you. Dany. You find me nice friend. She need nice clothes. Tomorrow we go shopping. O.K. Jiminy? All go shopping. You busy. She move in tomorrow night. You go to London tomorrow night, yes?'

'Yes. About the shopping....'

'Good shops, good clothes,' she cut in. 'You take your card. Then you leave us plenty of money.'

Jiminy looked appealingly at me. I looked away.

'Tracey take taxi back to campus, collect things. O.K. Tracey?'

'O,K, Greta.'

'I'll be going then. Glad to be of service.' I made for the exit.

**\*\*\*\***

I had just picked up the thriller I'd started, trying to

remember who was who, prepared for another lonely night, when Richard called.

'Meet for a drink at the hotel opposite the pier? We're not likely to meet students there. In half an hour?'

'Right.' I would have preferred Blanche, but Richard was better than nothing.

He was already installed at the bar when I walked in. He didn't have the air of a man who'd achieved his heart's desire.

'They tell me you scored.' I wasn't going to beat about the bush.

'News travels fast.'

'That kind of news does. So you weren't simply interested in her fine mind?'

'She doesn't have a fine mind. She has occasional brilliant insights, that's all.'

'You said she's the best student you'd ever come across.'

'An error of judgement.'

'Oh dear.'

'Disappointing. Her last piece of work was disappointing, childish, I've just reread it. I don't know what was wrong with me first time round.'

'Disappointing in bed too?'

'Inexperienced.'

'I should hope so. She's only eighteen, nineteen at most.'

'She was the one who suggested sleeping together. Practically dragged me into the bedroom. She was just trying to make that blond beast jealous. He didn't care, by the time we came up for air he'd gone off with one of her chums.' He finished his beer fetched another. 'It was all so humiliating. For some reason she found me intensely amusing. Whatever I did made her giggle. That's never happened to me before. She stayed the night. She was too drunk to drive back. We made love again in the morning. It wasn't much better. She didn't laugh, she just kept yawning. It was so absolutely meaningless. Still, that's got her out of my blood.'

'She won't be hurt?'

'Hurt? The whole episode has gone out of her mind already, no doubt. She called me Tricky Dickey when I was screwing her. "Go for it Tricky Dickey," she shouted.'

'Spare me the details,' I said dryly.

'How about you?'

'What about me?'

'You and Blanche. Didn't you go home with her?'

'My lips are sealed. A lady's honour is safe with me, Professor Bradshaw, particularly that of one of your colleagues.'

'She's a slick mover, that one. She's probably in line for a chair. I need you to sell my house. I might be leaving Sussex. Going to the States. A job has suddenly come up. I've been approached because of my reputation. I have to get the official application in quickly. I've had it in this country. Salaries are pathetic. So get on with the sale. I'll drop the price if necessary.'

He reminded me that our link was basically commercial, I wasn't his friend, I was an uneducated estate agent he had made use of in another way. Des having been tried and rejected, I was only good for selling his house.

'So long, Professor. We are at your service.' I abandoned him to his next pint of real ale.

****

On Wednesday morning, Mickey and I weren't speaking to each other, after I'd informed her that Tracey was to be Greta's companion. Ray was late in. He was apologetic and clumsy, dropping papers, losing his pens, bumping into his desk.

'What's wrong, Ray?' I asked. Mickey ignored him, tutting in annoyance every time he made a noise.

'Granny's not well. I called the doctor.'

Mickey stopped her typing to take notice.

'What's the matter with her?'

'She's been sick all night. Vomiting and diarrhoea. She

could hardly speak when I went in this morning, she was so weak.'

'What did the doctor say?'

'Probably a stomach bug.'

'You haven't been giving her any magic potions, have you?'

'Of course he hasn't, snapped Mickey. 'He wouldn't experiment on a fragile old lady, would he?'

'Oh no, I wouldn't, well, not until I was sure of what I was doing.' He knocked a pile of documents over. They scattered across the floor.

'Oh no! I'm sorry. I can't concentrate on what I'm doing.'

'Go home', ordered Mickey. Take the rest of the day off on full pay.'

'Thank you, thank you! I left her asleep. The doctor is sending a nurse, but I'd rather be with her myself.'

'I'll call by at lunchtime, if you don't mind.' I didn't like the sound of her sickness.

His absence increased the tension between Mickey and me. She was stony faced as she consulted her diary. No appointments until 11, the phone silent, the shop empty, it could be a good moment to make peace.

'Mickey.' No response, so I tried again. 'Mickey can we talk?'

'I'm busy.' She frowned at her screen.

'This hostility is ridiculous.'

No response. I went to stand in front of her. 'Mickey,' I shouted.

At last she raised her eyes from the computer. 'Well?'

'Put the "temporarily closed" sign on the door and let's go into the back room with a cup of coffee.'

We confronted each other for several seconds. It must have been my aggressive body language that convinced her. She did what I said. We carried our coffee into the back room, closed the door. First of all I resorted to my old trick of throwing a tantrum. I became threatening. I cried, (no more than a strategy), said how much her friendship meant to me. It was her turn to cry genuine tears. Everything was such a mess, she said. She couldn't cope with it all. She was useless with magic. Fran was useless with magic. I tried to comfort her by assuring her that she was excellent at selling houses. She cried even harder. It would have been better if she hadn't inherited all this money. It was a responsibility. She was too young to be so responsible. When I first knew her she wanted to be an International women's rugby player. She had no other ambitions.

'Dany, I just want to give it all away and go backpacking in India.' She sobbed into her handkerchief. 'In search of wisdom.'

'I thought you were doing that, here in Sussex. You want to forsake Wicca for Buddhism?'

'No! Wicca takes wisdom from many sources. It doesn't matter. I can't do it.' She blew her nose, shook my hand. 'If I felt better about myself, I wouldn't be so horrible to you.'

'Then we're working together? Buddies?'

'Yeah, buddies.'

We took the sign off the front door, the phone rang and we were in business again.

The eleven o'clock appointment was to take a couple of teachers to see Richard's house. Although I had planned to take them over myself, I asked Mickey if she could go instead. I had no wish to listen to Tricky Dicky impressing them with a list of his publications. It was a fortunate decision, for no sooner had they driven off together than I had a call from Roz.

'I have a spare ticket for a concert tonight, would you like to come? It was for Jim, but he's working his socks off in London.'

No use in asking who was playing what. I would accept whatever it was.

'Meet me outside the Dome at 7.30.'

A lot had been achieved already that day, Mickey and I had made peace again, and I had a date. The icing on the cake was that the teachers were buying Richard's uninspiring little box. Mickey had cheered up. In spite of her denial she was pleased that "*Her Place*" was doing so well.

'I'd take you out to dinner, except that I have to be with Fran every evening.'

'It's O.K. I have a date.'

'Lucky you! It's about time I had some romance in my life too.'

It wasn't romance, but I didn't disillusion her.

My lunchtime visit to Davina left me distressed. Drained of its usual vitality, her face was a withered mask. She had been sleeping all morning, Ray whispered. It was good for her. He had kept a mournful vigil beside her, watching to see if her breathing slowed down or stopped.

'She can't die. She mustn't die.'

'The best way to leave this life is to die quietly in your bed,' I said gently.

'She's not ready to do that.'

'You mean you're not ready for her to do it.'

'I'm not ready and she's not ready. She's worried about me being left on my own. I'm too young.'

'You have to face the possibility.'

'Stop talking like that in front of her! Go away. I won't have you sitting in her room talking about dying.' He kept his voice low, looking sideways at his great grandmother.

'If you need help, you know where to find me.' He was already pushing me out.

Whilst Mickey was inspecting some properties, I put my feet up for a while. All the files were up to date, there was nothing else to do. Instead of fantasising about Anita as I usually did in these circumstances, I conjured up an image of Blanche's soft body. My imagination was travelling down from her throat to her breasts when in she walked. At first I didn't recognise her, against the light I couldn't make out her face, and I had been dreaming of bare flesh, whereas she appeared before me in a spotless white linen trouser suit and a black satin shirt.

'Good afternoon, Danielle.'

'Good afternoon, Blanche. Strangely enough I was just thinking about you.'

'Pleasant thoughts, I hope.'

'Very.'

'Would you like to come round tonight?'

Oh damn, damn, damn. I sure would. If only she'd been a bit sooner with her invitation. Could I cancel Roz?

'An intimate dinner?'

'Well, I have an engagement, but I'd love to come round later. Don't worry about the dinner.'

'How much later?'

How long is a concert, I wondered.

'Half past ten?' I suggested.

'It's not what I had in mind.'

'I don't suppose you're free tomorrow night?'

'No. Nor the day after, nor the day after. It's O.K. Forget it. It doesn't matter.'

I panicked. 'I'll change my arrangements. I'll come round at eight?'

'I get too hungry for dinner at eight. Seven.' She sauntered out.

Roz was with a client all afternoon. I tried three times, each time her secretary answered. I had hoped to speak to her personally. It was difficult. I asked the secretary to give her a message, but I couldn't be sure she'd get it. Sometimes I knew that she would stay longer than the secretary and be incommunicado. What if she went straight to the concert hall? I tried at 5.30. There was no answer except a recorded message. I tried her home at 6. Again a recorded message.

Mickey was preparing to leave.

'Mickey, would you do me a big favour?'

'What?'

'Would you meet Roz Browning at 7.30 outside the Dome and go to a concert with her? Say I'm terribly sorry, I'd forgotten another engagement I couldn't break. I tried to let her know but she was unreachable.'

'You want me to pick up your date?'

'Could you?'

'What's the concert?'

'I don't know. Does it matter?'

'It it's contemporary stuff I can't bear it. Let's have a look at the paper.'

Fortunately it was a Russian Symphony Orchestra, playing Rachmaninof and Tchaikovsky, with an apparently world famous pianist for the Rachmaninof, so Mickey informed me.

'Are you sure you can't go, Dany? This woman is fantastic. The concert must have been sold out months ago. And aren't you rather keen on Roz?'

'I like her. I'm not really into classical music. You'll enjoy it more than me.'

'I'll have to leave Fran to her own devices. She'll understand, I expect. What's the alternative attraction?'

'An intimate dinner.'

'A good restaurant?'

'Her pad.'

'I see. Do I know her?'

'No.'

'Is she attractive? Of course she is or you wouldn't be letting Roz down.'

I didn't like her saying I was letting Roz down. I was already guilty enough.

'Cut it out Mickey. I'll be in at nine tomorrow.'

'Wow!'

The intimate dinner was ready made, three courses. Blanche confirmed that she'd never learned to cook. Why bother when you could buy such prepared culinary delights. She ate greedily, licking her lips suggestively every so often. Conversation flagged but then conversation wasn't what the evening was about. She had lived through a terrible day was all she said. The job was getting more and more pressured. She was expected to do far too much teaching. First years! They'd asked her to lecture to first years! She wasn't going to do it. She needed to finish her next book. She had star research status.

My eyes began to glaze. I stopped listening, since none of what she was rattling on about mattered to me. Instead I watched the gentle movement of her breasts beneath her silk shirt as she raised her fork to her mouth in between sentences. It was a beautiful sight, she wasn't wearing a bra, would she be wearing underwear at all? The shirt was tightly buttoned, the fabric stretched across her skin, rubbing softly against her nipples with every gesture. Surely she was as excited by this as I was? How would she react if I leaned across the table and took one of those hardening nipples in my mouth?

'What do you think of Richard?' She licked her ice-cream spoon. A big pointed tongue.

'Richard?'

'Richard Bradshaw. He's a prick. Typical chauvinist. He came on to me at first. When I wasn't interested, he ignored me except to make snide remarks at meetings. He can't bear the fact that my books are rated more highly than his. And he can't tolerate the possibility I might get a chair.'

Her arms were by her side. Her shirt fell in loose folds. 'Shall we go to bed?' she asked.

I have never chosen to make love straight after eating. Besides, my moment of desire had passed. The spark had to be revived.

'How about a digestif? A brandy? Or a port?'

She found an almost empty bottle of rum. 'Will this do? I brought it back from holiday in the Caribbean.'

'Excellent.'

She served us with bad grace, impatient for the real business to begin.

'Come and sit beside me. And don't talk!' I pulled her on to the sofa. 'Let's concentrate on the foreplay.'

She sank back. 'I love it when you're dominating!'

At half past two I got up, got dressed.

'Aren't you staying the night? She asked in dismay. 'I don't have to be in until lunch-time tomorrow.'

'I'm sorry. I have to be in at nine. I'm tired, I have to get some sleep.'

A one-night stand can be incredible. If you try to repeat it the edge disappears. I'm not saying it wasn't good with Blanche, we both had enough experience to make sure of that. But a couple more times and it would become routine.

'Dany, you do like me, don't you?'

'Sure I do.' As a matter of fact I wasn't sure. I supposed I did. Not enough for us to become bosom friends.

'We'll do this again soon? When term has finished and meetings are over?' She had switched on the bedside lamp so I could see her anxious face. I was the bit of rough she didn't want to lose.

'Yeah. Ciao.'

****

Ray stayed away for the rest of the week. We missed him. More than once we had to put the "Out on visits. Back soon" notice on the door.

Just before we closed on Friday evening, Ray bounded in, all smiles. 'She's better!'

His delight was infectious. We cheered.

'This morning I made her porridge with honey. She ate lunch, then I fetched her a meringue for tea. The doctor was amazed. I'm sure he'd given her up.'

He was bursting with excitement. He obviously had more to relate.

'I have to say, I'm responsible.'

'Ray, you haven't.....' It was Mickey's head girl self speaking.

'I have. I did. And I got it right. I got it right!' He blushed with pride.

'I told you not to. You could have got it wrong, terribly wrong.'

'I followed a recipe. I bought the right herbs, put in the right amount, recited the right words.'

'You cast a spell over a concoction you made up?' Thank goodness she's alive, I thought.

'I didn't make it up. It was one of Culpepper's recipes. I made the spell up. Aren't you impressed? I saved my Granny's life. Whenever she's sick, I'll make her better. Congratulate me! It's a triumph.'

'I'm not going to congratulate you. It could so easily have been a disaster. I'm glad she's better. Will you be able to come into work tomorrow?'

He was cross, disappointed. 'Not tomorrow morning.'

'Tomorrow afternoon. I can't be here.'

'Nor can I,' I slipped in. Saturday afternoon I introduced Julius to Craigie.

'Well, if you're absolutely stuck...'

'Fine. Two o'clock; you still have your key. Do you want a lift, Dany?'

'I'll be with you in a minute. I'll lock up.'

Whilst she fetched the car, I shook Ray's hand.

'Great stuff! In the end you might be a better witch than Mickey or Fran.'

'Oh no! Thank you, anyway.'

'He shouldn't administer potions to old women,' Mickey insisted, as we drove home. 'He was lucky. She would have come round naturally, I expect.'

I was tempted to tell her Julius had more confidence in Ray than she had, but that would have been provocative.

'You haven't had a chance to tell me about the concert.'

'It was fabulous. The experience of a lifetime. I hope your intimate dinner was worth it, because believe me, you'll never have that sort of opportunity again.'

She didn't know I'd come home. I'd deliberately set off before she did, wearing the same clothes as the previous day, had a full English breakfast at a greasy spoon café and pretended I'd spent the night on the tiles.

'Yeah. She was dynamite. Was Roz annoyed when it was you turned up?'

'Surprised. When I explained, she shrugged and said "Too bad". If I had been you, nothing in the world would have kept me away from that fabulous performance. A night of good sex isn't in the same league.'

'That's your opinion.' I retorted, grumpily. 'Sex isn't high on your agenda.'

She blushed. 'Right now I have more important matters to get on with.'

'Chacun à son gout,' I muttered.

I waited until late before calling Roz. After I'd listened to a long message from Ellie more or less saying goodbye for ever. She was moving north the next day. She was cut off before she'd finished. I rang back, she'd gone out. I left a message in my turn, wishing her luck, asking for her new address. The finality hit me hard. We had loved each other.

I shook myself, rang Roz.

'Oh hello Dany. Sorry you couldn't make it last night. The concert was amazing.'

'Mickey told me. I was so disappointed. I had completely forgotten my previous engagement. And the ticket was expensive, wasn't it?'

Silence. I felt wretched.

'How are you fixed over the weekend? I'd like to make amends. Take you out somewhere.' I offered.

'No need. I'm busy catching up with friends I've neglected recently. Aren't you spending the weekend with your girlfriend in London?

Better come clean, I told myself. 'We've split up.'

'Oh dear, I'm so sorry. I know what that's like.' She was professional rather than sympathetic. 'Maybe we could have a drink together one evening in the next couple of weeks.'

The next couple of weeks! Had I offended her so much? Had Mickey told her I'd chosen debauchery instead of culture?

'Love to. Monday? Tuesday?'

'Afraid not. Commitments. I'll call you.'

'Right.'

'Take care. See you sometime. Bye.'

'Bye.'

Would I ever learn? Or would I keep on shooting myself in the foot?

# Chapter 21

Saturday morning I was kept from brooding over my foolishness by phone calls and visits. I fixed up appointments to inspect properties all over East Sussex during the next seven days. Our fame was spreading. I was glad to be on my own for a change. I was acquiring a sense of power. I waited until Ray arrived at two before I left. He was more buoyant than ever.

'She's out of bed! I did some shopping and she cooked me lunch! I'm going to buy her a box of her favourite chocolates and we're going to sit and watch DVDs later. We often do that. She can't get to the cinema, so we hire all the new releases. I think it will be "*Spiderman III*" tonight. And then maybe "*Pirates of the Caribbean*" again. The first. We've seen it four times already, but we both love Johnny Depp. That probably does mean I'm gay.'

'Not necessarily. I love Johnny Depp and I'm a dyke. Have a good afternoon. Give my love to Davina. Have you tried the Harry Potters?'

'Yes. Interesting effects but ridiculous nonsense as far as magic is concerned.'

I left him to his first customers of the afternoon.

I hardly recognised Craigie. He had shrunk. Not only was he thinner, but also his presence dimmed.

'You're fading away!' was my spontaneous, tactless reaction. 'You need feeding up.'

The wretchedness was still in his eyes. I remembered how I'd warmed to those friendly dark eyes when we first met. 'You don't feel like eating much when your ribs are still mending' he said, with a hint of a smile. 'You're not looking on top form yourself, Dany. A bit peaky, I would say. I speak as a doctor.'

'Too many late nights, I expect.' I took his arm. Carefully, in case I hurt him. 'Are you up to this afternoon's events?'

'I hope so. I must face it. I have to sort something out with Fran. But this bloke you're setting me up with is another matter. Let's just go and have a coffee.'

'You'll be pleased afterwards. Trust me.'

'I no longer trust anyone, my dear.' He allowed himself to be led to Julius's house though. Simon answered the door.

'Julius is waiting. Go straight upstairs. Dany, would you like a cup of tea?'

In spite of his doubts Craigie, went upstairs. We could just hear Julius say 'Ah doctor. So pleased to meet you.' before he shut the door and blocked out any further sounds.

'Do you know what this is about?' I asked Simon, as we waited for the Earl Grey to infuse.

'Julius doesn't discuss his own affairs with me. I assume this is a Wicca business?'

'Sort of.' I was curious. 'You've never fancied becoming a witch?'

'Good heavens, no! I prefer the theatre. There's enough magic and mystery there, if you get the settings right. Milk?'

'No thanks.' I wondered what was going on upstairs. Craigie hadn't immediately backed out, which must surely be a good sign.

In order to keep me entertained, Simon played me a DVD of "*Wuthering Heights*" in which the young Laurence Olivier was at his romantic best, he said. I watched politely not wanting to hurt him. I'd never cared for melodrama. It was quite a long film and Craigie still hadn't come downstairs.

I looked at my watch. Craigie would be late for Fran. Should I ring her? She would be tearing her hair out. No sooner had this intention entered my mind than Julius's door opened and he and Craigie came downstairs together.

'I called Fran to let her know that Craigie is on his way. We'd both love a cup of tea, though.'

It was extraordinary. Already Craigie was transformed. I swear that he had grown again. The tension, the strain had vanished. He looked ten years younger. Julius could have earned thousands as a beauty therapist, was my irreverent thought. He came over and shook my hand.

'I'd give you a hug but it would be too painful.' He grinned. 'Thank you Dany.'

I travelled in the taxi with him as far as their house. He was calling it "home" again rather than "Fran's house". He and Julius had a totally frank exchange about Wicca, about Fran, about Craigie's obsession. It had been an incredible experience. 'The man's a saint or something. Not a saint, a holy man, a wise man, a healer'. He ran out of descriptive words. Julius had given him back his strength, restored him to himself.

'I'm an independent person for the first time since my marriage' he affirmed.

Did that mean he was out of love with Fran? Was he going to leave her? As if in answer to my thoughts, he said 'I shall see Fran with new eyes. I don't know whether I still love her, or even like her. But I shall be capable of acting with at least an element of rationality.'

I was dying to ask if Julius performed some kind of ritual or gave him a potion, but I decided against it.

'Do you want me to come in with you, for support? Mickey will be there.'

'No thank you. If Mickey is there, I'll ask her to leave. It will be between Fran and me.'

I gave him a kiss on the cheek, and asked the taxi to take me to the marina.

I did the shops. All of them. For no reason except that there wasn't much else to do. I walked to the end of the harbour wall. Looked at the range of yachts, big and small, then turned towards the open sea. There was a lock at the harbour entrance, a gateway to freedom, to the Mediterranean, to the great oceans. As I watched the lock was in operation for the exit of a motor launch, a glamorous craft that might well be on its way to Saint Tropez. It sped off gleaming white in the light. As it passed me I glimpsed a name *Pinocchio* which I wasn't sure I read properly because it was going fast. Too fast, I would have thought. Wasn't there speed limits on water as well as on the road?

I wondered whether Mickey would be home yet. I tried her landline then her mobile.

'Mickey, where are you?'

'In my car outside Fran's place. Craigie wouldn't let me stay. She'll need me when he's gone, so I'm staying put.'

'How long are you prepared to wait? What if he doesn't go?'

Silence.

'He might want to move in again.'

'You reckon?'

'Who knows?'

'It's true the owner of the Indian restaurant in the next street has just arrived with a take-away.'

'There you are! Go home. Or meet me for a fish supper at English's.'

'I don't like to abandon her.'

'Couldn't you be tempted to a Dover Sole? My treat.'

She gave in. She had to admit that eating together indicated that a degree of familiarity was being re-established between the estranged couple.

The first course had just been served when my mobile rang. Mickey clicked her tongue in annoyance.

'Why didn't you switch it off?'

I hadn't wanted to miss a call from Blanche, that was why. In any case, she was on red alert herself, waiting to hear from Fran.

'Danielle? I'm very worried about Greta.'

'I can't talk now, Jiminy, I'm, about to swallow an oyster.'

'I've been phoning her whenever I can during the day and there's no answer. I didn't trust that Tracey person to take care of her.'

'Look Jiminy. I'll call you back.' I smiled placatingly at the other diners, irritated by the disturbance. The waiter was heading in my direction.

'Please, Danielle.'

I took the phone outside.

'Will you go round? Check it out?'

'What if she won't answer, or more likely has gone out for the day? I don't have a key.'

'If she's out for the day she should have her mobile with her. She should take it everywhere.'

'Mr. Cricket, I have left my food and my companion. I'm hungry.'

'Will you go round? Michaela has a key. I asked her to keep a spare. I'll get in touch with you early tomorrow morning. Don't ring me.'

'If it's convenient, I'll go. Love to your wife and your father-in-law!' I added maliciously.

'Your Jiminy Cricket is a pest,' I grumbled as I sat down again. I filled her in about his demands and asked her if it was true she had a key. She said she had, back at the office.

'Then how about you and me fetching it later and paying a quick visit?'

'It's not the way I'd choose to spend a Saturday night.'

'Me neither. What else had you in mind?'

Since neither of us had plans we agreed to do as Jiminy asked. Not until we'd taken our time over the full menu, though.

'Not exactly jumping with vibrant life, this building, is it? I remarked as we alighted from the lift into a thickly carpeted corridor.

'Discretion is what it's about' replied Mickey, her finger on Greta's bell. You can often tell by the way a doorbell sounds whether there's anyone at home. Mickey pressed the button three times. There was a hollow echo. She produced the key from her bag, turned it in the lock.

We stood dumbstruck. It was empty. Not a stick of sump-tuous furniture was left. Even the carpets had gone. We went through the kitchen, the bedrooms, the bathroom, everything removed. The washing machine, the dishwasher, the refrigerator, all gone. Mickey sank to the floor. I followed suit. We'd half expected to find a body, instead there was nothing.

'Did Tracey do this?' Mickey whispered through white lips.

'Oh my god! What are we going to tell Jiminy?'

'We can't tell him anything until tomorrow morning. Should we go to the police?'

'No.' We both knew how jumpy he was about the police.

'If it's a kidnapping they'd leave a ransom note wouldn't they? We'd better have a good look.'

There was a note. Stuck on the inside of a fitted wardrobe. Big sprawling writing. It said *"Ciao, Jiminy. It was nice while it lasted"*.

'The bitch! The absolute bitch!' Mickey shouted. 'What a con artist!'

A con artist is exactly what she was, I agreed. That silly accent, that fabricated history about a family of "fieldworkers". She was the villain, not Tracey.

We locked up, went home. No message from Fran. I persuaded Mickey to leave them alone. There was a message for me from Robbie, inviting me for a picnic with her gang on Sunday afternoon. She left a number to ring back.

I was in the middle of a dream in which I was making love to Blanche when a removal van arrived to take away her furniture. "Don't take my chair," she kept screaming. Then her doorbell still kept ringing. When she went to the door naked, she found nobody there but the doorbell kept ringing. I woke up to find it was my phone. It was 3 a.m.

'Danielle?' His voice was hushed. 'My wife's asleep. I'm in the kitchen. Tell me quickly. Was she there?'

I was half asleep. 'No.'

'Was that girl Tracey there?'

'No.' I hesitated. 'Nor any of your furniture.'

'What! What are you talking about?'

'They've done a bunk with your furniture. Left a note saying goodbye, it was good while it lasted.' It was brutal, but I was in a brutal mood. I always am when I'm woken suddenly.

'I can hear my wife coming along the corridor. I'll call again.'

'I'm unplugging the phone, switching off the mobile. Sleep well.'

**** 

The sun struggled through the clouds on Sunday morning about the same hour as I struggled into consciousness, which was around noon. I remembered the student picnic. I plugged the phone in again, confirmed with Robbie that I would go.

'We've invited some of the tutors. You'll be pleased that La belle Blanche is coming and Tricky Dickey. And others you haven't met.'

Was I pleased to know that La Belle Blanche would be there? The news left me indifferent.

'The big gardens of the house in the University park at 4.30. Bring a cake.'

I hastily dressed in order to go on a cake search. There was a very good French patisserie near the station. I took the opportunity to buy an almond croissant, which I ate in the Pavilion Gardens, where I had last sat with Greta, the Greek/Albanian/British fraud. That was why she laughed at the jokes that night, why her gestures, her expressions when she was unguarded reminded me of women I'd known working in London bars. Had she lived in the East End? She'd done a pretty good number with poor old Jiminy. Her face and figure were her fortune, she could play the lady when she chose. There was this sinister pimp or whatever he was, in the background, getting his cut. Now Tracey was mixed up with these shady affairs. She didn't have the attribution of a call girl nor even of a mere ordinary prostitute, so it was hard to imagine what they would do with her. Had she gone along willingly? Would they do her in at the earliest opportunity, dispose of the body? Despite my aversion for her, shared, it would seem, by all who came across her, I wished her no harm. The best scenario was that they would teach her how to be a successful criminal, also how to present herself. Greta seemed to be the one person who initially liked her, but that could have been as much an act as the rest.

I had bought two cakes, one a pear tart with chocolate topping, the other a lemon meringue pie. One was for the picnic, the second for Davina. She could choose between them. I hoped she wouldn't have had a relapse. Ray could have been overconfident about her recovery, especially as he was claiming the credit for it. Strange how important she was to me. Like Ray I was willing her to live on and on, defying mortality.

'The pear and chocolate, I want the pear and chocolate.' She exclaimed, her eyes gleaming in anticipation of pleasure. Shall we have a piece now?'

'Granny, you've only just had your lunch.' Ray was hovering anxiously behind me.

'So what? Don't try to boss me around, I won't have it. Fetch a knife and some plates.'

'Davina I must be on my way soon. I'm invited to a picnic in the University Park, and I've just had breakfast.'

'Breakfast! I never breakfast after twelve o'clock. Breakfast is between seven and eight, lunch twelve and one, tea at four and dinner at eight. If you've only just had breakfast that means you got up late, which means you were up to something naughty. Am I right? Do tell!'

I assumed an expression which I hoped was coy. 'That's my secret.'

'How annoying. It wasn't Roz, was it? I would be so pleased if it were Roz.'

'No. Roz is busy.' I watched Ray cut three huge chunks of tart. 'Honestly, I couldn't.'

'You're too thin. This will do you good. And you have to have a piece with a whole half pear. That's why it has to be divided in this way. Isn't this fun? I thought I'd copped it, Dany. The grim reaper was by my bed sharpening his scythe. He's been here before, you know, and I've always sent him packing. He must be so fed up he won't come back. That big man in the sky will send an angel instead. Ray, make us a cup of coffee, will you, good and strong. And close the kitchen door behind you.'

He opened his mouth to protest, thought better of it, obeyed. She beckoned with a gnarled finger so my face was close to hers.

'I think it was him drove Comrade Death away. Death likes a bit of quiet and Ray kept weeping and carrying on. "Granny, Granny, don't leave me, don't leave me. I can't bear it." Very touching. He's a good boy. I have to see he finds a good woman before I kick the bucket. Or a good man, I don't care which.'

I drank the coffee, ate the cake, called a taxi and went off to the picnic feeling full but happy, mobile switched off.

The picnic was a disaster for me. Tricky Dickey was one of the reasons for my bad feelings. And Blanche was another. The last was Roz, who was seated on a blanket between Richard and Blanche, both vying for her attention. The three of them acknowledged me with a wave, before continuing their flirtation. I felt sick, not because of having devoured an almond croissant and a quarter of a pear and chocolate tart, but because Richard or Blanche would take Roz home to bed, which I suddenly desperately wanted to do myself. She was looking good, more attractive than either of her suitors, responding to their flattery. How did she come to be there? I had to break up the threesome. These two rivals were playing at scoring over each other, that's all. Richard had no idea how slight his chances were when up against Blanche. The idea of Blanche using all her tricks in bed with Roz drove me wild with jealousy. I tried to be casual as I flopped down the other side of Blanche.

'You know Roz, don't you Dany? She's dealing with my conveyancing. I invited her, thought she'd enjoy it,' said Richard.

'Oh it's great fun, takes me back to my own student days. Hello Dany.' Her smile was brief.

'Hi, Dany, how are you? Sorry you left so suddenly the other night. I was worried about you getting home safely in the small hours. You ought to have stayed until morning, especially as you'd managed to get out of your previous engagement to be with me.'

There were so many messages in that statement. She wasn't implying that she and I were an item, on the contrary, she would give a girl a good time with no strings attached, and she hoped Roz was this kind of girl. What she didn't know was that Roz had been my broken engagement, or did she? I was too ashamed to meet anyone's eye. I simply plucked daisies, started making them into a chain.

'I have to collect a book from my office' announced Blanche. 'Would you like to come with me, Roz? I have some stuff about law you might find interesting.'

'Why not?' Roz sprang to her feet, stretched out a helping hand to the other woman, whose tight skirt made getting up more difficult. I surreptitiously watched them whilst ostensibly concentrating on my garland. They made a handsome pair.

'You do know she's a dyke?' I asked Richard when they were out of earshot.

'Who Blanche? Of course.'

'No, Roz.'

'I didn't. She was married and has a son.'

'She lived with a woman who broke her heart.'

'Then she might decide that men are the better option after all.'

'Dream on, Professor Bradshaw. Let's see how long it takes to examine a few law books.'

'Give me that daisy chain.'

He took it from me, put it around my head.

'It suits you. You look like a Greek shepherd.'

He could be nice when he wanted.

'My father isn't well,' he said suddenly.

'He's going to have some pretty awful treatment. My mother will need all the support she can get.'

I blinked. Was there a caring son hiding beneath the ambitious intellectual?

'I can't leave the country. So I'll have to turn down the job in the U.S.A. My two brothers are already abroad. I'm the only one left.' He adjusted my daisy chain. 'That's better.' He plucked a stalk of grass, sucked on it. 'The old man and I never got on. It's my mother I care about. If he dies, I'll look after her.'

We joined in the games until a mist crept in. Neither Blanche nor Roz having reappeared, Richard and I went back to his house, where he managed to find a bottle of wine and a tin of spaghetti which he heated for us to share.

'I can't wait to get out of this house,' he said. 'I never liked it. I can go full steam ahead for the apartment now I've decided to stay.'

He showed me photos of his mother, father, brothers. He played me DVDs of a couple of his 'research' films. He opened another bottle of wine. When he'd drunk three quarters of it he said, 'You don't like me, do you? You think I'm shallow and selfish.'

'Does it matter what I think?'

'Yes. I like you enormously. It matters.'

'The truth is, I liked you, then I didn't, now I do again. I've changed my mind twice. I think you're a mixture, selfish and unselfish. Shallow no.'

'Let's drink to that.'

'And you don't mind that Roz went off with Blanche?'

'No. It was worth a try. Do you mind, yourself?'

'Yes. I mind very much. I don't blame her.'

'Blanche is hot stuff, I hear.'

From whom did you hear it, I wondered. 'You could say that. Would you call me a taxi?'

****

'Dany, they've made it up! They're together again!' Mickey grabbed me. 'Isn't it fantastic?'

'Stupendous.'

'Fran just phoned. They're going way for a bit, to rebuild the relationship, she said. I am just so relieved.'

So was I. Craigie had been on my mind whilst Richard subjected me to *"Terminator 2" and "Nightmare on Elm Street"*.

'She sent you their special love,' she said with some resentment. 'And Jiminy called. He wants you to meet him at the apartment at 8 a.m. tomorrow morning. He's catching an early train down. Seems he has to be back for a lunch-time board meeting. He couldn't talk much.'

'Why don't you go? It's too early for me.'

'He asked for you. See you back at the office as soon as you can make it. I'll be dying to know what he's gong to do.'

I trailed upstairs, set my alarm for seven o'clock.

# Chapter 22

At eight o'clock Jiminy was already pacing round Greta's apartment. He attacked me immediately.

'Danielle, you've destroyed me!'

'I expect you're insured against theft, Mr. Cricket.'

'Theft!' He exploded. 'Theft! What are you talking about? I don't care a damn about missing furniture, most of it came with the apartment anyway. It's Greta! How can I go on without Greta, my comfort, my solace? When I wasn't with her she was always on my mind, I'd have erections in the middle of meetings. It was the only way I could have sex with my wife, fantasising about Greta. How on earth will I manage?'

'If you don't mind me saying so, Mr. Cricket, fantasies are fantasies. Close your eyes, concentrate, and, bingo, you'll spring into life.'

'I never imagined you could be so heartless towards a broken man.'

'Ah, you don't know me at all.'

He was holding her note in his trembling hands, staring at the words disbelievingly, shaking his head.

'We'd better contact the police!'

'No. Leave the police out of it.'

'If you want her back, they'll put her on the missing persons list.'

'I said no police!' His vehemence was alarming. There was a violent side to him, I should treat him with more caution.

'What are you going to do then?'

'You're going to come with me to the marina.'

'Do you think she's somewhere down there?'

'I have a motor launch. I *had* a launch. Perhaps I don't have one any more.'

The image of a launch leaving the harbour at a danger-ous speed came back to me, the name flashing past, a name to match Jiminy Cricket.

'Is your boat called Pinocchio, by any chance?'

'Did she tell you about it? Did she take you out in it?'

'She knew how to drive it did she?'

'Of course, we went out in it together. She adored it.'

'Then this is the bad news. I saw it heading into the Channel. There isn't any good news, I'm afraid.'

The berth was empty. Jiminy was as distressed by the loss of his boat as the loss of his woman.

'I'd only had her a few months,' he moaned. 'I sold my old one and bought Pinocchio as a sort of gift for Greta. Not the boat itself, that was in my name, but the gift was the pleasure of using it. I was planning to take her round the Med.'

'That's probably where she's gone.'

'She knew how to drive it, she wouldn't have any idea about navigation. When I showed her the charts she fluttered her eyelids and said she couldn't make head nor tail of it.'

'Maybe she understood more than she let on. She conned you Jiminy, she conned you all the time. She may add blackmail to her list of crimes, who knows.'

'We need a drink.'

'I need a plate of scrambled eggs on toast.'

When I'd polished off a double helping of breakfast, I told Jiminy about the man I'd seen with Greta near Hove Lawns.

'She denied it, but I'm sure it was her. He was a nasty type. I also have to say that they were arguing in English although I was too far away to hear the actual words. You can tell by the rhythm and intonation.'

'How can you be positive it wasn't Albanian?'

'Albanian, my foot! Greta's a Londoner, I'll bet you. Wise up. You've been well and truly had. How much was your boat worth?'

'A lot of money. Too bad.' He rubbed his forehead. 'It's gone. They'll change the name, it will be like a stolen car. Why didn't you tell me about this man?'

'No point as she swore I was mistaken.'

'So they're in it together.' By now he'd recovered from the shock. Bitterness, self-recrimination was creeping in. 'How could I be so stupid? She was so vulnerable, my friends who took her in as an au pair were completely taken in.'

'Love is blind, they say.' I ordered a second mug of tea.

'She is dazzlingly beautiful, isn't she?'

I had to agree.

'So sexy. So skilled. I have known a few call girls in my time. None of them could match up to her. I would have taken her as my mistress wherever she was from. She didn't have to invent a false life.'

Now he'd aroused my sympathy.

'If you don't try to get her back you'll never know the truth. It could have been the man who made her do it.'

Jiminy was drinking brandy.

'I have to leave for the train soon. I can't miss the meet-ing. My conduct must be unimpeachable. My father in law suspects me of shady deals on the side. I have my own sidelines, you see. The boat was out of an account he does-n't know about. Greta's maintenance was from private investments. I have to provide for my future. When pa in law dies, little wifey will inherit megabucks. The stock market is rocky, as you know. I'll have to wipe the slate clean as far as Greta is concerned.' There were tears in his eyes. 'It's painful Dany. Terribly painful here.' He thumped his chest. 'I'll be lucky if I get through the rest of the day without sobbing my heart out.' The tears rolled down his cheeks. He blew his nose on a table napkin. 'Tell Michaela to put the apartment back on the market. At an increased price, naturally. Send me a contract.'

By extraordinary coincidence, Mickey had a client who was looking for an apartment just like Greta's.

I believe she's Swedish. Tall, slim fashion model type, maybe she *is* a fashion model. They earn fantastic salaries don't they? She's charming.

'She made me go quite weak at the knees' Ray chipped in.

'Oh, so you're not gay after all?' I teased him.

'Dream on, young man,' Mickey said. 'I don't pay you enough to afford her. It would cost you a week's wages just to take her out to dinner.

'Will Jiminy have to meet her when the sale is completed?'

'No. But perhaps he should.' We exchanged knowing smiles.

'I have a visit for you. Should be interesting. Ray can go with you if he likes. A boutique hotel.'

'What?'

'An old fashioned guest house turned into a top class luxury hotel. Small but perfectly formed. Exquisite taste, apparently. A beauty salon, sauna. Sure fire investment. Converted to the highest standard with attention to every detail. You deserve a treat after being up so early.'

'Can I take the camera? I'm not a bad photographer.' Ray was more eager than I was. I would have preferred to have an hour off to sit on the beach.

'This is the four-poster, black and white room. Marble bathroom. It's the biggest of our seven bedrooms. King sized bed.' He pulled aside the gauze drapes. 'All our bed linen is pure cotton. It's so much pleasanter for the skin than a polyester mix. Except that in the lilac room, which is the ultimate in luxury, the sheets and pillowcases are silk. We call that our bridal suite. Lilac is more for the girls than the boys, but boys don't seem to mind. Since we can all get married or the equivalent, we've had an awful lot of honeymoon couples.'

Ray had already taken at least fifty photos.

'This is our relaxation room, next to the beauty parlour. And the hot-tub is through that door. It's very pleasant to sit in the relaxation room in the mornings as it faces east. Come through the french windows into the courtyard.' We followed him. 'Total privacy, not overlooked by the surrounding buildings. We keep the fountain running because the fish like it. Get out of here!' He made a swipe at a ginger cat who leapt for safety on to a garden wall. 'He's always in here. Just sit on the bench for a moment. Isn't it sweet? I love this place to bits.'

'Why are you selling it then?' asked Ray when he'd finished clicking.

'I'm afraid my partner and I are splitting up. The whole business was too much of a strain. Living with a mess for two years, got on our nerves. We kept sniping at each other until we had a final blazing row and off he went, up North I believe. The hotel is in my name, so I'm free to sell. We didn't even have a chance to open for our first guests. We've started to get bookings from all over the world through our Internet advertisements. I'm selling a going concern here.'

'What'll you do afterwards?' Ray was taking the last few shots of the courtyard.

'Well, actually,' he blushed, 'I've met someone else. We're gong to Croatia together to set up something similar.'

'What a beautiful hotel,' remarked Ray on our way back to the office. 'And his own accommodation was super. Perhaps Mickey would buy it in Davina's name, make me the manager then I could move in there with Granny. It would be Wicca friendly. How about that? The first Wicca friendly boutique hotel!'

'Davina's not a witch, is she?'

'No but she isn't prejudiced. I think she'd think it was really cool. She'd meet some interesting people. As a matter of fact I felt an atmosphere inside that building. I'll bet a witch had already lived there. And it's all furnished, we'd be able to move straight in with no bother. Just close up our other flats and do furnished lettings. Did you notice at the other side of the courtyard there's a sort of a summer house?'

'I'm as observant as you are young man. It's in the details. Whilst you were photographing the kitchen he explained they hadn't quite finished that yet. It was to be a sort of relaxation room.'

'Perfect! We could put an altar in there.'

Mickey wasn't against it. A Wicca friendly boutique hotel appealed to her imagination. A new project. She put the pictures up on the screen, nodded at each one approvingly.

'You do realise you now have to make a full confession to your great grandmother? You'll have to come out to her,' I warned him.

'I was meaning to anyway, now I'm a priest.'

'You'd better take the afternoon off then.' Mickey gave a loud whistle when she saw the courtyard with the summer house. 'You're right. There are distinct possibilities. Go on then, Ray. Make your granny an offer she can't refuse. Take as long as it takes.'

He was off like a shot.

'A very old lady could be an added attraction.' She said, when he'd gone. She shrugged. 'You couldn't count on it for long, though.'

'You could always bring in another when she's passed on,' I suggested.

She blushed. 'I'll go and get a bite to eat, if that's O.K. with you.'

She was gone a long time. No-one came in, the phone didn't ring. The files were up to date, there was no clerical work to be done. Nothing to take my mind off my empty future. When Mickey finally returned I was sinking into depression.

'Cheer up,' she said 'It may never happen.'

I detest that phrase.

'That's the trouble' I replied. 'It may never happen.'

'Shall I make you a formal partner?'

'No thank you.'

'Would you like to be in sole charge, whilst I make my spiritual journey to India?'

'Absolutely not. I've had enough.'

'I could put it all in your name. You can see how well we're doing. You could buy yourself a super-duper apartment in that new complex on the Hove front.'

'Mickey, once and for all, I am not interested. Keep your business. Keep your money. I don't want it.'

'What do you want? Do you want to come to India with me? Discover yourself?'

'Leave me alone, Mickey, to enjoy my melancholy.'

Ray was away the whole afternoon. We hoped his confession and/or his plan hadn't given Davina a heart attack. Mickey left me alone as requested, except to tell me she had just received an e-mail from Fran to say they'd be back soon to rebuild their life together. It was brief but encouraging, she thought. What I didn't tell her was that I'd received one from Craigie more doubtful.

*"Dany, I don't know if it will work. I hope so.*
*Everything's different now. Love Craigie."*

I was ruminating on this when La Belle Blanche sauntered in. Designer jeans which suited her to perfection, knitted silk top in the kind of green which showed off the red of her hair. Her smile encompassed us both, but it was me she addressed.

'I'd like you to sell my basement.'

After her first sharp intake of breath at this vision of

beauty, Mickey concentrated on her computer and left me to deal with things.

'You are familiar with the layout. What do you think it's worth?'

I could sense Mickey's internal "wow!" as she jumped to the right conclusion.

'Lower ground floor apartments don't fetch such a good price. However, yours is spacious. The second bedroom, which you use as your study is unpleasantly airless.'

'Will you come round tomorrow morning to measure up? Take photos?'

'I'll have to consult my engagement diary. Do you know where you're moving to?'

'Probably America. There's a job that's almost certainly mine. Fits my profile easily. Half in Women's studies, half in Irish Studies. You know I wrote a series of articles about Irish women emigrating to the united States during the Potato Famine, based on diaries and letters?'

'No. How would I know that, ignorant little me?'

'You're an inverted academic snob, Dany. You'd find at least one of those articles interesting. You'd be surprised how many lesbian relationships were formed on board ship.'

Mickey went into the back room and shut the door.

'Is she homophobic?' asked Blanche.

'No she's leaving us alone so you can proposition me.'

'Clever girl. That's exactly what I was going to do. I'm serious about the sale though. The interview for the part will be a formality.'

'A chair is it?'

'A prestigious one. Will you have supper with me tonight?'

'Afraid not.'

'That's a real shame.'

I had to ask 'Did Roz find your law books interesting?'

She studied her beautifully varnished fingernails. 'Not as interesting as I'd hoped. Perhaps she's the wrong genera-tion. Are you sure you can't manage tonight?'

'Positive.'

'Ah well. You'll be round tomorrow morning?'

'Ten o'clock. Between appointments. I won't have much time to spare.'

'I can take the hint.'

'If I were you I'd take down your pictures before I bring clients round.'

She threw back her head and laughed. She had a magnificent throat. 'I didn't think you were a prude. *"Elle fait des tableaux couvrir des nudités, mais elle a de l'amour pour la réalité."* Do you recognise the quote?'

'No, but I understand what it means. I think it's closing time, Dr. O'Grady.'

'Until tomorrow then.' She blew me a kiss.

\*\*\*\*

The next two days were completely without incident. I was strictly professional with Blanche, who didn't care. Why would she? She could get whoever she wanted whenever she wanted. Ray was back in the office. Davina loved the idea of the hotel, she had been tickled pink that he was into witchcraft not drugs. Mickey made an offer in Davina's name. It was accepted.

Then I was faced with another dilemma. Fran and Craigie returned and invited Mickey and me to dinner. Roz, from whom I hadn't heard a word, invited me to accompany her the same evening to a ballet and supper afterwards, another of Jim's tickets. It was a sign of her forgiveness. Turn this one down and I'd blow it for ever.

'Craigie was particularly anxious that you should be there,' Mickey said. 'He wants to thank you for your support and friendship. You will come won't you?'

'Yeah,' I replied miserably. I'd described myself as his best friend, after all.

I called Roz's office. Busy with a client.

At the end of the day I went round to her office in person. The secretary was leaving.

'She'll be occupied for another half hour' she informed me. 'I have to lock up. I can't leave you here.'

'Would you just knock and tell her who I am?'

'Can't you call through? Don't you have an intercom system?'

'It's not worth it as I'm right next door,'

'Please knock.'

'No!'

'If you don't, I will.' I raised my voice, so Roz might hear. I guessed the walls weren't very thick. I took a step towards the door.

'Don't you dare!' There was a light of battle in the secretary's eye. She stepped in front of me, ready to grab my arm should I make a false move. The door opened.

'What's all this disturbance?'

'This woman was insisting on seeing you.'

'It's all right Mrs. Danvers, you can go. Dany will you wait here, please?'

Was she really called Mrs. Danvers, I wondered? She tossed her head, put her coat on, marched out, stiff necked. Roz went back to her client. I waited half an hour, willing it not to be Blanche in conference. Thank goodness it was a small, thin, worried man who finally emerged, wiping his brow.

'Come in,' invited Roz.

It was a very pleasant room, conducive to calm, reasonable discussions. Shelves of books and files interspersed with watercolours of Mediterranean landscapes. What was visible of the walls was painted a soft dove grey, matching her carpet. She indicated that I should sit in the armchair in front of her desk.

'You have something to say to me?'

Yes, I had, but I hadn't know what it was until I actually said it. I liked her very much, I had become increasingly attracted to her. I was desperately sorry about letting her down in order to spend the night with Blanche. I was ashamed. I told her about Fran and Craigie, the accident, the reunion, last of all the invitation to dinner. I was careful not to mention the spell, the Wiccan affair. She listened without interruption, I guess that's what a good lawyer does.

'Roz, what I would like most in the world is to go out with you tonight, but I have to be there for Craigie.'

'I understand. And this time I can't take Mickey.' She dialled a number.

'Simon, how are you fixed for tonight? Would you like to come to the ballet with me?' Pause. 'Yes, probably. They usually do at least one dance naked. See you 7.30 outside the Theatre Royal.' She looked at me with some amusement. 'See what you're missing. Perhaps not, it's usually the men who are naked. I have to go and change. Dinner, Saturday?'

The wave of relief which swept over me was almost overwhelming.

'Oh yes! Thank You! Nothing, but nothing will keep me from that, I swear!'

'Come to me at 6.30. We'll drive out somewhere.' She looked me straight in the eye. 'Blanche is too fast track for you, Dany. She's ruthlessly ambitious.'

I shifted uncomfortably.

'I must dash.' She came round to my side of her desk, kissed me on the cheek.

'Remember Dany, nobody has ever stood me up three times. You're handsome and charming enough to get away with it twice, no more.'

The kind of magic Julius must have performed almost converted me to witchcraft. Fran and Craigie sat holding hands, subdued but with no trace of anxiety or tension. After stating that they had discovered that they cared for each other enough to want to reconstruct their marriage, they turned to more general topics. We all spent a happy evening, eating, drinking a little, listening to music. At the end, as Mickey and I stood on the front doorstep, Craigie took me by the shoulders, and said 'We want to thank you specially, Dany. We'll never forget the role you played.'

I could read in his eyes the seriousness of the remark. Wretchedness had been replaced by understanding.

'And of course, I must thank Mickey particularly for supporting me.' Fran hugged her friend who had been looking quite put out.

Sipping a so-called "soothing drink" in her kitchen (I was sipping a whisky) Mickey said 'Are you going to join us then?'

'What?' I almost dropped my glass. She couldn't mean what I thought she meant.

'Are you going to become a Wiccan?' I hate to admit you might be rather good at magic. I thought that all along. That's one of the reasons I wanted you to work with me. Miranda was probably like you when she was your age. People are drawn to you. If you have special powers, you should use them, otherwise they may turn against you.'

'Listen, I do not have special powers. I just, I just..... What to say? 'I'm just an ordinary person who likes to help.'

'Julius took to you.'

'I took to him. So? Two individuals who like each other. There's nothing extraordinary about that.'

'Julius isn't just any old individual, he's a fount of wisdom.'

'Well I'm not. I'm the opposite. I'm ignorant. Once and for all, I'm not going to become a Wiccan any more than go back to Catholicism or become a Muslim, Hindu or Buddhist.'

'Forget the rest. Wicca is the oldest, truest religion, without dogma, in tune with the natural universe.'

'Goodnight Mickey.'

# Chapter 23

I dreamed about Anita all night, waking every two hours, falling back into yet another episode of a saga of love and loss, Anita flitting through a forest just out of reach, leading me on like some wood-nymph, Anita sitting cross-legged in the moonlight, gradually fading away to nothing, Anita dancing like a dervish, gypsy skirts flying, revolving frenetically until she was sucked into the hole she had bored in the ground, and, finally, Anita lying open armed waiting for me. Standing over her, I saw she was dead. I took out a wand, touched her forehead and she sat up slowly. I bent to kiss her, her lips were like ice. I woke up to relive my distress of the previous year.

My low mood lasted for several days. Mickey and Ray did everything in their power to cheer me up, without success. I visited Davina whose enthusiasm for the new hotel made me feel a little better. The expression "a new lease of life" was most appropriate to her situation. She was even delighted by Ray's Wiccan practices.

'Of course, we came across that sort of thing in the colonies,' she said. 'Actually I put more trust in witchdoctors in Africa than in the traditional medicine. They achieved the most astounding feats. I'm too old to learn magic, I'm afraid I might make dreadful mistakes. I look forward to meeting witches from all over the world. What fun!'

To take myself out of myself, I went to the cinema. Another complicated story about cops and robbers. In one scene the tough black cop was chasing the Hispanic criminal amongst the crowd gathered for Mardi Gras in the French quarter of New Orleans. It was noisy, violent, too oppressive. I was on the point of leaving when I recognised a face. I froze. The camera lingered on her face for a full minute before moving on to another exotic extra. My pulse was racing. She never appeared again. I went into the cinema foyer, bought an ice cream and went back for the later showing. There was no doubt that it was Anita. I tried to find a DVD of the film. It didn't exist. I returned the following day, sat through two showings, which was as much as I could possibly stand, came out full of doubts. The nose wasn't quite right, the lips a trifle less full than those of my beloved, lips that I remembered again. I went to bed very late in a state of misery and didn't sleep at all.

Saturday morning I was alone in the office just after nine. It was rare that customers came in before ten at the weekend but we opened earlier just in case. Ray and Mickey had gone together to look at a houseboat in Shoreham, belonging to a friend of Jim and Ernest, an actor who had concluded that he had reached an age where life on dry land would be easier. All our documentation was in order, my desk was tidy so I was on the point of taking up my long abandoned thriller when an e-mail came through from America.

"Hi Dany!
*My dear, it's already incredibly hot here. Not normal, they tell me, for May. I'm wrung out. Great jazz, you can't imagine. My other half is working his socks off. Attached is an article in yesterday's local paper. It might be one helluva coincidence. Ernest gets a few days off – long weekend. We're off up the Mississippi. I'm back Friday. See you.*
*Hugs and kisses*
*Jim.*

*P.S. Sweetheart, don't be too upset – closure is good.*
With my heart in my mouth, I brought up the article on screen.

### Double Murder in French Quarter
*A man has been charged with the stabbing of a couple in a back street of the French Quarter. The woman of mixed racial origin was dead when the police arrived, the man a white Caucasian believed to be Canadian, died on the way to hospital. The alleged murderer, Roberto da Silva, who contacted the police and stayed at the scene of the crime, was the estranged husband of the young woman, Anita da Silva. The other victim was described by da Silva as an evil demon who had taken possession of his*

*wife's soul. It is believed that Da Silva had already attacked his wife some years before in an attempt to "rid her of the devil." She had subsequently disappeared.*

*Da Silva also claimed that his wife and her companion had been members of a group of Voodoo practitioners and had put a spell on him. (See article on P6, Voodoo in New Orleans.)*

There was a photo of Anita and her husband on their wedding day. I couldn't take my eyes off it – they were a radiant Prince and Princess. I remembered the long scar I had glimpsed down Anita's back when she was in the shower. She wouldn't normally let me see her naked – we made love in the darkness and she was always dressed again by morning. Closure is good, Jim had said. Anita was dead. Stabbed to death by a crazy husband. The guardian who hovered around her in France was dead too. Complete closure.

I was still staring at the screen when Ray and Mickey came back, full of excitement about the houseboat.

'It was cool, Dany, really terrific. You know what? I think it would suit you. We can get someone else to buy it and then you can buy it from them.' She stopped in full flow, at the sight of my face.

'What is it? You look awful! Has somebody died?'

'Yes. A woman I knew last year.'

'I'm sorry.'

I deleted the e-mail and article – I could retrieve them later. I was incapable of further explanation.

'It was a shock, that's all. She wasn't very old. I can't talk about it.'

'Do you want to go home?'

'Yeah, maybe. Yes, please.'

I didn't go home. What would have been the use of that? I sat outside a pub on the beach, sipping a half of beer. I was numb. When I glanced at my watch I saw I'd been there for two hours. The numbness turned into acute pain. I thought of ringing Craigie, a doctor who would understand. No, I must leave him alone. It was instinct rather than reason led me to Julius.

Simon and he were watching a DVD *"La Cage aux Folles"*. Without me uttering a word he took me upstairs, gave me a spicy drink and listened. Then we talked until he gently suggested I should sleep. He gave me another drink.

'I have to go to Roz at 6.30. I must!'

He smiled, 'You have two hours to sleep. I'll make sure to wake you.'

No dreams this time. At six o'clock I was woken with a cup of tea. It was as if I had been reborn.

'I'll drive you round to Roz's' offered Simon.

'I interrupted *"La Cage aux Folles"* I said as I got out of the car.

'Darling, we've already seen it a dozen times. Have fun.'

The strange thing was I felt as though I could face the evening, even enjoy it. I saw Roz with new eyes. She was wearing a striped dress which must have been tailor made it fitted her so well. The colours were brighter, showing off her slightly tanned skin. She had jade earrings and a necklace to match. She was dashing. I was still wearing my smart business suit.

'Julius called me' she said. 'Told me you'd had very bad news. Do you still want to go out?'

'Yes, please. But I feel awkward in these clothes.'

'You look just right. I'll lend you something if you prefer.'

'It's O.K.' If she was happy, I didn't really care.

It was a good meal in beautiful surroundings, a pub beside the River Adur in West Sussex. Roz asked no questions, however, I wanted to share my experiences with her, as far as I was able. To Julius I had poured out my heart and soul, my account to Roz was more rational. We walked along the river bank as the stars came out, our fingers entwined.

'Do I take you home?' she asked when we were back in town. She put a hand on my arm. 'Thank you for spending the evening with me,' she added gently.

I didn't want to sleep alone, be alone. 'May I come back with you?' I mumbled looking away.

Oh, how comforting it was to lie in her arms, my head on her breast. That was all. For the time being. She stroked my body with a soothing touch. She let me weep, she rocked me like a baby until the tears dried. She kissed my hair. It wasn't until morning that we made proper love, when I opened my eyes to see this beautiful woman by my side. I think we were both surprised by how easy it was, how right it felt.

We didn't get up until lunch time. I rang Mickey to reassure her that I was fine. We had a sandwich went back to bed, devoting the afternoon to a slow exploration of each other. Then she made me supper. Neither of us had said "I love you".

'I have a spare room now Amelia's gone, if you'd like to move in.'

I wanted to reply "Yes, please". Instead I said 'Thank you, Roz, I think better not.'

'Perhaps you're right. The offer's open if you should want to take it up.'

Her hair was tousled, she was wearing a tee-shirt, nothing else. She had long slim legs. She was more like a teenager than the mother of a grown-up son.

'I have a fortnight's holiday fixed as from tomorrow. I have some work to do at home, stuff I can't leave, so I couldn't get away until Wednesday or Thursday. I'd planned to drive down to the West Country, find hotels, bed and breakfast as I went along. Would you like to come? Would Mickey give you time off?'

'She might now Ray is, helping. I've never been to the West Country.'

'You'll love it!' She served me a plate of pasta cooked how I like it with an excellent Bolognese sauce.

Fran and Craigie were waiting for me at Mickey's. I guessed Julius might have been in touch, to fill them in. I was glad that I had no need to say more. We sat close to each other, Craigie with one arm round my shoulders, the other round his wife. Mickey brewed us something pleasant and we made, light superficial conversations whilst the real communication underneath was our concern for the other's welfare.

'Dany, you know we're always here for you,' were Craigie's parting words.

I squeezed his hand. Fran hugged me.

'You're sure you're O.K?' Mickey asked anxiously, as I climbed my stairs.

'Don't worry. The cure's started without magic intervention.'

'Well, if you can joke about it, you must be all right.'

'Could I have time off? Ten days from next Thursday?'

'Yeah, no problem.'

'Thanks partner. See you in the morning.'

**\*\*\*\***

I had black moments, bursts of inexplicable panic during the next few days, but I began to look forward to the holiday with Roz. I wanted to handle our relationship, whatever it was, carefully. It was all too easy to take advantage of the comfort she was offering. She and I understood each other's grief, we would help each other heal, perhaps that would be all. No more that that. The closeness of our bodies would be part of it. That's what we both needed now. The future would take care of itself.

Lady Loxley's estate was sold to the family with horses. Mickey undertook to clear the spare room. A prospective buyer looked round Blanche's basement a few days before the professional interview in the States. Mickey told me the walls were bare, the desk tidy and the bookshelves practically empty. The prospective buyer was a lay preacher at a nearby church.

Davina had been most insistent that I call in, her great-grandson said. So I visited after work, bearing two meringues and an éclair. She was ecstatic.

'I hear you've done it at last! You made it with Roz! When's the wedding?'

'We're taking it a step at a time.'

'Rubbish. She's a good catch that woman, I've told you. Mind you, so are you, handsome as you are. Get on with it. Publish the bans.'

'We're starting by going on holiday.'

'Not a bad idea to have the honeymoon first.'

'If we wait a while we can have the reception at your new hotel.'

'Oh dear, I don't think so. I think that will be strictly reserved for Wiccan weddings. You're not going to be converted are you?'

'No.'

'Pity. We could all dance naked in the moonlight together if you did.'

'You're not becoming a Wiccan?'

'I'm going to have a go.'

What that meant I couldn't imagine. She was hopping about like a sparrow. She looked ten years younger than when I had last seen her.

'We're going to have such jolly fun.'

On Wednesday morning a letter arrived from Majorca. It looked like a letter. It was, in fact, a photograph in an envelope. Two bikini clad women lay on sun loungers under a parasol by a swimming pool. One was Greta, even lovelier undressed than dressed. It took us several minutes to recognise the other as a transformed Tracey, head back, wide smile, clean flowing hair.

'Can it really be that scruffy misfit?' wondered Mickey.

I turned the photo over. On the back in black capital letters was written,

I DON'T HALF LOOK GOOD, DON'T I? T.

'She's quite pretty actually' was Ray's comment. Then he

added 'Why don't we give this to a detective? They're crim-inals. They should be put in prison.'

'Leave it out Ray!' I advised him. 'Jiminy has written the whole business off. He's not spotless himself.'

'People shouldn't be allowed to get away with dishon-esty' muttered Ray. 'Dany are you going to look at that houseboat? A friend of mine will buy it in his name then you can buy it back.'

**\*\*\*\***

'Have you any suggestions as to where we should go?' Roz and I were heading towards Southampton.

'No. Take me where you like.'

'Then we'll start with Dorset. I know a little hotel in Lulworth Cove with a bedroom leading straight out on to the cliff path. What do you reckon?'

I leaned back closed my eyes. 'Perfect.'

We were on a dual carriageway with hardly any other traffic. She put her foot down on the accelerator.

'Let's go West then. Drive into the sunset.'

So we did.

## Author's note

Sandra Freeman lived and worked in Brighton for 30 years, with the painter, Faith O'Reilly. She taught French and Theatre Studies at the University of Sussex, wrote, acted in and directed 20 plays and she consorted with artists, musicians and all kinds of performers, as well as one or two more indefinable characters. She moved to France four years ago but continues to keep her finger on the Brighton pulse by visiting the city frequently. This is her fourth novel for Onlywomen Press.